# PROLOGUE

My foot slipped on the ice and I went down hard, the impact jarring every last bit of breath out of me. I lay there, unable to move, unable to get my breath back for a few terrifying seconds. But then my chest unlocked and I sucked in a cold mouthful of air, which burned my lungs and made my eyes water. I couldn't stop shaking, but a heavy feeling suddenly overcame me, like I was more tired than I'd ever been in my entire life. I could barely keep my eyelids open.

My eyes had almost closed all the way when a surge of anxiety shot through me, and with that anxiety came a jolt of adrenaline. I tried to scramble up, knowing that if I let my eyes close now, I'd probably never open them again. But my limbs didn't want to cooperate; it was like my brain was telling them one thing and they were doing the opposite. I flailed and thrashed but I couldn't get my feet underneath me. I couldn't get up.

I lay back, looking up at the dark sky. Another shooting star streaked across it. Was that my imagination? Had I ever even seen a shooting star before tonight? And now I'd seen two? You were supposed to make a wish when you saw one, right?

That heavy feeling returned, lurking like a stranger at the edge of my vision. All I could hope now was that Navan was okay, that nothing bad had happened to him, that he'd be able to continue the mission and be successful.

I made a wish that this would not be my final hour, but let my eyelids close, unable to fight their weight any longer.

1

---

"*R*emind me which genius suggested we put this off till midday?" My friend Angie's muffled voice drifted through the stalks of corn to my right.

"I believe the same one who didn't pack enough water," my second companion, Lauren—also obscured by giant shafts of corn—replied, from five feet to my left. Her naturally dry tone sounded more sarcastic than usual, probably because, thanks to Angie, we'd run out of water half an hour ago.

I smirked, taking a few seconds' pause from picking corn to wipe sweat from my forehead with the back of my wrist. Despite wearing a shirt and shorts made of cotton so light it was almost see-through and a wide straw sombrero, and religiously sticking to the shade of the corn stalks, this Texan sun was killing me. Still, I loved this kind of work, using my hands— it was cathartic —so I wasn't going to complain.

"Also the same one who suggested we spend our vacation on this delightful farm," Lauren added with a grunt. I pictured her tall, lanky form hunched over as she tackled a far too unripe cob, while her narrow, purple, librarian-style glasses glided slowly but surely down her nose.

"Oh, come on, Lauree." I couldn't resist teasing her, despite my resolution to save my voice for after we'd returned to the farmhouse and I'd downed a liter of water. "We know you *love* it here."

"'Course she does," Angie proclaimed, and I could hear her broad grin through her voice. "What's *not* to love?"

"Guess you have a point." Amid her heavy breathing, Lauren managed to force a note of thoughtfulness into her voice. "I mean, aside from the fact that we're off the grid, with no electricity or phone signal for *literally miles*—who wouldn't appreciate a welcome package of a heap of moldy towels, a sprinkle of roach droppings on their pillowcase, or... *a snake* in their toilet pot?"

Angie and I burst out laughing. From the tremor in Lauren's voice, I could tell she still hadn't gotten over last night's surprise. Trust Lauren to get dibs on the snake.

"*After* I had sat down, I might add."

"It was a grass snake," Angie retorted, "and a pretty cute one at that."

"Cute my ass," Lauren grumbled.

A span of amused silence fell between us as we returned to filling our sacks. This was the second of three assignments we had to complete today; the first had been running bed linens through a manual laundry machine, draining them through a ringer, and then hanging them up to dry outside, and the third would be picking fresh herbs from the greenhouse. Mr. and Mrs. Churnley, friends of Angie's grandparents and the owners and sole full-time residents of Elmcreek Farm, were to assign us three such jobs every day, in return for free board and lodging.

We had arrived only yesterday evening, having flown from New York to Austin, but I was already feeling a sense of calm about the place. Being without electricity, internet, or a working phone was a culture shock we were all still getting used to, but the lack of external distractions was exactly why we had chosen to come here.

This summer was the last chance Angie, Lauren, and I would have to spend quality time together for possibly a very long time, because after the vacation ended, we'd all be heading off in vastly different directions—Angie even to a different country. I was enrolled to begin a mechanical engineering course in Michigan, and Lauren was to study pre-law at Stanford, while Angie would be jetting off to Paris for an apprenticeship at a prestigious sports-fashion brand (thus combining her two biggest passions). If things worked out for Angie there, we'd see very little of her indeed.

She and I had known each other since kindergarten, while Lauren had known us since first grade, so we decided we needed to do something special, and completely different, this summer —something we'd never forget.

I also had a more personal reason for wanting to be in the middle of nowhere this particular vacation... unreachable. Before I left for Michigan, I knew my birth parents were going to try to get in touch—something I dreaded from the very core of me. My adoptive parents, Jean and Roger, could only hold them off for so long now that I'd turned eighteen, and the court legislation no longer had the same hold that it did during my earlier teen years. After I became an official adult three weeks ago, my birth parents had gotten the idea that they wanted to know me. I might have been more amenable to that if they hadn't spent the first decade of my life neglecting me to the point of abuse. Alcohol had always taken precedence over me in their lives, and I didn't see any reason that would change. Their addiction would've gotten me killed if I hadn't run away at nine, and I swore then that I was never, *ever* going back...

I let out a breath, forcing my consciousness back to the bright, beautiful world around me, allowing it to separate the past from the present.

Yes. Elmcreek was the perfect escape for all of us this summer.

"Oh man, my hat just blew off." Angie broke the quiet. "And —augh—I can't reach it. Could one of you guys help me?"

"I volunteer Riley," announced Lauren.

Exhaling, I stowed the cob I held in my hand in my sack. "Yeah, okay, shortie. Coming."

I waded through the field, batting away flies and pushing aside leaves until I reached her. The five-foot-five girl with curly

blonde hair was standing on her tiptoes, the hem of h
blue dress hiked high up her legs as she stretched for a floppy
pink sun hat that was ridiculously out of her reach. She turned
around to face me, her hazel eyes meeting mine. She had a
smile on her round, impish face, and her light blonde eyebrows,
so fair in the daylight they were almost invisible, rose in
expectation.

I eyed the hat again and tried to reach for it myself first,
given that I was a fair bit taller than her, but I couldn't, so we
ended up coordinating a balancing act with her on my shoulders, knocking my own hat to the ground in the process.

"Wo-hoah, it's like a whole other world up here," Angie
gasped as her head rose above the jungle of corn.

"Just be quick," I muttered from between her chunky thighs.
"Your butt is breaking my shoulders."

"It's all muscle and you know it," she retorted, before
stretching out.

Then she stilled.

"What's taking so long?" I asked, squinting in the glaring
sunlight.

"Hey, I thought the Churnleys didn't have neighbors on that
side of the woods."

"What?"

"Looks like there are people over there, sunbathing on logs."
She pointed northward, toward the direction of the woods that
bordered the Churnleys' portion of land. I realized she had

grabbed the hat already, and was now just staring straight ahead.

"Okay—I'm glad you're having a nice time up there, but if you're finished I'm gonna—"

Angie's knees suddenly clenched around my head. "Wait, Riley. They're *dudes*... Four of them. They look like lumberjacks or something. Here, you can see too." She dove a hand into the side pocket of her dress and slipped out her phone. "That's what a *zoom lens* is for... Still got a bit of battery left." A sharp click sounded as Angie's phone camera went off.

"Okay, geddown now," I growled, tugging at her ankle.

She acquiesced, sliding down me with a self-satisfied look on her face. She squinted down at her phone to check out the photo she'd just taken, but it was far too bright to see the screen properly.

"Well, now we all have an extra incentive to hurry up and get back to the house." She winked at me, before donning her hat and continuing to pick corn.

Smirking, I rolled my eyes and picked up my hat, then moved to return to my spot in the field, when Lauren suddenly materialized out of the bushes in front of me. Her faded blue dungarees looked decidedly grubbier than when we had started, and her coffee-colored ponytail was a tangled mess, but her brown eyes sparkled with mild interest. Adjusting her spectacles primly, she flashed us a sardonic smile.

"Did I hear someone say 'lumberjacks'?"

Water was more than enough of an incentive for *me* to finish the job quickly. After my little break, I worked at twice the speed and managed to pick enough corn to fill all three of our sacks within the next fifteen minutes. Then, lugging each sack over our shoulders, we traipsed back to the wooden two-story house that stood at the edge of the cornfields.

We mounted the steps to the porch, passing the Churnleys' three lazy golden retrievers, who barely raised an eyelid as we reached the door. It had been left on the latch, and Angie pushed it open with a creak. We stepped directly into the kitchen/dining area, where we were met with the pungent smell of Mrs. Churnley's cooking, and the short, podgy lady herself standing in front of a stove, her bouncy gray hair cooped up in a brown bonnet, while her bald husband sat at the dining table dutifully peeling potatoes.

Their eyes shot to us as we strode in and planted our sacks down on the wooden floorboards.

"Where should we leave these, ma'am?" Angie asked, panting.

"Oh, good girls!" Mrs. Churnley left the frying pan she had been monitoring and bustled over to examine our finds. "You got some real beauties here! I'll have Mr. Churnley skin some for lunch."

Mr. Churnley, who was of a similar height and build to his wife, waddled over to join her in examining the corn with his monobrow furrowed, while Lauren, Angie, and I hurried to the sink. We each grabbed a metal cup from the drainer and quickly served ourselves water from a large pitcher. Once we'd swallowed two cups in a row, Angie remarked to the couple, "Seems like you might have new neighbors, by the way."

Mrs. Churnley turned, her rheumy eyes widening as she made her way back to the frying pan. "Hmm?"

"Yeah," Angie replied, "we—or I—saw four guys lounging around in the field next door. They were shirtless, so I assumed they were sunbathing..." She set her cup down and dove her hand back into her pocket to retrieve her phone. But as she navigated to her photo app and touched the screen to zoom in, she frowned. "Huh. That's real weird." Her eyes narrowed to slits as she squinted at the screen.

"What?" Lauren and I asked.

"I can't, uh, make them out in the photo," she replied, still looking befuddled. "There's just logs. Odd. I could have sworn I saw dudes there too."

Lauren's lips twitched in a wry smile as she took the phone from Angie. "Yup," she confirmed. "Logs."

I peered over Lauren's shoulder to take a look at the photo for myself. A cluster of four logs lay near the edge of a flat field, right near the woods' border... Definitely no shirtless lumberjacks.

Mrs. Churnley chortled, nudging Angie in the arm with her elbow. "Seems we all react to the heat differently, eh? The only 'shirtless dude' I've seen around here in the last twenty years, other than Mr. Churnley, is Mr. Doherty, our neighbor on the southern side of the fence, and I wouldn't say he's anything to get excited about—unless curly white chest hairs are your thing." To our alarm, she threw us a salacious wink.

"Now, Nora," her husband spoke up in a gruff voice, "don't get the ladies too excited."

I felt myself turn as red as the tomatoes on the kitchen counter as Mr. and Mrs. Churnley erupted into raucous laughter. Angie, Lauren, and I cleared our throats in an attempt to join in, before inching toward the door.

"We're just gonna go and rest a bit before lunch if that's okay," Angie said with a plastic smile.

"Of course!" Mrs. Churnley replied, and the three of us swiftly took our leave. "It'll be ready within the hour!"

I let out a breath as we entered the narrow corridor. They were definitely an unusual couple. Apparently they used to live in the city, and worked as bankers before they got so burned out on metropolitan life that they had a midlife crisis and swung the other way—completely the other way. They bought this patch of land decades ago, and judging by the state of the house, they probably hadn't renovated it since they moved in.

We climbed the rickety staircase that led to the second floor, where the three of us shared a bedroom fitted with three single beds. Although the Churnleys had space for guests, it was quite obvious they weren't used to having any. There were two other bedrooms on our level—one belonging to the old couple, and another that had fallen into disrepair. Angie suspected the latter had belonged to their only child, a boy who had died at the age of thirteen from a rare form of cancer.

Angie's grandmother was convinced they were terribly lonely, but would never admit to it, since they'd "rather rot" than go back to living like the rest of the world. So when she learned that Angie, Lauren, and I wanted to do something memorable this summer, she had been quick to think of her old friends, and had contacted them by snail mail.

Lauren was the first to use the en-suite bathroom when we entered our musty-smelling room, while Angie and I flopped back on our creaky beds. The shower started, and we sniggered as Lauren stepped in and sighed to herself, "Ah, luxury."

It was kind of amazing the things you appreciated when everything got stripped from you. I imagined I'd feel utterly spoiled when I returned home in a month.

Angie blew out softly, staring up at the bare wooden beams strutted across the cobwebbed ceiling. "I could have *sworn* I saw dudes there," she mumbled.

I smiled to myself. "It was an illusion, Angie," I said in a dreamy voice. "A *mirage*... Where normal people would see an oasis of water in a desert, you would see an oasis of, well..." My tone dropped. "I do kind of worry what that says about you."

She chucked a pillow at me. "Shut up."

"Hey," I said, changing the subject, "why don't we go visit the creek this afternoon? After lunch, we can gather the herbs quickly, and then have the rest of the day free."

"Suits me," she muttered. "We'll see what Lauren thinks."

I stood up to stretch out my arms and, yawning, caught sight of myself in the stained mirror near the window. My brown hair was hardly in better condition than Lauren's or Angie's, even though I'd braided it and then wrapped it in a tight bun, and the corners of my blue eyes were tinged reddish—they were feeling a little irritated, come to think of it. I wasn't used to being so close to nature.

The shower stopped abruptly. Lauren emerged from the bathroom a moment later, clutching a towel around her bare body, her shoulder-length hair foaming with shampoo. "So, the water just stopped," she announced, her toes curling on the wooden floor as water pooled around her feet.

"Ah." Angie threw her an amused, yet apologetic look. "Maybe—"

Before we could hear her speculation, Mrs. Churnley's voice boomed up from the bottom of the staircase. "You used too much water at one time, dear—whichever one of you was in the shower just now. I'll have Mr. Churnley come up and show you how to manually work the pump—"

"Oh, don't bother, ma'am," Lauren replied quickly. "I'm sure Mr. Churnley has enough to do."

She looked back at the two of us with tight lips, and I frowned, assessing our options. "Maybe we should just save our hair washing for the creek and use this bathroom only for quick showering—Angie and I were gonna suggest we go there this afternoon anyway."

Lauren blinked, taking a moment to process my suggestion.

"Hair washing in the creek," she repeated, almost robotically. "Right. Okay. So, I'll just... wrap up this sticky slop of hair and wait then. That's fine. No problem."

With that, she turned and marched stiffly back into the bathroom. Exchanging glances with Angie, I laughed. It seemed Lauren was getting past the stage of expecting things to work and surrendering to the experience. And that was good.

It was the first step toward us all having a lot of fun.

"So where is the creek exactly?" Angie asked Mrs. Churnley. We stood on the porch after eating as quick a lunch as we could manage, with the couple for company, and finishing our duties in the greenhouse.

Mrs. Churnley prodded a chubby finger toward the tractor path that ran in front of the house. "Just take a right turn once you're out of the gate and follow that track. It'll lead you to the creek after about a thirty-minute walk. Do make sure you're back before it's dark, since there won't be any lights to lead you."

"Sounds simple enough!" I said brightly.

"Thanks, ma'am," Lauren said, adjusting her towel-turban, beneath which the shampoo had mostly dried and turned her hair into a curious blend of stiff and sticky.

As we turned to leave, passing the lounging dogs and heading down the steps, Mrs. Churnley added, "Oh, and watch out for leeches in the creek! Neither Mr. Churnley nor I have been down there since last summer, but they're usually around at this time of year."

Lauren's jaw tightened. "Thanks."

"Leeches beat snakes though, right?" Angie snickered as we stepped through the gate and began our journey along the track. Breathing in through her nose and setting her gaze straight ahead, Lauren chose not to comment on that.

I was carrying a large bag stuffed with towels, two jumbo bottles of shampoo and conditioner, and enough drinking water (I'd made sure of it myself this time), and we all wore our bikinis beneath our clothes. Lauren, being Lauren, was also sporting green jelly shoes.

"This place really is in the middle of nowhere, isn't it?" I remarked, both admiring and feeling kind of intimidated by the endless sprawl of no-man's land that surrounded us. Having been brought up in the city and not traveled much in my life, the largest stretches of nature I was used to seeing were city parks. This was something else. It made me feel small and insignificant, like a tiny piece of a far greater existence that really didn't care about my life plans or problems.

"Ya know," Angie said, her tone taking on a distant quality as she joined me in gazing out on our surroundings, "I wish we were here for longer than four weeks."

A melancholic silence fell between us. Even Lauren didn't remark. None of us had to ask why Angie wished for that. Despite our proclamations that our friendship would stay the same in spite of the distance, deep down I was sure we were all doubtful about how the next stage of our lives would really affect it. If I was honest with myself, I didn't see how our dynamic wouldn't change. It seemed inevitable that we would drift apart, no matter how much we loved one another. We would meet new friends, be exposed to different ideas, and the little quirks we'd come to know each other for would change along with our habits.

We would grow into different people; there was no escaping that. The friends Jean and Roger were closest to now, in their mid-forties, were not the same as those they'd had in high school.

The thought made me feel insecure, but also all the more fiercely grateful that we had come to this place, so stupidly cut off from everything that could distract us from *us*.

Glancing at my friends, whose eyes, like mine, had turned to the gravel crunching beneath our feet, a renewed determination rolled through me to make the most of the next four weeks that we possibly could.

I allowed a toothy grin to spread across my face as I set my gaze on the entrance to the woods, where the track was leading us.

"Last one to the trees is a roach dropping," I announced, before rocketing forward. Lauren yelped as I caught her arm and dragged her along with me, her jelly shoes slapping on the ground. Angie didn't need an assisted head start—she might have been the shortest of the three of us, but she was the fittest.

She quickly caught up with us, and it was, predictably, Lauren who earned the unfortunate title, Angie and I just about tying in first place.

We skidded to a stop once we were over the woods' threshold, and looked around. It was cooler and darker than I had expected it to be in here—I was surprised by how thick the trees were. Faint birdsong drifted down from the canopy of branches overhead, and the air was still, with very little breeze.

"Kinda creepy," Angie said in a hushed tone.

"Beautiful creepy," I replied, just as softly.

We walked on in silence, and I relished the peace, the woods' quiet energy thrumming around us. Direct sunlight touched our faces only intermittently as we followed the path straight ahead.

Then Angie stopped abruptly. "Hey," she whispered. "Do you hear that?"

Lauren and I halted and listened. I was confused at first as to what exactly Angie was referring to, but then I heard it—a distant *thunk, thunk, thunk*. Like the sound of metal against wood.

We met each other's gazes, and I knew exactly what Angie was about to say from the triumphant gleam in her eyes before she said it.

"Lumberjacks!" she whispered. "Maybe I wasn't imagining them after all! They could've spotted my head above the crops and just rolled off the logs before I took the picture, or something..."

Lauren frowned at Angie, looking dubious, but then shrugged. "I would've done the same if I noticed some perv watching me."

Ignoring Lauren's comment, Angie strayed from the track and began to creep through the undergrowth toward the noise, leaving the two of us staring after her.

Lauren's thick eyebrows rose high above the rim of her glasses as she exhaled. "So, are we going dude hunting now, or to the creek? Because they're in two opposite directions, and as much as I would—"

Lauren faltered as Angie turned around and held a finger to her lips.

The noise had stopped.

There was a pregnant pause as we waited another thirty seconds to see if it would start again, and when it didn't, Angie let out a sigh and ambled back to us.

"Seems they're shy," she remarked with a droll smile.

"Okay, let's keep moving," Lauren said firmly, taking the lead. "Some of us have crap to scrape off our heads."

As Mrs. Churnley had promised, the creek was easy to find. We heard gushing about five minutes before we reached it, and quickened our pace to arrive before a beautiful, gently flowing basin of water enclosed by stooping tree branches and bordered by bushes of white and purple wildflowers.

"Well, this is nice," Lauren admitted, her expression almost suspicious.

We approached the bank, searching for the best place to set up. We found a little patch of grass, and I dumped the bag there before pulling out the items we needed. We stripped to our swimwear, examining the ground more cautiously now that we were barefooted, and then approached the water. It was surprisingly cold, but a welcome contrast to even the relatively cool forest air—we had all grown sticky during our walk.

Goosebumps ran along my skin as I waded deeper, the soles of my feet slipping along the smooth stones of the riverbed. Our eyes darted around the murky water, searching for leeches. When the water was up to our waists and we'd spotted none, I bit the bullet and submerged myself all in one go—Lauren and Angie following suit.

I billowed to the top, gasping for air. "Awesome!"

Lauren quickly set about scrubbing all the dried and cakey shampoo off her hair, and I moved back to the bank to grab the shampoo and conditioner bottles. After the three of us had completed the ritual—which actually took less time than it would have in a regular shower or bath, due to the movement and volume of the water—we started frolicking about like graceless mermaids, and things soon descended into an all-out splashing war. We were only vaguely aware of the time passing from the amount of sunlight that trickled through the treetops, and by the time I pulled away to check my watch on the bank,

CHAPTER 2 | 21

we needed to start heading back, unless we wanted to get trapped in the woods after nightfall.

"Oh, dang," Lauren said as Angie and I were leaving the water. "Where's the shampoo?"

We whirled around to see her pointing toward a stone jutting out into the center of the creek, where we had set down the bottles while we swam. Angie and I had totally forgotten they were even there, and now only the conditioner bottle remained standing.

"Oops, that sucks," I said. "One of us must have knocked it accidentally. Looks like we'll be stuck with Mrs. Churnley's homemade shampoo for the rest of the trip..."

With that prospect ringing in her ears, Lauren surged toward the stone, snatched up the conditioner and threw it to me. "You two get everything packed up," she ordered. "I'm looking for that shampoo."

"Need your glasses?" Angie offered with a smirk.

"Just pass me a long stick," Lauren muttered, staring down.

Angie and I left the water and hunted around for a broken tree branch until I found one that seemed thick and long enough to be useful. I chucked it toward Lauren, and then Angie and I turned away from the water and began drying off.

Lauren's shriek a minute later made us whip back around.

"*What the*—" She swore.

"What?" Angie and I called, staring at her as she splashed toward us, her eyes set on a patch of water about five feet away from the rock where we'd kept the bottles.

"I dislodged something!" she panted, still backing away from whatever it was she'd spotted in the water.

I was expecting it to be a leech, or a group of them, but then I saw it. Something was rising from the depths of the creek. A long, dark shadow at first, but as it broke the surface, it was... My eyes bugged. It took my brain several moments to put a name to what I saw.

"A *wing*?" I blurted.

It was a huge, black, shimmering thing—several feet across —with protruding veins and a startlingly pointed tip. It looked like... some kind of giant, prehistoric bat wing.

Angie was already wading into the water for a closer look, passing Lauren and grabbing the stick. By the time she reached the thing, Lauren had climbed out of the water and snatched up her glasses so she could see in detail past more than a few feet. Angie used the stick to guide the wing to the bank, and once it was close enough, I wrapped the edges of my towel around my hands to act as gloves and kneeled over the edge. I gingerly got a hold of the edge of the wing and, in spite of how offputtingly heavy it was, managed to haul it up onto the grass. We gathered around it, our mouths hanging open.

"It must've been stuck between some rocks on the riverbed," Lauren breathed.

"What *is* it?" Angie mused, bending down. She cautiously poked a bare finger against its leathery surface, and it gave way at her touch. Her nose wrinkled. "Ew... Feels supple."

I hesitated to ask why that might be. Was there some kind of rare bird species inhabiting this area that could have shed such a thing? If there was, I sure didn't want to come face to face with it. Now that the thing was out of the water and I was looking closer, I could make out the reason the tip looked so sharp—there was a gnarly hook attached to it... It looked predatory.

Our gazes slowly raised, in unison, to the treetops above the creek, as if expecting to suddenly spot the owner of the wing perched among the branches and glaring down at us with red demon eyes.

Lauren gulped. "I, uh, think Mr. and Mrs. Churnley should see this."

"I agree," Angie said, her voice slightly hoarse. "If there is some kind of weird animal living around here, they ought to know."

Our eyes returned to the wing, and silence reigned once again. Judging by my friends' expressions, it wasn't just me who found the idea of lugging this back with us through the woods, bringing it back *home*, creepy.

I cleared my throat, realizing we had wasted too much time already. Perhaps it was just my imagination, but the atmosphere suddenly seemed a lot darker than it had only a few minutes ago.

"Let's get going," I mumbled.

I slipped on my shorts and top over my dry-ish swimwear, and we hurried to pack up our things—Angie and Lauren not bothering to waste time drying off, just wrapping a towel around themselves. That left my towel and two of the other spare ones we'd brought with us to use in carrying the wing. We wrapped them around our hands to prevent direct contact. Angie lifted our bag over one shoulder, taking her turn to carry it, and we gingerly grabbed hold of the wing and started to tug it away from the creek.

I knew I was stupid for getting spooked over this—there was probably some perfectly rational explanation for what the wing was—but somehow I couldn't shake the feeling of eyes watching us as we trekked our way back home.

"Wﾠhat on earth?" Mrs. Churnley gasped.

We reached the house just as the last slivers of light were disappearing from the sky. Panting and sweating, we lugged the wing into the center of the kitchen/dining room and dropped it on the wooden floor. My hands were aching from having clutched the thing for so long; extra strain had been applied from squeezing tightly to keep the towel in place.

"Yeah... We really don't know," Angie said, wiping her brow with a towel.

Mr. and Mrs. Churnley rose from the table where they'd been sipping iced tea and hovered over the wing, their faces set in utter confusion.

"*Any* clue what it is?" I prompted.

"It looks like a giant bat wing!" Mr. Churnley exclaimed, voicing my initial impression of it, his eyes bugging with awe.

"*Where* did you get it?" Mrs. Churnley demanded, bending down and slowly reaching out to touch it.

"Lauren, uh, excavated it from the bottom of the creek," Angie replied, the shadow of a smirk on her lips.

"My, my, my," Mrs. Churnley blustered. "I have absolutely no idea what it could be, or why it would be sitting at the bottom of the water. It definitely does look like a wing, though."

"I'll go visit Mr. Doherty tomorrow," Mr. Churnley said, making his way back to his seat, his eyes remaining glued to the specimen. "Bring him here to take a look at it."

"Good idea, cupcake," Mrs. Churnley said. "Maybe he'll have a better idea. In the meantime, girls, maybe stay away from the creek?"

Lauren let out a dry laugh. "I do think so, ma'am."

We eyed the wing a few tense moments longer, before Angie made for the staircase. "Not sure about you, Lauren and Riley, but I'm pretty exhausted after all the fresh air and surprises we've had today."

Lauren and I nodded, saying goodnight to the old couple before following Angie to the staircase. Once in our bedroom, we collapsed in our beds. I *was* exhausted after the day's events, and all the physical activity I wasn't used to, but at the same time, the last thing my mind felt like doing was shutting down. It was still downstairs, stuck in that kitchen, mulling over what the heck the strange wing belonged to.

"I wish we had internet right now," I muttered, rubbing my forehead. I lay on my back, facing the shabby ceiling.

"Yeah. Could've Googled... "giant bats of Texas", or something..." Lauren mumbled, trailing off. I could hear the fatigue in her voice. Unlike me, she did sound ready to drop off. I guessed that cool water had really gone to her head.

Angie, taking the hint, switched off the light, and we lapsed into silence, listening to the distant murmuring of the Churnleys' conversation downstairs, then the sound of something heavy being dragged across the floor. They were probably moving the wing to one corner of the room, where it would wait for us till morning... Then came the creaking of stairs, the Churnleys retiring to bed.

Lauren's first snore of the night filled my ears, followed shortly by Angie's, and I turned over on my mattress to face the open window, to which I was closest. The moon's rays filtered through the thin curtains, casting pale light upon my face, and a gentle breeze caressed my skin.

I closed my eyes, hoping to begin coaxing myself to sleep, and slowly, my thoughts pulled away from the externals—from the weird wing, the creaky old farmhouse, and this crazy vacation I found myself on with my two best friends—and withdraw deeper into my subconscious, and the thoughts that I had locked away there, waiting for me just beneath the surface.

It wasn't a surprise that my parents were the first among those thoughts. Their faces, drained, and looking... so much older than the day I'd left home. It was a memory of the last time I'd seen them face to face—a little over a month ago, before my eighteenth birthday, when they'd appeared illegally outside my school, claiming that they just wanted to see me. That they'd brought me a gift. Jean had already arrived to pick me up, so I hadn't stood there behind those school gates, facing them, for long. But it was long enough to receive their little brown parcel in my two shaking hands, and the sight of them remained burned in my brain as if it were yesterday.

*You should see them*, a small part of me whispered, as it often did when the lights were out and the night was still. *They're your parents, and they won't be around forever, especially given their lifestyle. If you deny them even a simple meeting after all these years, and something happens... you'll live with that for the rest of your life.*

My parents had conceived me late in life, and I was a shock to them as much as I was to the doctors, when my mother checked into the hospital with a stomach complaint. My parents would both be sixty-one next year and were already riddled with various medical issues.

It was nights like this when I felt like a terrible person. I hadn't even opened the gift they'd come all the way to my school specially to give me. It still sat under my bed at home, where I'd shoved it to try to forget about it... because I feared what it would hold.

Because I *knew* what it would hold.

Its contents were the same as the last little brown parcel they'd sent me, six months prior. I'd rattled it to check; it sounded like photographs. Opening the previous set had left me a trembling mess. There had been almost twenty of them, snap-shots of a little blue-eyed girl, ranging from two to five years old, a toothy grin always plastered across her face—often eating ice cream or some other treat—and enveloped in the protective arms of her parents.

It was as if they thought sending me these photographs could rewrite history. Erase the childhood they had given me—everything that had happened in between the moments when a smile crossed my face for the camera—and replace it with the one they were presenting... and make *me* feel guilt. Make *me* seem like the monster.

The worst part was that it had worked. I hadn't been able to sleep that night, and barely functioned the next day at school. I'd suddenly found myself battling with doubt. I hadn't even remembered them taking photos of me as a kid, and I'd been nine when I left home. So very young. Could I have been exag-gerating things, in my immature little mind? Could there have been another side to things that I just couldn't see? They were my parents, after all. Surely they loved me? Why would they have bothered to take pictures of me if they didn't care?

Thankfully, Jean had been there for me when I returned home from school that day. It had been a difficult conversation for her to have with me for sure, because on the one hand she didn't want to demonize my parents, but on the other, she cared deeply for me, and she didn't want me suffering further because of a toxic relationship. In the end, she had simply stated facts: the police had found them guilty of physical, alcohol-fueled abuse and consistent neglect of a minor. They had gone to jail for it.

After she'd calmed me down, I had been able to remember why I was staying away from them, remember that it wasn't out of hate or vengeance, like they might have me believe. I wasn't doing it *because of* them, but *for* me. It would be a lie to say I didn't resent them at all, but that had faded, like a scar fades with time. I was keeping my distance because I was carving out a new life for myself. By genetics and upbringing, I was fated to follow the same path as them—just like so many young adults with dysfunctional childhoods who fell by the wayside later in life. But, by God, I wasn't going to let that happen to me. I wasn't going to be the repeat of an old song; I was going to be the damn definition of avant-garde.

That's why I avoided talking about my past life with my friends—even Lauren and Angie. I never told them that doubts still haunted me from time to time. Because they were my future. The people I had chosen to let mold me, with their happy childhoods and bright futures. They were part of a painting I was creating, stroke by painstaking stroke, of a beautiful spring morning, and I didn't want any black ink seeping into it.

I wasn't sure the niggling doubts would ever fully go away. Maybe one day I'd actually feel ready to face my birth parents again, but I couldn't pressure myself—or allow them to pressure me. They'd made their choices, and I'd been forced to make mine.

A sudden grating noise broke through my thoughts. It sounded like the gate bordering the yard outside. My first thought was that it must be one of the Churnleys, but why would they be leaving the house's compound at this time of night? And I hadn't heard any creaking stairs either. My eyes shot open, and I turned to look over at Angie and Lauren. They were both still sound asleep.

I slipped out of bed and crept closer to the window, looking out in time to see a tall, dark masculine silhouette moving with alarming speed toward the house.

The next thing I knew, there was a loud bang downstairs, and the dogs erupted into barking. Lauren and Angie woke with a start, eyes wide and gazing around.

"Wh-What was that?" Angie murmured.

I was already halfway across the room. "Shh! Stay there!" I hissed.

My brain was in a haze of panic, and all I knew was that my instincts were telling me to keep quiet. If this person was a burglar, then we should just let him come in and take what he wanted, rather than try to fight him off. There was literally nothing to take anyway—which made the situation even more bewildering. Who would break into an old shack like this? Whatever the answer, for all we knew he was armed.

The Churnleys' door opened as I reached the landing, and Mr. Churnley stepped out wearing nothing but a long nightshirt and underwear, his eyes bleary.

"Which one of you—?" he began, but I quickly held a finger to my lips, cutting him off.

"What's going on?" Mrs. Churnley emerged wearing a cotton nightie, her hair in curlers.

"Someone broke in," I breathed. "We need to stay quiet."

"Riley?" Angie whispered from behind me. She and Lauren were standing in our doorway, looking pale and utterly terrified.

"J-Just stay where you are," I repeated, barely daring to breathe as I inched toward the staircase, a shaken Mr. Churnley following me.

"What the devil," he cursed beneath his breath. "My guns are downstairs."

I prayed none of the floorboards creaked too loudly beneath my feet as I lowered myself and craned my neck to look down in between the banisters, trying to catch a glimpse of what the intruder was doing.

From my mostly obscured view of the kitchen, I caught a blur of black sweeping past the edge of the dining table—heard rapid footsteps pounding across the floorboards, and then, to my confusion... head outside. The gate groaned seconds later.

My heart was in my throat, and I stayed frozen in my position for several moments, wondering what on earth had just happened. Had I heard what I thought I'd heard? Had the intruder seriously already left? It remained quiet downstairs—save for the barking of the dogs—so I could only conclude he had.

"I think he's gone," I managed, my voice raspy as I rose to my

CHAPTER 3 | 33

feet. My knees felt shaky from the shock and the adrenaline still coursing through me, so I kept gripping the banister for support.

"Maybe he heard us wake up," Lauren said, her voice uneven.

Swallowing hard, I proceeded down the staircase, and the others followed. Arriving in the kitchen/dining area, we analyzed the room, looking for signs of disruption and anything that might be missing.

Nothing looked immediately out of place. The chairs were still drawn neatly around the table; all the kitchen cupboards and drawers were closed. He'd been down here for barely a minute, and clearly hadn't had time for any rummaging around.

*Then what had he been—*

"He took the wing!" Mrs. Churnley suddenly exclaimed.

Everyone stilled, scanning each corner of the room.

Indeed. The wing was gone.

*W*e barely slept two hours that night. We sat around the table, fruitlessly trying to make sense of the situation. The most absurd suggestion came from Mrs. Churnley: "Maybe it was someone's homemade Halloween prop that they'd left curing in the river, so they just came in to take it back."

To be fair to her, the suggestion was made at about seven in the morning, by which time we were all complete zombies. And it wasn't like we'd come up with any better alternatives—or really any alternatives at all. We went around in circles until I couldn't take it anymore and slumped my head down on the table.

After a bit of sleep, we all felt more human. We showered, and I was expecting the Churnleys to want to get in touch with the police as soon as possible, but Mr. Churnley decided to head out and talk to their closest neighbor, Mr. Doherty, instead.

"It's not like the man took anything that was ours, anyway," Mrs. Churnley said as she bustled around the kitchen cooking us all a late breakfast. "He clearly didn't mean any harm. Just took what was... apparently his, and left."

Angie, Lauren, and I argued against it, saying that there was no harm in calling the police—since we'd had a break-in after all, and they might be able to get to the bottom of the mystery— but it seemed that the morning had brought newfound confidence to the old lady, and she wasn't having any of it.

"We've lived here for decades without needing help from the police, and we don't need it now—whoever it was won't come back. Just don't go picking up any foreign objects and bringing them home!"

I knew it was futile to argue. Even if her stubbornness sprung from nothing but prejudice against relying on "the system,", this was her home, so the decision was entirely hers to make.

She offered to have Mr. Churnley drive us in the truck to the nearest town so we could talk to our parents about what had happened, if we wanted, but ultimately we decided not to. I didn't want to worry Jean and Roger, and Angie and Lauren felt the same about their folks. What was the point? Mrs. Churnley was right, in the sense that the intruder was highly unlikely to come back. It was clear he'd visited for one thing and one thing only; otherwise, if he was a petty thief, why go for such a weird, heavy object, out of all the other knickknacks in the kitchen he could have swiped?

As we ate breakfast, my mind wandered back to that journey home through the woods... that sensation I'd felt of eyes watching me. I shuddered. *Had* there been someone watching us? *Who?*

Mr. Churnley strolled into the house just as we were finishing our meal, clad in blue dungarees, sweat staining the pits of his shirt. He dabbed a napkin to his forehead and sat down in a chair with a creak, while his wife hurried to prepare a plate of food for him.

"I'm not ready to eat yet, Nora," he said, helping himself to a glass of water. "Just a few minutes and I'm off again."

Mrs. Churnley swiveled around from the kitchen counter to look at him. "Hm? What do you mean? How did it go with Brendon?"

Mr. Churnley laughed dryly. "He's no police sergeant. Was as clueless as us. But he did serve me a grand portion of his wife's hash browns...which is one reason I'm not ready for your lovely cooking just yet." He gave us three girls a wink. "But on my way back, I noticed someone's building a fence on the other side of the cornfields."

Angie sat up straighter in her chair. "On the other side of the cornfields?"

Mr. Churnley nodded. "Mhm," he replied, finishing his water.

"But we have no neighbors on that side!" Mrs. Churnley exclaimed. "Not for miles."

Her husband rose to his feet. "Well, there's a fence being built as we speak. I'm going to go see what's up."

Angie looked at me and Lauren, and I could tell what she was about to ask from the expression on her face. "Can we come with you?"

"'Course you can," Mr. Churnley replied, heading out the door.

We followed him, leaving Mrs. Churnley behind to finish her meal.

"Do you think…" Angie began as we walked across the yard toward the truck, a few steps behind Mr. Churnley.

"That the *lumberjacks* are building a fence?" Lauren finished, her dark brows raised.

Angie shrugged.

"This is all so weird," I said.

We had yet to even lay eyes on these mythical lumberjacks, so before we mulled over the strange twist of events any further, that was the first step—find out if they actually existed.

We piled into the truck, and Mr. Churnley drove us down the track toward the forest. As the new fence came into view, my eyes widened. When Mr. Churnley had reported that a fence was being built, I'd figured perhaps a dozen feet or so would have been set up by now, given that there had been nothing standing there at all yesterday. Instead, I found myself staring at a fence that must have spanned at least a mile in circumference, cornering off a large enclosure of the forest.

"How on earth—" I paused as three tall figures came into view, surrounded by strips of wood. The men must have been at least six feet in height, and they... definitely matched Angie's description. They were shirtless, the sun beating down on their bronzed skin, and held tools in their hands—a hammer and nails, while one of them held an axe aloft over his shoulder.

They went still, staring at us, as we trundled toward them.

Mr. Churnley sped up. "Hey, fellas!" he called out of his open window, the sound carrying clearly through the noiseless afternoon.

He pulled the truck to a stop a few feet in front of them, and as we all tumbled out of the vehicle, I laid eyes on the strangers —all apparently in their early twenties—properly for the first time.

The man holding the axe, who was also the tallest by about an inch, stole my attention first, and it took my brain a few moments to process his appearance. His eyes reminded me of winter, twin whirlpools of harsh steel and ice blue, while every-thing else about him screamed pool parties and picnics on the beach.

His sun-kissed skin had a radiant glow to it, and his hair was black, cropped close at the sides in an almost military style. He wore black pants that hugged him low around the waist, exposing a chest that was clearly the product of years of wielding axes. It belonged to a swimsuit model, a perfect canvas of sculpted pecs and abs... except for the scars that criss-crossed it, one even extending over his heart. I couldn't help but wonder what kind of terrible accident had caused those. His strong jawline also bore a scar.

I suddenly realized his gaze was on me and I had been gawking way too long. I quickly looked away, glancing toward his two companions. The man to his right was probably his brother. His hair was of the same color and style, and though his eyes were less steely and closer to sapphire, there were other marked similarities in the shape of their lips and broad facial structure.

The third man, the shortest of the three (though by no means short), had fairer features, with long blond hair tied back in a ponytail and pale brown eyes.

"*Dang*," Lauren breathed, voicing my general thoughts appropriately.

It even seemed to take Mr. Churnley a minute to collect himself, his eyes bugging slightly as he eyed them, before he cleared his throat, seeming to remember what we'd all come here for.

"Good afternoon! I'm Geoffrey—Geoffrey Churnley—and I'm from the other side of the field, Elmcreek Farm. Are you our new neighbors?"

The taller man's slate eyes rested on Mr. Churnley, and he nodded. "Not exactly, sir. We are here to work." His low voice rumbled up from the depths of his chest, and it was... definitely not Texan. I couldn't put my finger on what the accent was

CHAPTER 4 | 41

exactly. It was neutral and clear but had a slight foreign twang, almost British but... not. I wasn't great at discerning accents anyway, given how little I'd traveled. Maybe he was an immigrant.

"Oh, I see," Mr. Churnley replied. "And what sort of work are you doing here?"

"We've been hired to renovate the old farmhouse within this patch of woodland," the man replied, his expression stoic and his eyes wandering casually to the fence. "We won't be staying long."

"Is the owner planning to move here, then?" Mr. Churnley asked.

The man shrugged, still avoiding direct eye contact. "We wouldn't know, sir. We're simply here to do a job."

"Aha, naturally," Mr. Churnley murmured, squinting in the sunlight as he took in the length of the fence. "You sure put this up quick."

The man gave him a faint, perfunctory smile that told me he was quite done with the conversation. It seemed Mr. Churnley picked up on it too.

With the three of them working together, I guessed it was possible to put up a fence that fast—especially with a team as fit as this one. Not that I had any experience putting up fences...

"Well, thanks for your time," Mr. Churnley said. "We'll—"

"Um, one moment, if you don't mind," I interjected, not quite prepared to leave these guys yet. Mr. Churnley seemed to have forgotten what I considered to be the most important question.

I set my eyes on the taller man, who was now looking right at me. Focusing on my train of thought became suddenly way harder than it should have been. "I, uh—we had a break-in last night," I explained, furrowing my brow and shifting my attention to the other two men. "Someone came in through the front door and... didn't really take anything of value, but it was quite worrying. I guess this is a long shot, but I wondered if you'd seen anyone or anything out of the ordinary in the past day or two?"

I dared return my gaze to the taller man, and his dark brows drew together in a frown.

Then he shrugged, and responded with a single word: "No."

"Right, okay." I felt myself flush slightly, and exchanged a quick glance with Angie and Lauren, who looked like they didn't know what to make of the situation. Which was basically how I felt.

I hadn't been able to see much of the intruder last night, but the one impression I had been left with was that he was male and he was tall. How tall, I couldn't pinpoint—it had all happened so fast—but it was probably stupid to suspect these guys. Millions of men fit that descriptor, and from the looks on these men's faces, they really just wanted to get on with their work and get out of the heat. I couldn't imagine why they'd bother to break into an old shack to steal a... wing.

Honestly, I was beginning to think we might just have to lay this whole incident to rest as some unexplained mystery in our lives. Something so bizarre that there probably was some funny and complicated explanation for it, but one we'd likely never unravel. As long as the guy didn't come back, it really didn't matter.

After spending more than half the night talking about it, I was kind of done with the subject anyway.

"Well, we'll leave you to it," Mr. Churnley said courteously, nodding and backing away toward the truck. "Good luck with the renovation, and if you need anything, give us a yell! Happy to help."

"Thank you," the tall man murmured. His eyes passed over me one last time before he turned his attention back to the fence, his two companions swiftly following suit.

Lauren, Angie, and I returned to the vehicle, and seated ourselves all in the back seat. Angie harrumphed as Mr. Churnley turned the car around and we began rolling in the opposite direction.

"Well, that was... interesting, I guess," she said, her gaze taking on a dreamy quality as she stared out ahead through the windshield. "They sure were *fine*. Could any of you make out that accent?"

I shook my head, and so did Lauren. They hadn't traveled that much abroad, either.

"You said you saw four guys yesterday, didn't you?" Lauren asked, rubbing her forehead and looking befuddled.

"Yeah," Angie replied. "I guess he must be in the enclosure somewhere."

I heaved a sigh as the Churnleys' farmhouse came into view, replaying the brief encounter we'd just had over in my head.

The timing of everything was definitely odd—how the first break-in the Churnleys had ever had coincided with these workers arriving here, and—

I caught myself before I could venture further down that rabbit hole, reminding myself that it was pointless and would probably end up giving me a headache if I dwelled on it much longer.

*It was all a coincidence,* I simply reaffirmed to myself. *Just an odd coincidence...*

5

*I* managed to avoid thinking about the wing incident for the rest of the day, though it was hard to get the lumberjacks completely out of my head, partly because of just how damn good looking they'd been, but also because the noises they were making back in their enclosure echoed over to our land throughout the rest of the day. It sounded like they'd finished putting up the fence—the banging and chopping of wood had stopped—and they'd started shoveling something, perhaps rocks or cement, or upturning the ground itself.

We didn't talk much more about them, though, after our visit, and generally tried to distract ourselves with other things —which Mrs. Churnley made fairly easy, once she'd doled out our tasks for the day.

We set to work digging out weeds from the vegetable patch and then we took the dogs out for a stroll, walking them in the opposite direction of the woods, until we spotted Mr. Doherty's farmhouse. The old man was sitting out on his porch and noticed us before we could turn back, so what had started out as a short stroll ended up as a rather long outing, by the time we'd had tea with him and his wife. They were both exceptionally friendly, and due to the day's high temperature, much to Lauren's dismay, we were given ample opportunity to verify Mrs. Churnley's statement about the curly white chest hairs.

Once we managed to extricate ourselves, we headed back, and by the time we'd helped with some vegetable peeling and laundry hanging, the sun was already setting.

We had a small dinner with the Churnleys out in the front yard, and when darkness set in, we snuffed out the dining candles and went indoors. Angie, Lauren, and I made for the stairs, and since it was dark, there wasn't much else to do other than get an early night. The heat of the day still hung heavy in the air, and I was looking forward to splashing some cool water on my face in the bathroom. But Mrs. Churnley called out to us as we were mid-way up the stairs, bringing us to a halt.

"Hey, girls. I just realized we never showed you the tree-house, did we?"

We turned around to face her, and shook our heads.

"No, you didn't," Angie replied.

"Well, why don't you let me show you? It's just near the house."

"Now?" I couldn't help but ask. Nighttime didn't seem like the best time to admire a treehouse.

"I was actually thinking you might like to sleep up there tonight, given how hot it is indoors. There's mosquito netting and—" She paused abruptly, her voice faltering for a moment. "We used to sleep up there with our Ethan, around this time of the year. I-It really is lovely."

My voice caught in my throat as I realized who Ethan must be, and Angie immediately softened. "Oh, of course. We'd love to check it out!"

Mrs. Churnley's round face lit up as Angie grabbed our hands and pulled us back down the stairs toward her. She waddled into the kitchen, pulled open a drawer beneath the counter, and retrieved four flashlights. She handed one to each of us, keeping one for herself, before leading us outside.

Cricket song filled the night and the gentlest of breezes touched our skin as we crossed the porch and rounded the house. She took us to a tree-lined enclosure around the back that none of us had paid much attention to since our arrival.

She stopped at a tree with a ladder running down it, and as I tilted my head upward, beneath the light of our collective flashlights, I laid eyes on a quaint little treehouse, square in shape and lined with flower vines. It had four glassless windows covered with meshing, and the construction showed its age. It was also at least twenty feet up, though the promise of the view that it would afford was enticing, and I couldn't imagine Mrs. Churnley suggesting we go up there if it wasn't safe.

"Why don't you all head on up and I'll send Mr. Churnley out with some suitable bedding," she said. "You'll find mattresses there already— three of them." She sighed wistfully, then chortled, running a hand over her ample stomach. "These days Mr. Churnley and I wouldn't make it halfway up the ladder."

With that, she turned and left, leaving the three of us to decide which one of us would head on up there first. Predictably, it was Angie who volunteered for the challenge, and mounted the creaky ladder, while Lauren and I shone our flash-lights to light her way.

"First thing you gotta do is clear the area for snakes and spiders," Lauren ordered. She was already getting antsy about being outside in the dark, shifting from one foot to the other, and scratching at invisible itches on her arms.

"And for cockroaches, rats, termites, moths, earwigs, weevils —" Angie extended Lauren's list of horrors as she climbed, until Lauren told her to shut up.

Once Angie had actually reached the top, however, and pushed through the door to look around inside, she reported back in the affirmative. "Wow, looks amazingly pest-proof!"

"You'd better be sure about that," Lauren replied suspi-ciously.

"Pinky promise. The wood is well sealed, with no gaping holes, and I think this mesh stuff really works. Seems to have kept everything out over the years... except for dust... and maybe the odd patch of mold. But hey, we've got mold on our ceiling inside too." Angie's head suddenly disappeared from sight, and the floorboards creaked. "Woah!" she called a minute later. "The view up here, it's... ah-mazing! Get up here, girls!"

I didn't need asking twice. I gripped the ladder and scaled it, and when I reached the top, I realized exactly why Angie was gushing. The view was absolutely breathtaking. We could see for miles across the fields from up here, thanks to the moonlight. It bathed the landscape in a stunning pale hue, making it look surreal in its beauty, almost fairy-tale like.

I heard a grunt behind me and turned to find Lauren clambering up the last of the steps and staggering inside—careful to immediately shut the treehouse's door behind her. I thought the first thing she'd do was make sure Angie wasn't lying about there being no pests, but her attention was stolen by the view too.

"Okay," she said, standing next to us as we gazed out of the windows, "this is pretty awesome."

We admired the view for another minute or two, before directing our flashlights to our more immediate surroundings. There were three mattresses, propped up by wooden blocks on the floor, and one little bedside table with a cupboard, whose interior was empty. If there had once been a more elaborate set up here, I guessed they'd stripped it down after Ethan had passed away.

"Special delivery!" Mr. Churnley's cheery voice drifted up from the ground.

Angie hurried out and down the ladder to collect a large

shoulder bag stuffed with bedding from the old man, before thanking him and climbing back up.

He'd brought thick sheets for us to cover the old mattresses with, as well as three pillows, a water bottle, and a black waist bag containing keys in case we needed to return to the house. The water was an especially thoughtful touch, considering we probably would get thirsty during the night. We made our beds, gawked at the view one last time, and settled down for the night, enjoying the fragrant breeze wafting through the mesh and over our skin.

All in all, I was grateful for Mrs. Churnley's suggestion. It was so much more pleasant out here than in that stuffy wooden house.

"Maybe we should sleep out here every night," Angie said.

"Well, let's not be getting too hasty there, Miss Angelica," Lauren replied. "The night is still young." I snorted. "*But*, I'll concede," she went on, holding up a hand in the air, "I am more optimistic for a good night's sleep tonight than I have been since we arrived. This netting is quite comforting."

"I would've sold my brother for a treehouse like this, growing up," Angie said wistfully.

"You would've sold him for much less," I chuckled, recalling how mad her little brother used to make her. Up until the age of twelve, his favorite pastime had been setting booby traps for her around their house, which more often than not resulted in her showing up to school late, with globules of glue in her hair, or in some other similarly unfortunate state.

"Okay, probably," she conceded, "but my point stands."

"We actually *had* an old treehouse in our backyard," Lauren said, "at least, in the first house we lived in. My parents are the literal opposite of handy, though, so we never got it fixed up."

"You wouldn't have had much of a view anyway in that place," Angie added.

Lauren laughed. "Heh, yeah that's true. Just the train tracks."

My two friends continued their small talk for a bit, before falling quiet, allowing me to relish our surroundings. I listened intently, and discovered that the chirping of crickets was only the surface of the myriad of sounds that ruled the night. A soft, gentle cooing drifted over from the direction of the woods, along with the creaking of tree trunks and the whispering of leaves. I could even make out the tinkling of chimes in the distance— coming from Mr. Doherty's home.

I let my eyes fall closed as I dug deeper into the layers of serenity, trying to identify each unique sound, each instrument in the night's chorus. Mr. and Mrs. Churnleys' snoring soon became a part of it.

And then a loud shout pierced the air.

At least, I thought it was a shout. It was a booming, yet short sound, which had just been too humanlike to be a bark.

I was turning over to look at my friends when I heard it again, but louder and longer this time, drifting over to us from the woodland area.

"You heard that, right?" I asked, staring at Lauren and Angie.

Their eyes were wide, concern etched across their faces. "Yeah," Angie said. "Someone shout—"

It came again, longer and more urgent than before.

We all stood up and moved over to the window. "It's coming from that direction, isn't it," Lauren murmured, pointing toward the mass of trees.

"Yes," I replied. "I wonder who—"

When it happened a fourth time, it was closer to a scream than a shout, and there was no doubt in my mind that whoever was making the noise was definitely in pain. The near silence of the night amplified the noise, carrying it to us with unnerving clarity.

"Who else would it be but one of those guys?" Angie said after an anxious pause. "I think we should go and check it out. Make sure they're okay."

Lauren and I looked at her, and I swallowed, gauging the distance between our treehouse and the beginning of the fence bordering off their patch of forest. It was really no more than a ten-minute walk, and we had our flashlights out here already.

"Okay," I said. "I think we should too."

Lauren bit her lip. "Shouldn't we let the Churnleys know first?"

We paused again, looking toward the farmhouse.

"Honestly," Angie replied, "I feel bad about waking them up. If it's serious, we'll obviously rush back and figure out how to get help to him, but—let's just find out what's wrong with the guy. I mean, for all we know, it could just be a really bad stubbed toe..." She gave us a sheepish smile, and I grinned in spite of myself.

"Okay, I guess that makes sense." I raised a brow at Lauren, who was still looking dubious. "What do you think, Lauree?"

"I guess I'm just a little nervous about wandering around out there in the dark."

"Well, you don't have to come," Angie said, already rummaging around for our flashlights. "You can leave the initial recon mission to Riley and me."

"No way," she replied, frowning. "If you guys are going, I'm not gonna be left behind."

"Okay, well—let's get going then," Angie said, handing Lauren and me our flashlights. Lauren readjusted her dark hair in a tight bun, as if she was preparing to go to war or something, and then grabbed the waist bag Mr. Churnley had brought us and fastened it around her waist. "In case we need water." She flashed us a knowing look before we piled out of the treehouse and clambered down the ladder.

There was definitely no harm in bringing water, given how sticky the night was, but I didn't anticipate our being gone for much more than twenty minutes. Especially if we jogged, which I suspected we would, given how intense the shouts were becoming.

As we touched down on the ground and hurried toward the gate, I had to wonder if the noise would end up waking up the Churnleys after all. Then again, they were deep sleepers, so it wouldn't surprise me if they slept through it.

We pounded down the track leading to the woods, aiming our flashlights ten feet ahead of us, though the moon on its own was almost bright enough we didn't need the flashlights.

We didn't say much as we ran, since we were preserving our breath to get there as quickly as possible, but once we reached the beginning of the fence, we paused and looked at each other. The shouting was definitely louder now, meaning that it was, without a doubt, coming from within the fenced enclosure. But, now that we were here, we were faced with the predicament of —

"So, what do we do exactly?" Lauren asked in a hushed tone. "Climb over the fence?"

"No," Angie replied, eyeing the fence with a slight wariness. "I think we should just yell and hope they hear us."

And so we began to call out. "HELLO?"

"ARE YOU OKAY?"

"DO YOU NEED HELP?"

But the shouting continued undeterred, as if he couldn't hear us at all. Even when we yelled at the top of our lungs, it was as if it fell on deaf ears.

Angie huffed, her gaze passing along the top of the fence again, pausing at a few low-hanging branches.

"So maybe we should climb over after all," she muttered.

Lauren looked nervous, her lips twitching, but she nodded. I didn't actually think it would be a big deal. Several of the trees looked easy enough to climb, with many low branches. It wouldn't be any harder than climbing a ladder.

Angie went first, with Lauren and me giving her a boost, and I went second, climbing just high enough so that we could drop our legs over the other side, and leap down. There were other trees on this side that looked easy to climb, too, so I didn't worry about us getting back out—in case we didn't end up finding whoever we were here for, or he couldn't unlock the fence's opening for some reason.

Once all three of us were safely on the ground, we headed through the trees, guided by the ever-present shouting...which had finally grown a little softer, and now sounded more like groaning.

We hurried, careful to dodge brambles and fallen trunks— as well as a large pit that had been dug in the ground. I wasn't sure why they'd been digging a hole here, but the sight of it confirmed the shoveling noise we'd heard earlier.

After five minutes of walking, an old wooden house came into view, and my eyes widened. It was much bigger than I'd expected it to be — bigger than the Churnleys' home, with four stories rather than two, and about twice as wide. As we drew closer, I also realized that all the windows had been boarded up — and it was with new wood, which meant that it had been done only recently, probably in the last day or so. Which confused me somewhat, given what the guys had told us earlier. If they were here to renovate this old house, why had they boarded up the windows?

I shrugged the thought aside as we reached the porch. Five low steps led up to it, and twin wooden columns rose up on either side of the door, which certainly looked like it had seen better days. Like the rest of the house's exterior, the wood was roughened with age, and discolored by moss and mold.

"Am I the only one getting a creepy vibe from this place?" Lauren said quietly.

I shrugged. Yeah, I guessed the fact that it was built in the woods, and we were approaching it at nighttime, did give it a Hansel and Gretel vibe. Though I imagined that in the daytime it looked quite picturesque.

Angie reached the door first and was about to knock, when it gave way slightly under her touch. It glided open, creaking softly, and Angie looked back at us with a questioning expression.

Lauren and I said nothing, so she continued pushing it, until there was a large enough gap for the three of us to slip inside.

Once we were through, we found ourselves standing at the beginning of a long, dusty hallway. Everything was wooden, from the walls to the floors, and completely bare, except for a few dusty gas lamps fixed at odd intervals against the walls.

More than anything, I was taken aback by how high the temperature was. It felt like a wave of hot air had washed over us as we stepped in, and I found myself stilling for a moment, trying to adjust to the temperature as my mouth went dry. It definitely was a good thing that Lauren had brought water.

"Okay, yeah, this is pretty creepy," Angie whispered, eyeing the general decor—or rather, the stark lack of it. She pulled back a bit, so that she was level with Lauren and me, rather than ahead of us.

I refocused on the groaning, which sounded like it was coming from the other end of the hallway.

"Hello?" I called softly.

Still no response.

I wondered where the other men were, and from the confused expressions on my friends' faces, they were wondering the same thing. Were they all sleeping in this place? It seemed so... bare. But where else would they be? We hadn't noticed any kind of camp on our way here, unless it was set up around the back of the house.

I poked my head through the open doorways on either side of the hallway as we passed them, and each of the rooms beyond, also bathed in dim gaslight, looked equally derelict. Most were scattered with furniture, covered with thick layers of dust, and none of it looked like it had been used in years. Perhaps upstairs was nicer?

It was the strangest thing, but as we crept deeper into the house, I realized it was becoming hotter. By the time we were two-thirds down the corridor—having passed a set of stairs leading up to the higher floors—we had to stop and take a sip of water.

"Seriously, it's like an oven in here," Lauren gasped, stowing the bottle away once we were done with it.

I brushed away the sweat that was quickly forming on my brow with the back of my hand, and set my focus on the only door in this corridor that was closed — right at the end, and now only about five feet in front of us. This house was far deeper than I had anticipated; the hallway had seemed to stretch forever. I guessed the heat also had something to do with that impression.

As we closed the final feet between us and the last door, my ears picked up on something other than the persistent protests of pain. There was murmuring coming from the room—which meant other people were in there—but there was also the sound of... crackling?

It sounded like the crackling of flames.

"It's all right," a deep voice spoke from within. "It's almost over."

"Just think," a second voice added, "one more day, and it will be done. You'll never have to go through this again."

"You're doing better than we could have hoped, Ronad," a third voice spoke. "Hang in there."

*Ronad?*

More groans interspersed the comforting statements, and my curiosity reached the breaking point. I strode forward, gripped the handle, and pushed the door, springing it open wide and granting the three of us full view of the room.

Nothing could have prepared me for what we saw.

I had to be hallucinating.

I frowned, then closed my eyes and blinked several times, trying to shake myself to my senses, but when I opened my eyes, the scene was unchanged.

I glanced at Angie and Lauren, and from the look of utter shock on their faces, I realized they saw it too.

A fire roared in a hearth in the center of the room, beside which stood a small stand holding a round glass container, filled with reddish orange liquid. Huddled near the stand and in front of the fire were four men, bare from the waist up. At least, "men" was the first term my brain spat out for what they were. Unlike any man I had ever seen—or unlike any human for that matter —these men had skin the shade of ash, literally gray in color, and... wings. Two broad, black wings that protruded from beneath their shoulder blades, except for one man who was lying on his back closest to the fire, supported by some sort of stretcher—he appeared to have only one wing.

Lauren let out a string of curse words and stepped back, while Angie and I remained rooted to the spot. All we could do was gape.

The men whipped around at Lauren's movement, and I recognized three of them instantly—the three men we'd met earlier, outside the fence. Only, earlier they'd looked like bronzed gods, rather than some kind of ash demons from hell.

My gaze locked on the taller man, whose eyes had darkened to thunderous storm clouds. His jaw went slack as he stared at us, apparently as shocked to see us here as we were to see them, and a hard look came over his face, one so stony and unreadable it frightened me.

The next thing I knew, an arm as rigid and strong as iron had locked around my waist, pushing me backward, and then the floor disappeared from underneath me. I felt the sensation of intense heat around my midriff, where the arm was holding me, as well as against my back, which was suddenly pressed against something smooth yet rock hard. It was all I could do to not cry out at the surge of heat flooding through my veins, before my stomach dropped, and the last breath was knocked from my lungs.

I soared off the ground and flashed through the corridor and into one of the open doorways at what felt like lightning-speed, then landed with a thud that caused whatever strength I had left in my knees to leave me. The iron arm released me, the heat relinquishing along with it. I sank to the floor, gasping for air, and felt my two friends collapse on either side of me.

When I looked up barely a second later, the door to the room slammed shut, followed by the sound of a bolt being drawn.

We'd been thrown into one of the dusty rooms cluttered with old furniture. I scrambled to my feet and darted to the door, slamming against it, yanking the handle. It wouldn't budge.

"Help me!" I wheezed, panic setting my brain alight.

This couldn't be happening. We couldn't be stuck in here. With these... I didn't even know what they were.

My friends rushed to help me, but no matter how hard we slammed our fists or kicked against it, the door wouldn't move.

I paused, holding up a hand to indicate to Angie and Lauren

to do the same. I took a deep breath and pressed my ear against the door, listening, half fearing what I would hear.

Someone was murmuring. Were it not for the heated tone of the conversation, I doubted I would be able to make out the words. As it was, I could, just about...

My friends followed my lead, pressing their ears against the wood, and I gazed at them with wide eyes, one finger over my lips as I strained to hear.

"It doesn't matter," one of them spoke. "They've seen us, Navan!"

"I am aware," came the growled response.

"So what do we do? We can't keep them locked in there forever."

"We have no choice for the time being," a distinct third voice replied, similar in tone to Navan's. They all had similar, hard-to-place accents.

"I wonder how much of a problem it would be if we just... smothered them," a fourth voice added, and our breath caught in our throats.

"Forget it, Ianthan," Navan's deep growl returned. "You *know* that's against my code... We'll have to give them Elysium."

"Elysium? Do we know if that will even work on humans?"

"It will. It just requires the right concentration."

*Elysium? Work on* humans? *What* are *these men?*

It seemed that Lauren couldn't take it anymore. "Please, let us out!" she cried, and began banging against the door with her fists. "I swear, whoever you are, we won't breathe a word! Just let us go!"

The voices had fallen quiet. There was the sound of a door opening, and then swift footsteps just outside, moving toward the far end of the corridor. Another door creaked, and then all was completely silent, save for the soft crackling of flames.

It seemed they hadn't been aware that we could hear them. Which left me with the terrifying question of why they wanted privacy.

*What are they talking about now?*

*What are they going to do to us?*

I sensed those questions trembling in my friends' eyes, too, as we inched away from the door and gaped at each other.

6

*I* didn't know what was happening—all I knew was that we needed to get out of here before whatever *they* were, returned.

We raced around the dingy room, picking up any objects we could find that might help us break the boards covering the windows. But there was nothing we could do to get the wood loose. We'd need at least a hammer to have even a chance, and there was nothing close to that in here.

I had been afraid to try the door again, because it would make a lot of noise and draw their attention, but it seemed we had no choice. I hurried back to the door, Angie and Lauren right behind me, but we had no better luck than before in trying to pry it open. Not even a minute had passed when the sound of footsteps returned.

My chest constricted as I staggered back, instinctively gripping the arms of my friends and tugging them with me. Whatever those four were, they weren't human. There was nothing human about that experience of being picked up like I weighed nothing, then flung through the air so fast I couldn't breathe. Not to mention that unworldly heat that had coursed through me the moment he touched me. The rational part of me didn't want to believe it, even though I knew it was true.

A bolt drew on the other side of the door, and it opened ominously. I wanted to look away, close my eyes, but I stood there, rooted to the spot, and stared. The tallest man—Navan?—entered first, followed by two other young men, all of whom we had seen just a matter of hours ago, outside, by the fields.

I blinked hard, realizing there was something different about them compared to when we had walked into that fiery room. I was sure, absolutely positive, that they'd had wings— the same kind of black wing we'd found down by the creek—but now there was nothing shadowing their backs. Nothing at all. They donned black shirts, and the only evidence proving that my initial vision hadn't simply been a hallucination was their skin: it was still ashen.

"Wh-Why's your skin that color?" Angie stammered, apparently hoping—like I still was, deep down—that they were human after all, and perhaps simply part of some weird cult.

Navan took another step toward us. His gray-blue eyes took us in, one by one, before settling on me. His lips tightened, and then he held out his right hand, palm up. Resting there were three small cylindrical containers, each about the size of my thumb. I had no idea what was inside them, because the walls of the little containers were opaque, made of some type of metal—and the fact that he was holding them out toward us, like I should know what to do, just made the whole situation even more confounding.

He continued to stare at me as though I were the only person in the room, a hard frown on his face.

"We're not going to hurt you," he said suddenly, startling me. He had been so still, I hadn't even been sure that he was going to speak. "But you weren't supposed to see this. We cannot simply let you go as you are."

"As we are? What have we discovered?" Lauren croaked from behind me.

"Something I don't think you'll be able to comprehend. All that matters is you get out of here, right?"

"Yes," Lauren, Angie, and I said in unison.

"Then it's simple—each of you take a vial from my hand and drink its contents."

I stopped breathing for a moment. "Wh-What? What is it?" I asked, recalling that allusion to something strange called *Elysium*. For all we knew, it was some kind of poison or dangerous drug.

Not that I had any idea why they would want to poison us, or give us dangerous drugs. Then again, I didn't have any idea about anything in this scenario.

Navan's intense eyes bored into me, and it felt as though

everything else in the room fell away. I blinked, my heart pounding.

"You don't trust me?" he asked, and to my surprise, the tiniest of smiles curved the corners of his lips. I really hadn't been expecting that from this growly man, and I wasn't sure how to respond for a moment.

"I-Is that supposed to be a joke?" I stammered. "Of course we don't *trust* you. Who *are* you? Why are you keeping us captive like this?"

It was hard to read the expression on his face, though if I were honest with myself, there was a part of me that didn't mind having to stand there and scrutinize him... he was undeniably handsome.

*Stop it. That is completely* not *the thing to be thinking about right now!*

But it was almost as if he could read my thoughts, because that curious smile deepened, just a little bit, and his eyes seemed to sparkle as he held my gaze.

"Captive? I believe you were the ones who broke into this house."

"We didn't *break in*," I snapped. "The door was open and the only reason we were out there was because we could hear someone in pain and we thought maybe you needed help."

"How thoughtful," he replied, raising his dark brows and ignoring my initial question. "So let me return the gesture. Drink this and it'll wash your memories of approximately the last twelve hours. It will knock you out for about thirty minutes, during which time we will return you to your beds, and you will wake up with no memory of entering this house."

"N-No memory of tonight?" Lauren sputtered. "I'm down for that."

"Wait, wait." I held up a hand, frowning. I shook my head, trying to force my frazzled brain into some semblance of order. "Who are you, first of all? Why is your... *skin* like that?" I couldn't quite get the question, *And why were you wearing wings before?* out of my throat, so I settled on that for now.

He sighed. "You have a lot of questions. Now, there are few things more attractive to me than an inquisitive mind, but in this case—you're better off doing as I say."

*Attractive*? To my annoyance, my brain couldn't help but register the adjective, but I shoved the thought aside. I opened my mouth to argue back, but before I could, the guy I had guessed to be Navan's brother spoke up from his right, and now I could place it as one of the voices I had heard during our eaves-dropping. "Ladies," he said, clearing his throat, his voice almost the same tone and depth as Navan's. "You won't be getting anything out of us, so if you *would* like to get out of here, I suggest you take up our offer. Rest assured, we won't be letting you leave with memories of tonight."

Navan stretched his hand farther, pushing the vials closer toward us. I heard Lauren gulp as she stared down at the silver tubes, and I had to admit, the idea of being let out of here made it tempting to just grab one and down it, but... that would be really stupid. That would be something I would do in a panic.

And acting based on panic was never a good idea. Everything about this just felt so *wrong*.

I looked to Angie, wanting to gauge her thoughts, and, assuming I read her frown right, she was having the same doubts as me. Sensing Lauren was close to snatching up one of the tubes, I clutched her hand, and pulled her closer toward me, drawing the attention of all three men to me directly.

I glared back at Navan, trying to infuse my posture with confidence.

"We're not going to agree to drink some random substance," I stated, attempting to keep my voice even. "And you can't keep us here—that's a criminal act. I suggest you let us out now, or believe me, you *will* get into trouble. We have friends and family who will notice our absence very quickly, and there are only a few people in this complete wilderness who could be culprits. Given that you literally just arrived here, it won't take long for the cops to narrow it down to you."

I realized, as I stared into Navan's rugged yet very humanlike face—save for the gray tint of his skin—that I was talking to him as if he were a normal person who would be scared of such things as the police force. Given that my brain hadn't offered a better alternative yet, I was going to have to continue that hopeful train of thought... Which was probably a good thing for my sanity.

There was an agonizingly long pause as the men looked back at me with unchanging expressions.

"Guys," Angie ventured, her voice shaking slightly. "You

really just need to let us go. Please. We have family who love us and—"

"I would hate to have to force you to drink this," Navan cut in, once again completely ignoring what Angie and I had just said—and I became suddenly very aware of just how imposing he was. From the hardness of his stubbled jaw to the lines of his torso showing through his thin shirt, I realized he could easily follow through with that threat. His companions were not exactly pushovers either.

And yet, despite the threat in his words, there was something about the condescension in his tone that made me want to reach out and slap him. Whoever the hell he was, he had no right to thrust some arbitrary rule upon us, when all we had done was come here to see if they were all okay. They'd refused to answer even a single question of ours, and he expected us to just drink whatever crap he shoved beneath our noses?

"Sir," I began, planting my hands on my hips. Anger was rising in my veins and making me feel suddenly bolder, stronger. "There is no way we are drinking anything in this house, and there's nothing you can say to change that. It's not like you're exactly trustworthy, either. You told us you were workers, come here to fix up this property—and yet, it doesn't exactly look like you've been doing much fixing up around here, does it?" I gestured around the dilapidated room. "Why the heck have you boarded up the windows? That doesn't sound like *fixing something up*. Why were you all... crouched around that fire? What was that guy doing lying on the floor, groaning? Why is your skin gray, and why were you wearing wings?" There, I finally said it, and I could tell from the exhale Angie gave that she'd been hoping someone would finally voice that too. It *hadn't* just been our imagination, I was sure of it. "What are you, really? What you doing here? And why the hell is this house the temperature of a sauna in the middle of freaking summer?" My pitch rose at my last question, as I became aware of just how horribly hot I was. My clothes were drenched in sweat—which had been cold at first, from the panic and the adrenaline, but was now as hot as my temper.

As Navan and his companions stared back at me, I realized that I probably should've been more strategic in my questioning, and not spat out a barrage of questions at once, but my temper had gotten the better of me.

"I assure you that it's safe," Navan replied evenly after a moment, his hand still outstretched. "It is, as I say, a memory potion."

"A memory potion?" Angie cut in, her voice also stronger than before. "Seriously, what do you take us for? Kindergartners?"

Navan clenched his jaw, and although his face remained mostly controlled, there was the odd muscle twitch that told me we were testing his temper too. But I could hardly care anymore. This whole situation was *absurd*.

Now that I thought about it, they hadn't even asked us why we had come in here in the middle of the night in the first place. All they seemed to want was that we drink this potion that would knock us out. Ha. No way. It was dodgy as hell, and I was becoming more and more convinced that they were druggies who were members of some weird cult. That didn't explain the superhuman strength with which I'd been thrown into this room, but then again, maybe the drugs they used gave them such power.

"Yes, a memory potion," Navan replied, and I could tell from his expression that he believed what he was saying—and fully expected us to believe it too. "As I thought I made clear already, we do not wish to harm you, simply to expel you from this place. Think of it as us doing you a favor. A big favor. Because my next move is going to be something a lot less pleasant than this *scintillating* conversation we've been having."

"Look," I said, frowning. "I apologize that we barged in here —but I assure you, it was only because we heard someone yelling and we thought one of you might need medical assistance. You seem to not want any help, so let us go now, and I give you my absolute word that we won't tell anybody, not even the pol—"

Before I could complete my attempt at negotiation, Navan's outstretched hand suddenly retracted, withdrawing the vials, which he stowed in the pocket of his pants. His shoulders convulsed, and there was a ripping sound, and then something rose behind him... wings. Large, black, hooked wings shot out from behind his shoulders, and then...razor sharp *claws* emerged from his fingertips. He bared his teeth, revealing a pair of white pointed fangs. His very skin seemed to darken, along with his eyes, as his whole being turned into what I could only describe as a beast.

We were so stunned that it took us a few seconds to remember to scream. Lauren's went off first, then Angie's, followed by mine. We rushed to the back of the room, pressing our backs against the wall as if we could sink into it and emerge on the other side.

The creature before us growled so deeply, the noise rumbled through my very core, before he spoke, in the same voice that... Navan had just been speaking in.

"I told you this was going to be a lot less pleasant. So we're going to have to do this the hard way, it seems... Perhaps a night in here will help you reconsider."

He remained standing before us a moment longer, as if he wanted us to drink in his monstrous form and burn it into our brains. Then his wings, claws, and fangs retracted as suddenly as they appeared. He turned, revealing the shredded back of his shirt where the wings had burst through, and stalked out of the room, the others following him silently. The door slammed shut and was bolted once again.

"*R*emind me which genius suggested we go chasing strange noises in the middle of the night?" Lauren wheezed, about five minutes after they had left the room. It took us that long to discover our voices again.

There was no humor in her tone, just pure shock, and neither Angie nor I could bring ourselves to answer.

The first thing I did was grab hold of my friends' shoulders, squeezing them so hard they yelped, as my brain just wanted to be triply sure that we were not dreaming. We weren't.

We had stumbled upon some kind of supernatural creature. Not even my rational mind could doubt that any longer. What I had just seen was far too real, far too visceral—no amount of special effects could have pulled that off.

Then what on earth were they? And what were they doing here?

"T-These men are not human," Angie finally said.

"Glad I'm not the only one who noticed," Lauren murmured, removing her glasses, which had misted up, and wiping them on her shirt. "So, maybe we should stop referring to them as *men*."

I looked around the room again, desperately hoping to find some loophole we had missed the first time.

"We've got to get out of here before they return," I whispered.

It was maddening to think that there were less than a few inches separating us from the outside; if only we could figure out how to break through the damn windows. I used my flashlight to amplify the light in the room given off by the two gas lamps on either wall, trying not to miss a single detail.

I walked around the room slowly, examining everything—from the clock on the wall that had frozen at 9:05 AM, God knew how many years ago, to the chintzy floral green sofa, blanketed with dust.

An idea slowly occurred to me, and I gazed directly up at the ceiling.

It looked rickety, to say the least. There were fifteen long beams, stretching from wall-to-wall, and on top of that, it looked as if there was nothing but the floorboards of the room above, no plaster or cement. If we could somehow...

"We need to build a tower," Angie whispered, and I looked at her, realizing she had followed my gaze to the ceiling.

"A tower," Lauren repeated, now also staring at the ceiling. "You really think those wooden boards are loose enough?"

CHAPTER 7 | 75

I let out a breath. "We can only try. And we'd better do it fast."

Navan had said we would stay the night here, but that didn't mean they wouldn't visit us again to intimidate us.

And so we scrambled about the room, deciding the best way to go about this—which furniture to use, and in what order. We chose the small dining table first, then a coffee table, and above that, a basic dining chair. We were lucky the ceiling wasn't very high.

I took a step back, staring at the end result. It really didn't look safe, and I had no idea whether it could take my weight. But there was no time to doubt.

"I'll climb it first," I said, figuring that Angie was a bit too short for this, and I was more athletic than Lauren and would do a faster job.

"Are you sure?" both of my friends asked.

I nodded curtly, and then stepped onto the table. I climbed slowly, wincing each time the tower wobbled, but managed to make it to the top without the whole thing tumbling down.

Breathing heavily, I looked up at the ceiling and stretched out my hands, beginning to feel the floorboards, my flashlight clenched between my teeth. It was as I had hoped—they were loose—and from here, I could even see gaps, directly exposing the room above.

I just had to hope nobody was up there. When the guys had left us, it had sounded like they had retreated deeper within the ground floor of the house, so hopefully that was where they were staying.

I fumbled with the floorboards within my reach. They all felt pretty weak, like a hard enough shove could dislodge, maybe even crack, them. The wood had gone soft with age, the nails rusty and loose. This old house really was a wreck.

Lauren handed me up a piece of wood Angie had found in one corner, which had probably broken off from some piece of furniture. I gripped it hard, and pressed its tip between one of the cracks, using it as leverage until the board loosened and gave way, creating a hole directly above me. I then worked on the boards on either side, until I had created just a large enough gap for me to squeeze through. Given how fragile I had just proven the floorboards to be, I felt nervous about trusting them with my weight but... *Here goes.*

I placed my hands through the hole and gripped its edges, and managed to haul myself upward, until my head and shoulders appeared above the floor. I gazed around anxiously at this new room. It was dim, except for the light trickling through from the hallway. The windows were boarded up here too.

I lifted myself the rest of the way, until I was up through the hole and on all fours, floorboards groaning beneath my weight. I looked back through the hole, and my friends gazed up at me, their eyes shining with fear.

"There's nobody up here that I can see," I whispered down. And then I paused, realizing that it made no sense for them to come up, too. Not only was I worried about the floorboards' strength—perhaps they were the reason those creatures appeared to be sticking to the lower floors?—but also, we were much more likely to be caught with the three of us lumbering around.

"What is it?" Angie asked.

I hesitated, unsure of how they were going to react. "Guys, I think you should stay down there for now." They opened their mouths to respond, but there was no time to argue, and the more we spoke, the more likely it was the creatures would hear us. "Trust me on this," I whispered. "I'm gonna try to figure out where they are in the house, then locate an exit. If... If I think I can make it out, I'm just gonna run for it and get help, okay? There's more chance one of us will make it out of here than all three at the same time."

Their faces fell, and I could see what a hard pill that was to swallow. I felt it too, but it was the only way to go about this.

They looked at each other, then back at me, and nodded.

"Okay," Lauren said. "Just *please* be careful, Riley."

I sucked in a deep breath and nodded, then backed away from the hole, staying on my hands and knees as I crawled to the open doorway. Once I reached it, I stilled, listening. Everything seemed quiet. There wasn't even the faintest sound of the injured guy—perhaps he had fallen asleep.

Straight ahead was the staircase, and I moved toward it. I peered down cautiously until I was certain it was empty. I wasn't ready to attempt going down the stairs yet, as I worried about how much noise that would make. As I had told my friends, the first thing I had to do was pinpoint the monsters' location, assuming they were still in the house. I passed the staircase and crawled deeper along the corridor. Splinters wedged into my hands as I moved, and the floor was rough on my knees, but none of that mattered—all my brain could focus on was the location of our strange neighbors.

After a couple of minutes, I detected the sound of deep voices. I was sure they were coming from below the room directly opposite me, so I crawled into it, more careful than ever to move slowly and avoid creaking, until I was positioned directly over the room. I pressed my ear against the floorboards, and held my breath, listening.

"I can't believe we didn't sense their arrival," a voice muttered.

"Navan already warned us of this," a voice I had not heard before spoke up. It sounded older than any of the others—which made me realize that there were more of these creatures than we had seen. His voice held a maturity that I would attribute to a human in his late fifties. "This level of heat renders a coldblood's senses practically worse than a human's."

*Coldblood?*

"Anyway, what's done is done," the older voice continued. "There's not a lot we could have done to prevent it, and I would rather focus on deciding what to do next."

"What if, come morning, they still refuse to take the Elysium?" another voice asked. It sounded like Navan's brother. "It's not like we can bring them back to Vysanthe."

*Vysanthe?*

"They will take it," said the deep voice I now clearly recognized as Navan's. Chills shot down my spine as I recalled the demonic vision of him.

"They're going to have to take it within twelve hours of their arrival here," the older voice pressed, "or even the Elysium won't be an option, and we *will* have no choice but to knock them off."

"That is *not* an option," Navan replied pointedly, and in spite of all the other questions crowding my brain, I wondered why he appeared to be so against "knocking us off." Maybe he was afraid of the police after all? I couldn't imagine why he would be, when they could all just apparently fly away.

My curiosity burned, wishing I could better gauge his expression, and that of everyone else in the room. I lifted my head, searching the floor for cracks. I spotted one that I figured might just be large enough to peer through, a few feet away, and cautiously made my way over to it. The floor was thin enough that I could see through the hole and still hear what they were saying at the same time.

The room was small, about the same size as the one we had been locked in, and lit by three gas lamps. It was bare, except for three long sofas positioned around the edges, and some sort of coffee table in the center, which held a round steel bowl filled with a large pile of the same silver vials Navan had showed us earlier.

Navan, in his humanoid form and still wearing his ripped shirt, was prowling around the room, while three other men were reclining on the sofas. The three men consisted of Navan's brother, the fair-featured man with long blond hair who I guessed might be Ianthan, and another man with similar fair features, but clearly older... though not nearly as old as his voice sounded, which was odd. He looked perhaps in his late 30s or early 40s. I wondered if he and Ianthan were related.

Silence engulfed them as Navan continued to prowl, and I tried very hard to breathe only as much as necessary. My eyes bulged slightly as Navan's brother leaned forward and plucked one of the vials from the bowl, opened the lid, and downed it. Ianthan did the same, which made me realize that those silver tubes were probably just general containers they used for various liquids—in this case, some kind of beverage. Surely, *they* wouldn't be taking Elysium.

The older blond-haired man, after reaching for his own silver container and drinking from it, interrupted the quiet. "Killing them might *have* to be an option, unless you force the Elysium down their throats," he stated. "We simply can't afford to have leaky holes. Those girls will not keep quiet, despite what they may promise you now—especially not after your display, Navan."

Navan stopped walking, and I could make out the deep scowl settling over his face as he looked at the older man. "Jethro, this conversation is going around in circles. Just leave this mess to me—I'll deal with it, one way or another. In the meantime, I suggest you all get some sleep."

With that, he headed for the door and left the room, closing it sharply behind him.

Panic suddenly washed over me, as I feared Navan might be heading upstairs and would find me, but his footsteps did not reach the staircase—rather, they seemed to be heading deeper through the house, in the opposite direction. Hopefully, he was retreating to another room downstairs to rest.

I refocused on the room beneath me. The two younger men exchanged glances, and then sighed, before settling themselves down on one sofa each. The older man, Jethro, on the other hand, looked a little twitchy, like he wasn't quite done with the conversation. But after a few moments, he too sighed, before dimming the lights.

I waited for the sounds of him settling into his own sofa, and then dared to crawl out of my room and back into the hallway. When I reached the staircase, I waited, listening. My heart twisted as I thought of my friends, still waiting helplessly in that stuffy room, but I didn't want to risk going back there now to check in with them—it would only waste time and, after the conversation I had just witnessed, time was something we didn't have a lot of.

Once I'd gathered enough courage, I dared to broach the stairs, moving down them painfully slowly. My mind fixated on what Jethro had said about their "senses" being impaired by this level of heat, and I just hoped that would work to my advantage every time I hit a creaky floorboard.

When I reached the bottom, my blood was pounding in my

ears. I looked right toward the closed front door, and then left. My heart leaped into my throat as I saw moonlight trickling in from that end. The back door... it was open.

Balling my fists to keep my hands from trembling with anticipation, I moved at a snail's pace toward the door, my eyes fixed on the moonlight. As I neared, I felt the cool breeze slinking through the gap. I followed it, stepping out into the fresh night air. It felt incredible on my skin, after the intense heat of the house.

Feeling my racing heartrate slow a little, I looked around. A dense line of leafy trees surrounded a backyard, leading into the same woods that connected with the creek and the edge of the Churnleys' property. Tucked away in the shadows, the moonlight caught the edge of something... peculiar. I squinted, wondering if my eyes were playing tricks on me.

There, half in the trees, half out, was a beautiful, perfectly circular globe, bathed in the silvery glow of glinting moonbeams. It was large, the back end buried in the edge of the wood, though still managing to take up a quarter of the yard itself. Letting my eyes drift over it, I felt my jaw drop.

The design was sleek and elegant, and unquestionably foreign. Had it been a solid block of metal, it probably could have passed itself off as a human-made sculpture, but this was something else entirely. The outside looked as though it should mirror its surroundings, but it didn't. Light seemed to dance off it, and the reflection of the trees could not be seen within the polished metal of the globe. The normal rules of physics didn't appear to apply; I didn't know whether to be impressed or afraid.

My eyes traveled over the top curve of the globe, and I had to clamp my hands over my mouth to keep from gasping. Sitting atop the silvery surface was a figure, almost entirely camouflaged by the darkness. Where my skin reflected light, his seemed to absorb it. He was turned toward the woods, his upper body bare. His shoulders were sloped, his dark wings out, framing the scarred gray skin of his muscular back as they hung by his sides, his head bowed. Navan.

I watched him breathlessly, trying to keep my nerves at bay. He hadn't seen me yet, at least. I just thanked God I had spotted him in time. Now I needed to back away, and try the front door —I hoped I'd be able to get out that way.

I retreated into the shadows of the doorway, yet something about the sight of him gave me pause. If anything, it was morbid fascination. I wanted to get a look at this creature while his guard was down, while he didn't know he was being watched.

*What are you?*

I'd heard the term *coldblood*, but that didn't bring me any closer to understanding. If anything, it confused me more, as I remembered the heat that had flooded through me when Navan touched me. These men were hot as hell.

I watched the slight heave and sigh of his broad chest, the only movement he made as he sat up there so still, like some kind of dark predator, waiting for his prey... And yet, his posture exuded a sort of melancholy. Whatever the case, he appeared to be in a different mood than earlier.

*What is your story?*

*Where have you come from?*

I wished I knew, but I had run out of time to stand here and stare. I disappeared back into the stifling house, hoping that none of the other 'coldbloods' would come out of their rooms as I made my way back along the corridor, toward the front door. As I passed the room where we had first stumbled upon them, I heard the sound of deep breathing—and I guessed the injured guy was asleep after all.

He had been missing a wing, which by pure accident we'd discovered in the creek. Why had it been in the creek to begin with? By now, there was no doubt in my mind that it was one of these guys who had come into the house to re-collect the wing. Possibly Navan, judging by his height. Dammit, as much as I wanted to escape this place, my mind felt like it had been blown open, and I seriously needed answers. Hopefully, the police would help us get to the bottom of this—assuming they didn't think we were completely insane. At least there had been other witnesses to the wing—Mr. and Mrs. Churnley... not that they were the sanest people in the world.

Reaching the front door, I pulled the bolt to one side and was relieved to find that was enough to open it. I'd been half fearing I would need a key—and that would've been a real problem, since I didn't even have any hairpins on me to attempt to pick a lock.

*Easy does it*, I thought as I pulled open the door, inch by inch, until there was just enough space to slip through. As I emerged outside, I sucked in a lungful of air while pulling the door shut behind me. I winced, thinking again of my friends. *I'm coming back for you, Angie and Lauren, I promise.*

Then I bolted. It was dark, with so many trees hanging over this fenced enclosure, but I was too afraid to use my flashlight, in case it drew attention. I just ran, tolerating the scratches I sustained as I brushed past brambles and fallen branches. I kept my eyes focused in the direction of the nearest edge of the fence, which I could just about make out, thanks to the moonlight. My panting was loud in my ears, accompanied by the cooing of an owl somewhere in the treetops above me, and the occasional scurrying of some nocturnal animal in the undergrowth.

*Almost there.*

What felt like two minutes later, I was barely six feet from the fence. I sprinted ahead with renewed speed, when my ears picked up a different kind of noise. It sounded like...wind being displaced.

Wings beating.

"No!" I gasped, whirling toward the direction of the noise. I didn't even manage to see the approaching coldblood before it was upon me, an arm binding once again around my waist, crushing my rib cage as my back slammed against a hard chest, and my feet left the ground.

"NO!" I screamed, as the familiar heat surged through my skin from where his body touched mine, making me feel lightheaded. But then the air swiftly left my lungs as we hurtled through the trees at alarming speed, back toward the house.

I wriggled and struggled as much as I could, but the arm held fast. I was expecting him to fly me right through the front door and lock me back up, but instead, he was shooting for the roof. We landed with a thud, and I stumbled, terrified as I scrambled to find my balance on the mossy wooden slats. Once I'd obtained some semblance of stability, I raised my head to find myself face-to-face with Navan.

I cursed silently. Had he heard me running? Maybe his senses had become sharper again, having cooled down outside the house?

"Where do you think you're going?" he asked, his brow furrowed and toned arms crossed over his chest. "You do realize you're basically a mouse trying to escape from a hawk."

I glared at him, trying my best to ignore the painful lump forming in my throat. I was *not* going to cry right now—there was no way I was going to let him see my tears. Yet I'd been so close to escaping, only to be caught at the last minute. The frustration of that, more than fear, forced the tears to pool in my eyes and I turned my back to him, blinking furiously.

He spoke up again. "Well, I'm fine with the silent treatment so long as that includes you drinking the Elysium."

I wiped at my eyes quickly before whirling around to face him. "You basically just threatened my life!" I shouted. "You're telling me and my friends we have to drink some substance that's going to erase our memories!" My voice sounded strong, but to my horror, I could feel tears starting to fill my eyes again, and no amount of blinking this time was going to hold them back. But I kept yelling, because at least if I did that, I might not break down into sobs.

"I'm not drinking your stupid potion! We don't even know who you are! Or *what* you are! Or what that potion is! Who are you to even make such a rule?! You have no right to hold us here!"

He looked at me curiously. "You're crying," he said finally.

I wiped at my eyes again. "Yeah, no kidding," I snapped.

He paused, eyeing me closely, as if deliberating his next words, before informing me, "I don't like making girls cry."

I blinked, once again confused by his manner. "Oh, really? You could've fooled me. Just let us go, okay? That's all we want. We just want to leave without having to drink that weird potion of yours."

"I understand," he replied after a moment, his voice low.

"W-What?" I spluttered.

He sighed, rolling his eyes. "I said I *understand*. I understand that we have no right to detain you or your friends like this, but you're just going to have to trust me when I say there is a reason behind our actions."

"What reason?" I demanded, tears dangerously close to escaping from my eyes again. I choked them back, absolutely refusing to let this stranger see me cry again.

He started to say something but then stopped, pressing his ashen lips together.

"Please," I urged, my voice thick. "You can't keep us in the dark like this!" I couldn't bear the thought of being thrust back into one of those dust-choked rooms, probably with two of these coldbloods guarding us this time to make sure we didn't escape again.

I felt Navan's wintry eyes scrutinizing my face, as if debating whether to finally give in to my request.

I drew in another uneven breath, and repeated, in what I hoped was a calmer tone, "Please."

He ran his tongue over his full lower lip, then finally nodded ever so slightly. His voice was much softer when he spoke again —and once more it confused me what an utter contradiction his attitude was compared to the fearsome display he'd given us barely an hour ago. For that matter, his general demeanor was far more light and conversational that I would've expected—not just from a fanged monster, but from the stiff man he'd introduced himself as yesterday, when we'd first come across him and his two companions by the fence. I was still trying to place his personality.

"I see my attempt to scare you earlier didn't exactly work," he muttered, almost ruefully.

I frowned, surprised that he'd admit that out loud. He broke eye contact with me and his gaze passed casually over the empty roof surrounding us.

"In any case," he continued, "all I really want is to get all three of you out of my hair. I may be willing to make... certain compromises, in order to achieve that." His eyes finished their wandering and returned to me, imbued with concentration. "Are you saying that if I agree to tell you about ourselves, who we are, and why we are here, you will agree to drink the formula?"

I bit down hard on my lip, considering his words. It didn't exactly seem like a fair question to ask—our agreement to drink his potion would depend on his answers, of course, but... I was desperate now, and the idea of finally getting answers was too tempting for me to turn down.

"Yes," I replied bluntly. Though in my mind, I added, *I'll consider it.*

"Is that a promise?" He took a step closer toward me, close enough that I could feel the heat emanating from his imposing form, and it made me feel lightheaded again.

I took a step back, needing to place more distance between us, but I took a misstep on a patch of moss and slipped. His arm shot out to grab me before I could fall, and I gripped it hard, using it to steady myself again. I met his intense gaze as his nauseating heat flowed through me, his face a few inches from mine. *Close enough to kiss,* a voice whispered in my mind, and I shook my head in alarm, trying to banish it. Clearly, this was how my brain dealt with stressful situations—by suggesting the most ridiculous, outlandish thing it could think of. Kissing Navan—whatever he was—was the last thing I was ever going to do.

Swallowing, I nodded. "It's a promise," I croaked.

"Good girl," he said, the muscles in his face relaxing.

I frowned at his response, unsure of whether it was meant to be condescending or just... good natured, but before I could remark, he put his arm around my waist and lifted me up again, engulfing me in another wave of heat that made my head spin. He soared with me over the roof and down to the back of the house, where he planted me on the ground, near the back door.

As I found my footing and re-orientated myself, I was alarmed to see Lauren and Angie through the open back doorway, struggling in the grips of Ianthan and Navan's brother. The girls' hair was disheveled, and Lauren's glasses were askew and loose on the bridge of her nose.

"Hey!" I exclaimed. They all looked over—Lauren, Angie, and the two coldbloods.

"What's going on?" All four of them asked a variation of the same question in unison, which I probably would've found amusing, in different circumstances.

Navan stepped around me, and I gaped as his wings retracted beneath his shoulder blades... This was the first time I was witnessing it with his back facing me, and it was like one of those vacuum cleaners that sucked up the cord after you were done cleaning—the wings folded into compact lengths, before whipping back within his body. Where did he even have space to store them? I mean, their backs *were* broad, but... I shook my head, pondering their bizarre anatomy while Navan picked up his torn shirt, which was resting on a log near the door. He shrugged it on as he approached his brothers. "You can let them go," he said, gesturing to my friends. "I struck a deal with their friend, in exchange for them drinking the Elysium."

Angie and Lauren's eyes bulged as they stared at me. I nodded back at them, trying to give them a reassuring look—which was hard, considering I did not feel in the least bit reassured—before I hurried to them, grabbing their hands and pulling them out of the house, into the backyard beside me. Their skin felt hot, just like mine did, and I assumed it was the effect of the coldbloods' touch on them.

"We heard you scream," Lauren explained unevenly. The poor girl was shaking. "We climbed out of the room to come look for you—and we probably would've made it out if I hadn't dropped my damn glasses!"

"You really need to try wearing contacts again," Angie muttered, brushing down her shirt and shorts to straighten them.

"Guys," I said in a hushed tone, glancing hesitantly at Navan, who was muttering something to his brothers, his back turned toward us. "You're just gonna have to trust me on this one... At the very least, we're going to get some answers."

*a*fter Navan had finished talking with the other two coldbloods, he retreated into the house with Ianthan, while Navan's brother approached us. Angie and Lauren moved a little closer to me, and we all eyed him warily. He stopped a few feet in front of us and crossed his arms over his chest, looking us over.

"Since it appears we're all getting into the spirit of sharing information, I'm Bashrik," he announced, a genial expression on his face. Apparently, he had another side too.

"Um, okay," I murmured.

"Hi... Bashrik," Angie added uncertainly. He was the one who had been manhandling her just now, so I more than understood the hesitancy.

"And your names are?" he asked, smiling as if we had just met up for a first date.

"Uh . . ." I glanced at my friends, and they looked as befuddled as I felt. "I'm Riley—and this is Lauren and Angie."

"Riley, Lauren, Angie," he rolled our names around on his tongue. "Interesting."

"Not as interesting as your names," Lauren said.

Bashrik sighed, his eyes traveling back to the house as Ianthan and Navan re-emerged, carrying four chairs. "That's all a matter of perspective." Then he went over to where his brother and Ianthan were placing the chairs on the grass, about ten feet in front of the back door.

"A matter of perspective," Lauren repeated. I realized that she had also noticed the strange steel globe tucked beneath the shadows in one corner of the yard, and was gaping at it.

Bashrik followed her gaze, and smiled. "Ah, yes... That, I imagine, will be a part of our conversation."

"What the hell!" Angie exclaimed. "What is that thing?"

Navan took a seat directly opposite me. "We really weren't planning on having a bunch of teenagers crash our place tonight," he informed us. "So... I'm sure you'll forgive us if our hospitality isn't exactly on point." He gestured to the little gathering of chairs.

"Uh... it's okay," Lauren said absentmindedly, still completely distracted by the globe.

Bashrik seated himself next to his brother once Ianthan returned with two more chairs, while Ianthan sat on the other side of Navan. The older coldblood, Jethro, appeared in the doorway, glancing uncertainly toward us, but he made no move to come out.

Now that we were all seated, Bashrik introduced us by name to Navan and Ianthan, who nodded curtly. Navan sat up straighter and looked right at me, a resigned expression on his handsome face. "Well, *Riley*? Would you like to start this impromptu—and very *unexpected,* might I add—question and answer session?"

Of course I had a million questions, but now that I was being given the chance, my mind couldn't narrow it down to just one. I couldn't seem to get my mind to focus on anything... and the way he was looking right at me wasn't helping.

"What are you?" Angie blurted out before I could say anything.

Navan leaned back in his chair, contemplating Angie for a few moments, before replying, "We are known as coldbloods— although you humans would likely refer to us as vampires."

"*What?*" I spluttered. Though, now that I really thought about it, they *did* have that whole bat thing going on, at least with the wings. I had definitely read stories in vampire lore where vamps and bats had close ties, I just... never imagined that they actually looked like this... or existed.

"Vampires? *Cold*bloods? But why are you so hot?" Lauren asked, her face scrunched up in confusion.

"*That* is a long story," Navan replied somberly, and his eyes became clouded, distant, as if he were sifting through a long and troubled history in his mind.

He then cast a glance toward his brother and Ianthan. "Where do you think I should begin?"

Ianthan shrugged.

"You might as well start at the very beginning," Bashrik replied. "We still have time."

Navan rolled his eyes. "I don't remember signing up to be the leader of story hour." He then clasped his hands together, leaning forward in his seat, and cleared his throat as though he were bracing himself for something. "So... I suppose the first thing you ought to understand is that the life forms you humans are aware of, and who live amongst you on this earth, are not the only life forms in the universe. There are others... many, many others. Coldbloods are just one. We come from a place called Vysanthe—it is a world in a far corner of the universe where the sun barely touches." He looked at Bashrik. "This is stupid. I feel stupid."

"You're doing great," Bashrik said.

"Whoa, whoa, wait. Wait," Angie interrupted. "Another *world*? You... You guys are aliens?!"

The faintest smile touched Navan's lips, and his whole face seemed to light up. My stomach fluttered at the sight, much to my annoyance. "We are aliens to you as much as you are aliens to us," he replied.

"Mind. Officially. Blown," Lauren breathed, her eyes bugging as she continued to stare at the strange silver sphere. Yeah, that thing definitely looked like it came from another world.

I pressed my fingers to my temples and returned my attention to Navan. "So... You're not from Earth. Why are you here?"

Again, Navan shot a look at Bashrik. "They're not going to understand," he said.

Bashrik nodded encouragingly. "Just try to explain."

Navan huffed, almost petulantly, before resigning himself to continuing. "We are highly advanced," he said, "in ways that a human probably could not even comprehend. We are light years ahead of you in terms of otherworldly travel, and our rulers are constantly pushing their citizens for further innovation, in all fields of life... their current obsession being life extension."

"But . . ." I looked at Angie and Lauren to see if they had picked up on that. "If you're vampires, aren't you immortal?"

"We are trying to be."

"Uh, please explain," Lauren said, staring at him blankly.

"Your vampire lore is not accurate. We do possess some of the qualities featured in your stories—such as enhanced speed, strength, and sensual awareness. But we are born the same way humans are born—through conception—and we die the same way humans die, after approximately one hundred years, assuming external factors don't claim our lives sooner."

"Wow. So your lifespan is no longer than that of humans?" Angie reiterated.

"Our *natural* lifespan is more or less the same as humans," Navan corrected, casting his brother a grim look.

"If we consumed nothing but the blood of animals native to

our planet," Bashrik explained, "then we would die after about a hundred years."

"So you do consume blood, then?" Lauren asked. "Only blood?"

"Blood is our preferred meal," Navan replied. "And though we can drink other substances, too—especially for medicinal purposes—our bodies are not designed to eat solid foods."

"So... are you, like, sitting there lusting after our blood right now?" Lauren ventured, a morbid look on her face. "I'm totally not offering it to you," she added quickly. "Just curious."

Bashrik chuckled.

Navan looked less amused. "Your blood is too foreign to be immediately tempting to us," he said, looking at me even though it was Lauren who had asked the question. "It would have to be synthesized in order for us to benefit from it. After synthesis, however..." His expression grew dark as his voice trailed off. He looked away, toward the woods, focusing on no specific thing. "After that... your blood could prove to be very valuable to us, indeed."

His words hung ominously in the air, and for a few moments, no one said anything.

"What Navan means is," Ianthan said, breaking the silence with his higher-pitched, nasally voice, "your blood is most likely what our race has been seeking for the past four years."

Angie jerked forward. "Our blood?"

"Human blood in general." Navan's gaze had returned to me, and there were so many layers of emotion glimmering there that

I could only wonder what he was thinking. "Four years ago, one of Vysanthe's most... esteemed alchemists put forward what became known as the Immortality Theory. The basic essence of the theory is that the right type of blood could extend our lives indefinitely, as long as we kept taking it. For decades, we have known the effect that certain foreign species' blood can have on us—we have already figured out how to extend our lives for up to fifty years past our natural expiration with the use of blood from neighboring planets. So, immortality is naturally the next step.

"The theory posed that the farther the planet, the harder the blood is to synthesize, but the more effective it is once we have figured out how to absorb it. The alchemist argued that there was likely some planet in the universe whose predominant species' blood held the right potency and balance of chemicals to achieve immortality—we just needed to venture far enough."

He paused, and I realized I was hardly breathing.

"And you believe that blood is ours," I said slowly, the pieces suddenly falling into place. "You never planned to return us back home after we drank the Elysium—you were going to kill us and drink our blood!" My muscles tensed and my eyes shot to the doorway, where Jethro still stood.

Navan held up a hand and shook his head.

"Our *race* is out for your blood. We, however"—he gestured to his small group—"are not."

"Then why are you here?" Angie asked, her blue eyes narrowing.

"Navan would never take credit for this, but he personally discovered Earth about a year ago," Bashrik said.

"As far as I am aware, nobody other than the coldbloods with me here on this patch of land are even aware of Earth's existence yet," Navan said, ignoring his brother.

"How did *you* discover Earth then?" I asked. "And how can you be sure you're the only ones?"

"Because I am a man of high rank back on Vysanthe—one of two Chiefs in charge of exploration missions. I know the type of technology that is available to our teams... and none of it is yet advanced enough to reach this far into the universe. My ship is unique." He added this last part haltingly, almost shyly, as if he didn't want to let on how proud he was of the ship. He glanced at the silvery sphere, a flicker of fondness in his eyes. "It's the only one capable of traveling the distance. Jethro is a gifted mechanic as well as an experienced medic, and together, we figured out how to build what our fellows couldn't. At the time, I just wanted a ship better than anyone else so that I could... well, get as far away from Vysanthe as possible."

"Why is that?" I asked, frowning.

Navan looked truly uncomfortable at the question, and my fear that we were about to be devoured ebbed. "I'm sure you've got your ideas about who we are, what we're like," he said. "I'd venture to say they're probably all wrong. Let's just say I'm not proud of my species. I was originally trained as an alchemist, but about midway through my training, I decided to become an explorer instead—mainly because it afforded me frequent opportunities to get away from a culture that I honestly *despise*."

He practically spat the last word, and I was taken aback by his emotion. It felt like a very personal thing for him to share with us, and I wasn't expecting him to go this deep into his personal history. Now that he was, however, I'd be damned if I didn't make the most of it. "Why do you hate it so much?" I pressed.

He looked up at me, and it suddenly felt as if everything else had fallen away, that we were the only two in the room. "I'm not sure if this is included in our little question and answer session," he muttered.

"It's a question," I said. "So you have to answer."

"Do I?" he asked softly—his tone somewhere between curious and dangerous. "I'm not used to being told what to do."

I held his gaze, swallowing. "Yes," I said. "You do."

The seconds ticked by, and I found myself uncertain of how he was going to respond. His stare sent an almost electric shiver through me. My surroundings seemed to blur as the world narrowed down to just the two of us, existing in our own private universe. I had never experienced anything like it before—was it some sort of mind trick? I'd had trouble holding his gaze when we'd first met in the fields, too. It felt as though we had some sort of connection, though I knew how crazy that sounded. He was a creature from another planet—why the hell would I feel a connection with something like that?

He took a deep breath, breaking eye contact, and rubbed his

hand across the lower part of his face. "Well... Where do I start?" he said, resuming his former conversational tone. "In a nutshell, what I hate most about my kind is that their every accomplishment has been earned at the cost of others. They take pride in what they can plunder, rather than what they can create. I don't want to be like that."

"What do you mean?" I asked. "I'd think if you were so advanced, you'd be able to create plenty."

"They build their furniture from the bones of species they have driven to extinction and display it with pride in their homes; they boast cellars of blood from foreign creatures far too full for them to ever consume before expiry; they leech resources from planets on a whimsy, regardless of the consequences it might have for the local population. Once Vysanthe discovers a land that possesses something it wants, it will keep gnawing at it like a dog gnaws at the leg of a deer, piece by piece, sinew by sinew, until there's nothing left." He paused and drew in a deep breath. "Basically, I needed an excuse to get away; buy myself periods of time where I could just float in a vacuum without bumping into anyone of my own kind, clear my head, under the guise of embarking on missions to discover new species for our leaders' plans. And so... I'm thankful that Jethro helped me build *Soraya* over there." He cast a meaningful look at the older coldblood, and then another fond look at his ship.

"Well," I murmured, feeling quite speechless. "*Soraya's* a beautiful ship."

"For the longest time, Navan didn't tell anyone about his

discovery of Earth," Bashrik said. "He didn't even tell *me*. Can you believe it?" His eyes widened, as though we should be shocked by that. "Though, he discovered quickly after his arrival here by taking a blood sample that human blood held the properties we were seeking. He should have returned to report his findings to our authorities—if he's found to have kept Earth hidden, it would result in a level of punishment you couldn't imagine but... you didn't report, did you, Navan?"

Navan sighed. "I couldn't."

"Because you didn't want to be responsible for the damage your people would do to yet another planet—and you'd rather risk punishment?" I asked.

"Something like that... It's nothing I'd expect you to understand."

"Why is that? Because you're so much more advanced than we are?" I asked, frowning. "And why are you and your brother and friends here so different from the rest of your species?"

Navan shrugged, a muscle in his jaw twitching. "Every creature in the universe is born with free will. We can choose to be different, even if we share the same anatomy."

That... was true.

"What are you all doing here, exactly?" Lauren asked.

"We're trying to help Ronad," Navan replied, casting a furtive glance toward the house.

"So is Ronad one of your brothers, too?" Angie asked, looking from him to Bashrik.

"In a way, yes. He's not a blood relative, like Bashrik, but I do see him as a brother. I've actually got nine brothers, but only two whom I actually trust."

"I see," I said slowly, wondering how that must feel, to have so many brothers yet be unable to trust them. I was an only child, so I had zero experience of what it was like to have even one sibling, never mind nine.

"What happened to him?" Angie asked. "How did he get injured?"

"Injured would be the wrong word," Bashrik replied. "He is, uh, undergoing a transformation—for which we all decided to come to support him."

"Transformation?" I repeated.

Navan stood up and started pacing. "When I got here, I conducted a few experiments. Mostly because I was curious to know how a creature like myself might blend in better with Earth's environment, should I decide I'd like to spend a few days at a time here. I used my alchemy skills to develop a formula that would allow us to better adapt to Earth's atmosphere. Our bodies naturally conduct coldness—we are freezing by nature—but the formula I developed allows us to absorb warmth, and essentially become a conductor of heat. The more exposed we are to the heat, the hotter we become—and the daylight has an effect on our skin. It absorbs its rays and turns golden."

"So you're kind of like . . . a reptile," I said, blown away by everything he was saying. To have the knowledge and skills to invent a formula that could have that level of transformation... It was impressive to say the least.

CHAPTER 8 | 105

"And Ronad?" Lauren prodded.

Navan turned his back on us to face the house. "That's a story for another time. We've suffer—I mean, he's suffered a great loss and can no longer bear to live in Vysanthe. Let's just leave it at that. I want to do whatever I can to help him. We are in the process of giving him a treatment that we hope will have a more permanent effect. It would allow him to adopt a warm-bodied, human-like form on a permanent basis, so he can stay on Earth full time. He would live off the blood of wild animals and keep to himself. A side effect of the treatment is losing the wings... and a lot of pain. But by tomorrow night, we should have finished our business here."

"And then where will you go? And why come here, to this place in particular? Why were you digging a hole out the front?" I asked. There were still so many questions racing through my brain.

"I'm touched by your concern, really," he replied somewhat sarcastically, "but you don't have to worry about where we're heading next. Probably back to Vysanthe, because our absence would be noted otherwise, and we cannot afford to arouse suspicion. We will take one of Ronad's wings back with us and claim he suffered a fatal accident during an excursion, and the wing is all we have left of him." Navan and Bashrik exchanged a glance, and I could sense the sorrow between them at having to leave Ronad behind.

"As for why here?" Navan continued. "This area is particularly hot, so conducive for our purposes. I had landed in the vicinity a while ago, and discovered this abandoned house. I had left some money and supplies hidden underground around the front of the house—which is why there's a hole."

"So you threw your brother's wing into the creek?" Angie said.

"And then broke into our house to steal it?" I said.

"It's not stealing if it belongs to you," Navan retorted, and I could sense that he'd finally lost his patience. "And no one was supposed to find it in the creek. It's best for everyone that humans remain unaware of us, which brings us to the conclusion of this enlightening question and answer session." He reached into his pants pocket and withdrew the three silvery vials of Elysium. "I held up my end of the bargain," he continued. "Now, it's your turn. Trust me when I say our world is not something you want to get mixed up in."

His wintry gaze found me again, and I suddenly felt a dull ache in my chest. If I drank the Elysium, everything about tonight would be wiped from my mind... Everything.

*I* stared at the silver tubes, a wave of dread washing over me.

I was *not* just going to forget everything.

My mind had been expanded in ways I could never have predicted, and the thought of going back to complete ignorance was just... unbearable. It would feel like something had been taken from me, something precious.

But I had made a promise to Navan, and he was right—he had held up his end of the bargain. He hadn't tried to lie, and he'd been patient in his explanations.

"Okay," I said, my voice hoarse, my eyes glued reluctantly on the little vials. "Since we're going to lose our memory of the past twelve hours, can I... can I have a quick, private word with my friends?"

I didn't have a plan; I was just trying to stall the inevitable.

Have at least a few more minutes to get my thoughts in order before they were wiped out.

Navan looked as if he were about to say no, but then he relented. "Five minutes," he said, nodding toward the house. He met my gaze. "Don't get any ideas about trying to escape again," he added. "You're the mouse, remember?"

I swallowed, and headed toward the back door, Angie and Lauren behind me. Jethro stepped out of the doorway, silently watching us enter. The heat swallowed us whole as we made our way along the corridor. I ran a hand along the wooden wall and pushed against the first unlocked door that we reached.

"Mouse?" Lauren asked, confused. "What is he talking about?"

"He basically snatched me off the ground like a hawk would a mouse," I replied, remembering the feel of his arms pressed against me. I pushed the memory from my mind... If I wanted to keep *any* of these memories, I needed to focus. I had an idea, but it would be risky to pull off.

We were in the same room I had witnessed the coldbloods' earlier conversation in, with the three sofas and the bowl of silver vials sitting on a coffee table. I looked at my friends, my throat dry. "Guys," I said, my voice barely louder than a whisper, "do you really want to forget all this?"

If I'd asked that question a few short hours ago, the answer would have been a resounding YES, but now, I could see from their expressions that they felt the same way I did.

*How could we forget it all?*

Lauren sighed. "I don't want to forget. I mean, if there really is some deadly species out there in space looking for us all, I kind of want to know about it... But I also want to get out of here. I want to go home."

Angie nodded anxiously. "Ditto. And there's no telling what they'll do to us if you refuse to uphold your end of the deal."

I held my breath, my eyes returning to the bowl of vials.

"Riley?" Lauren said, her gaze following mine to the table. "What are you thinking . . .?"

I approached the bowl and picked three vials up, then turned toward my friends. I held out the silver cylinders in my palm, identical to the ones Navan was waiting outside with. "Since we all seem to be on the same page... What if we did a little hide-and-swap trick?"

They blinked, staring at me blankly.

"I know for a fact it's not Elysium in these vials," I said. "I haven't had a chance to tell you yet, but I did some eavesdropping and saw Ianthan, Jethro, and Bashrik drinking from this pile."

Their eyes widened, but I could see the idea sinking in, and they realized the same thing I had—it actually wouldn't be that difficult. The vials were small enough for us to hold discreetly in our palms without even looking like we were carrying anything. We'd just have to slip the real Elysium vials somewhere out of sight, while we pretended to fall unconscious.

"But . . . what is in *these* vials?" Lauren asked as they each took one from my hand. We unscrewed the tops and took a sniff.

I could barely pick up any scent, and the liquid inside seemed thin.

"It must be some kind of drink," I said, closing the lid.

Lauren's lip curled in disgust. "It must be blood."

"It doesn't smell coppery, though," Angie said.

"Whatever it is, it's not Elysium." We didn't have time to stand around debating. I wanted us to be out of this room before they came looking for us, in case they ended up putting two and two together. "And I'm guessing it won't kill us since I saw them drinking it. It could make us sick, though, given that our immune systems are different from theirs... The question is, is this something we're willing to risk? We need to hurry and decide."

*Were* the rewards worth the risk? It might have been reckless, but in that moment, I truly felt that they were. Remembering everything we'd just learned seemed worth risking an upset stomach. I didn't want to pressure my friends, however; this was a decision they had to make all on their own.

After a moment, Angie nodded, as did Lauren. They looked as uncertain as I felt, but also resigned.

"Okay," I whispered, and then quickly explained how we could make the switch.

Then we returned outside. The four of them were sitting on the chairs, though Navan stood the second we came out.

"Glad you didn't get any ideas in your head to do something foolish," he said, and I clutched the "fake" Elysium tighter in my hand. He outstretched his own hand, with three vials on it. I took one, my heart pounding, knowing if I slipped up, it could be all over for us. Navan was watching me, but I smoothly switched the vials in my palm, keeping my gaze on him the whole time. I unscrewed the fake Elysium containing who knew what substance, and, closing my eyes, tipped it into my mouth.

To my alarm, a rush of darkness flooded through my brain almost as soon as I had swallowed the slightly salty substance, and I wondered in a panic if I had messed up and drunk the Elysium after all. I barely had time to stuff both vials into my pocket before darkness claimed me, and Navan's piercing slate eyes faded to black.

*I* woke up to the smell of something deep-fried, and I could detect bright sunlight from beneath my closed eyelids. Someone was talking downstairs—two people— and I was lying on... a bed.

I managed to un-glue my eyelids and sit up, feeling completely disorientated. I was in our bedroom, in the Churnleys' house, my two friends sprawled out in the beds next to mine, still asleep.

For several long minutes, I couldn't remember anything. Then, the previous night's memories suddenly came rushing back.

I hadn't forgotten. I had not taken the Elysium, as I had feared. It was a coincidence that whatever it was I *had* drunk, also knocked me out almost instantly—and kept us asleep for... I glanced at the clock. *Geez.* For twelve hours. Granted, I didn't know exactly what time the coldbloods had returned us, but it was already 2:30 PM.

I swung my feet off the bed and stood up, before a wave of nausea forced me back down. I wasn't sure if it was because I had stood up too quickly, or if it had something to do with the after-effect of the coldbloods' beverage. A salty aftertaste lingered in my mouth, and the thought of it being some type of blood made me want to gag.

I dropped to the floor and crawled to the bathroom, using the sink to prop myself up so I could rinse my mouth out. After a minute, I felt ready to try and stand again, and this time I did so successfully, without all the blood rushing from my head.

I stared at myself in the mirror. My blue eyes were blood-shot, and my brown hair looked like I had been dragged backward through a jungle. My clothes were torn, and my shins and knees were covered with cuts, scrapes, and bruises.

I returned to the bedroom, glancing at the window sill. The coldbloods couldn't have known that we had been sleeping in the treehouse, and must have slipped us in here through the open window. I was surprised to see each of our flashlights resting atop the sill, along with the black waist bag Lauren had been wearing. It was thoughtful of them to return those, too.

"Hey," Angie said from behind me, rubbing her eyes and holding her head like she had a hangover.

"Hey," I replied as I sat back down on the bed and folded my legs beneath me. "How are you feeling?"

"I've felt better," she croaked. "But I remember everything. And I don't feel like I'm dying—yet."

She leaned over to Lauren's bed and shook her awake.

"No! Stop! Wha-What are you—" Lauren babbled, as she rose to consciousness. She bolted upright, her dark hair pointing every which way. She stared at us blearily before reaching for her glasses, which had been left on her bedside. Another thoughtful touch, I noted.

"Are you okay? Do you remember?" Angie asked.

Lauren groaned, closing her eyes again. Her brow furrowed, and then she nodded. "Yeah. I remember. And I... I think I feel okay. Just like I could sleep for another six hours."

"Okay, good," I said. At least we hadn't gotten sick from whatever we had drunk—not yet, anyway.

"Girls? Are you awake?" Mrs. Churnley's voice called from downstairs.

Guilt gripped my chest as I remembered what it had meant to her that we sleep outside in the treehouse—after all the trouble she had gone to show it to us, and Mr. Churnley bringing up special bedding. I felt awful.

I stumbled to the door and opened it, calling down, "Hi, Mrs. Churnley. Yeah, we're awake. I'm-I'm sorry we—"

"Slept so long?" Mrs. Churnley asked, and I was sure there was a slight note of disappointment in her tone.

"Yeah, we, uh..." I looked back over my shoulder at Angie, struggling to come up with a reason why we had come back indoors.

She came to my rescue. "We got a bit chilly out there in the treehouse, surprisingly, once early morning kicked in. We would love to sleep there again tonight, with some heavier blankets. We didn't get a great night's sleep, which is probably why we slept in so late."

"Ah, I see." That seemed to placate Mrs. Churnley. "Well, lunch is almost ready."

"Thank you so much," I replied. "We'll be down soon."

We closed the door and backed into the bedroom, turning to look at Lauren. I stuck a hand in my pocket and pulled out the two silver vials. My friends retrieved theirs, and a long moment of silence passed between us. I was sure we were all realizing the same thing.

Pretending last night hadn't happened was going to be hard.

***

My friends and I were so quiet during lunch it prompted Mrs. Churnley to ask us several times if we were okay. A part of me wished we could tell them the truth, but I felt bad enough about breaking my promise to Navan and not taking the Elysium, and it did seem that he and his companions had Earth's best interests at heart—given their mostly gentle treatment of us, and the fact that they were keeping Earth a secret from their race. They could've been lying about that, I supposed, but they had seemed genuine. Otherwise, why would they have let us go, instead of abducting us back to their homeland for our valuable blood?

I shuddered as I recalled Navan's description of his home-land; I felt sure he had good reasons for wanting coldbloods to remain a secret from humans. Besides, nobody would believe us anyway. The police would think we had lost our minds, and we didn't even have the wing anymore for them to analyze. We had never even thought to take a picture of it.

We ate lunch quickly and then set about our chores for the day. We began with the garden, doing some general mainte-nance, and then swept and mopped around the patio where the dogs spent most of their time.

There wasn't much we could talk about as we worked, since we were so close to the house. All the windows were open, and the Churnleys could hear us. But when Mrs. Churnley sent us to the overgrown blackberry bushes at the border of their land, near the woods, we eased up a little.

"A part of me still thinks it was a dream," Angie said, bending down to pluck a cluster of plump blackberries by her knees.

"I'm past that," I replied, dropping a handful of berries into my plastic bowl.

"Me too," Lauren said. "It doesn't feel any less weird though."

I nodded, sighing. My head was still reeling, and the consequences of last night were beginning to hit me. We would have to spend the rest of our lives with this incident living in our brains. With our minds expanded and blown open, in a way nobody else's on the planet was. It would almost feel like we were living in a different reality to the rest of Earth's population, everything seeming suddenly so... terribly mundane.

*You should have taken the Elysium,* a small, nagging voice whispered in my head. *Then you could have simply resumed your life, carefree and normal.*

I couldn't entirely dismiss the voice, because it held a note of truth. Sometimes ignorance *was* bliss. And yet, even now, in hindsight, I still couldn't bring myself to regret our decision to throw the vials away. Yes, ignorance could be bliss, but sometimes the truth was simply too illuminating to let go of, in spite of the consequences.

At least I had Angie and Lauren for company. Without them, I probably would have been a lot more worried. Maybe a silver lining existed in all of this—maybe this incident would turn out to be the thing that kept us close in our adult years, even if physical distance tore us apart. That was the only comfort I could cling to as the aftermath of last night overwhelmed my brain.

We let ourselves fall into silence and focused on picking, and the steady, rhythmic activity helped to soothe me. Physical activity almost always did.

As I neared the edge of the bushes, however, I heard a noise coming from the woods. It sounded like voices—male voices.

I placed my bowl on the ground and waved my hands to get Angie and Lauren's attention. When they looked, I put a finger to my lips and gestured that they follow me. Together we crept to the edge of the bush and peered around it as much as we dared.

It was hard to find them amongst all the trees, but my eyes finally settled on two tall, dark, winged figures, standing on a thick branch, about seven feet off the ground. I couldn't make out their faces, because their backs were to us, but as I listened more closely, I realized it was Jethro and Ianthan. They had come some way from their enclosure, as the beginning of their fence was at least a ten-minute walk from here... well, probably only a few seconds of flying at their speed. But I wondered what they were doing out here, away from their plot of land.

If we weren't in the middle of nowhere, I wouldn't have been able to hear them from this distance, but the almost deafeningly quiet atmosphere worked to my advantage. I could just decipher their words, and from the tone of their voices, it sounded like they were having an argument.

"—didn't think it through," Ianthan said.

"You had plenty of time to think this through!" Jethro retorted.

"You *pressured* me, Father. And things seemed different when we were back home, with distance between the plan and its actual execution. I'm telling you now, I don't...I *can't* go through with this. Navan is my best friend! I'd rather face the consequences than betray him."

"Fool boy! Navan will get caught sooner or later for deceiving Queen Gianne, regardless of our actions. You really think he can keep up this charade forever? Besides, we don't even have to blow the whistle on him. All we need to do is follow the blood sample back to Queen Brisha—if all goes to plan, we won't need to see the face of Queen Gianne ever again. Queen Brisha will grant us immunity from her sister's wrath and—"

"Wha—What do you mean *follow the blood sample?*"

"I extracted a blood sample from one of the girls last night—hardly difficult to do while I was flying her back to their house—and sent off the sample in a pod, early this morning before Navan woke up. It's on its way to Vysanthe now, waiting for us to follow in the ship—"

"*What?* That wasn't part of the plan!"

"No, it wasn't. But neither was those girls barging into the house. It was the perfect opportunity to get a sample on its way discreetly."

"But—"

"Look, Ianthan. I'm *sick* of arguing with you. Vysanthe will discover humans at some point, whether we're involved or not—it's only a matter of time before they figure out how to build a ship like Navan's. We might as well derive some benefit from Earth's discovery. Think of your future, of your wife and children... Which side would you prefer to be on, when it all goes down? Brisha's or Gianne's? If you possess half a brain you'll answer Brisha, because she *will* become Empress. She will be the first to bring war to Gianne's gate, and she will be the one to unite Vysanthe. You will thank me for getting us on Brisha's side when that happens, mark my words."

My heart was in my throat.

*Betray Navan?*

*Two Queens?*

*A blood sample taken from one of us, on its way to Vysanthe?!*

Nausea rippled through me, and I looked in alarm at my two friends. All of us began frantically checking our bodies for any signs of pricked skin. I checked my arms, legs, stomach, but found nothing, then asked Angie to check the parts I couldn't see without a mirror, while I did the same for her.

"Your neck!" she suddenly gasped, running a finger along the skin near the base of my throat, just above my collarbone. "You see that, Lauren," she said, pulling Lauren closer to me. "Two tiny pricks—they look so small they could be mosquito bites. I guess they must be from his fangs."

My stomach plummeted, and I suddenly felt imaginary pinpricks all over. That guy... he had bitten me while I'd been asleep. I felt utterly violated. But that was the least of my worries.

"He took my blood and—" I stopped abruptly as their conversation resumed.

"Navan and Bashrik leave in less than an hour for town, to procure more basic provisions for Ronad after his transformation," Jethro said. "We have to leave with the ship then. It'll be painless, I promise. Ronad still can't walk. You won't even have to look any of the brothers in the eye."

There was another pause in which every part of me prayed that Ianthan would resume his moral ground and refuse to be swayed by his father's words.

But instead he replied, in a low, resigned voice, "All right. Let's get this over with."

*How can you say that?!* I screamed at him in my mind. *You said Navan is your best friend!*

The two coldbloods shifted on the branch, spreading their wings to take flight. We scrambled backward to conceal ourselves behind the bush. We froze, listening to the sound of their rustling wings transporting them back to their base.

And then we stared at each other, wide-eyed and panicked.

e had less than an hour to try to do something —if anything could even be done. Jethro already said that the pod was on its way to Vysanthe. Even if we somehow managed to warn Navan and Bashrik before they left for town, and they thwarted Jethro and Ianthan leaving with Navan's ship, wouldn't it still be too late?

"Maybe Navan could go after the pod in his ship and catch it before it reached Vysanthe and... whoever 'Queen Brisha' is," Angie said. "His ship might be faster than the pod."

"Right," I said, trying to steady my racing mind, and tamp down the nausea that kept rising in my throat. "Yes, th-that's possible. So... what do we do?"

The thing was, we weren't supposed to remember anything about the coldbloods. Even if we managed to reach Navan, and got a word with him in private, who was to say he wouldn't slit our throats before we could warn him? I had broken my promise, and that might be what he'd focus on. I couldn't shake the vision of him bearing his fangs and claws at us, soon after we'd arrived at the house. He had looked downright ferocious, like he could tear us to shreds in a matter of seconds. Who knew how he would react?

But there was simply too much at stake not to try.

Angie cast a glance toward the Churnleys' house, and I followed her gaze. It was bizarre to look across the pretty garden surrounding the couple's home, flowers strewn and buzzing with honeybees—so at odds with the turbulent world within my brain.

"We could take some guns with us," Angie said, her voice coming out as a croak.

"Guns," Lauren murmured. "How will they help, exactly?"

"Well, obviously we've got to go back to that house and warn Navan and Bashrik," Angie said, running her tongue over her lower lip. "And with guns, at least we won't be as helpless as we were last time, against... whatever obstacles we might face."

"Do you know how to use a gun, Lauren?" I asked, putting my hand on her shoulder, trying to comfort her.

"My uncle showed me how to use one, but..."

She didn't need to finish her sentence. Angie knew how to work a gun, and so did I, though I wouldn't say either of us were experts. "We have no choice but to do our best," I whispered.

We rose from behind the blackberry bush, checking the sky briefly to be sure that the coldbloods were truly gone, and then raced toward the house. Luckily, the Churnleys weren't downstairs, so we hurried over to the wall opposite the kitchen counter, where Mr. Churnley kept a collection of rifles. We each grabbed one, and then stocked up on ammunition, which Angie found in one of the kitchen drawers.

I did worry what would happen when Mr. Churnley came downstairs, if he noticed that three of his guns were gone—but I couldn't think about that now.

We left the kitchen as quietly as we could, keeping the guns positioned in front of us, in case one of the Churnleys looked through a window and spotted us. As soon as we were out of direct view from the house, we broke into a sprint toward the coldbloods' fence.

This time, at least we had the advantage of knowing how the enclosure was laid out. I knew approximately where the house was situated, in relation to the fence, as well as where the backyard was. Instead of breaching the fence at the same point we had the night before, we traveled along the length of it, keeping our heads low, trying not to pant too loudly, until I sensed we had made it far enough to be approaching the backyard.

I peered through a crack in the fence, and was relieved to find my prediction accurate. Half of me had feared that we would arrive too late; that for some reason, Navan and Bashrik had decided to leave earlier—perhaps encouraged by Jethro— but I could see *Soraya's* peculiar metal surface shimmering beneath the canopy of leaves.

Apart from the ship, the yard was empty. For how long, there was no guarantee, but for now, it was a good sign.

"Okay," I whispered, so softly that I could barely hear myself. "The ship is still there. Now..." I'd been trying to figure out our next step, and though I was far from confident my idea would work, it was all I had. "I was thinking," I continued, "you two should watch the backyard. Climb into one of these trees,"—I gestured to the low-hanging branches by the fence—"and if Jethro or Ianthan show up, you... do whatever you need to do to stop them from getting into the ship. I'm going to try to get inside the house and reach Navan or Bashrik." *Without bumping into Jethro or Ianthan myself.* If I did, we'd all be dead. Jethro had made that perfectly clear.

"My God, Riley, are you serious about going in there?" Angie gasped, horror filling her and Lauren's eyes.

Their expressions did not exactly help with my nerves. "I'm not sure," I replied, my voice uneven, "but I-I have a gun." It had to be me—I wasn't about to volunteer one of them.

None of us took much comfort in that last statement, but we didn't have time to sit around and argue. I turned to leave but they grabbed me and hauled me back, giving me a tight hug.

"Be careful," they whispered.

"You too," I whispered back. Then I nodded, and took off, keeping my head low and my footsteps light as I traveled back along the fence.

*This idea had better work, or I might have just sentenced us all to death.* The thought played over and over in my mind like a broken record while I jogged. I stopped once I figured I had arrived about level with the front of the house, and glanced behind me. My friends were no longer standing outside the fence, which meant that they had already positioned themselves in the trees. *Good.* I hoped that they had managed to find spots to perch in that were well concealed.

I reached for the tree branch in front of me and, after securing the gun over my back using the strap, climbed up and over the fence. The moment my feet hit the ground, I sprinted toward the house, my eyes darting in all directions.

I reached the porch and found the front door had been left ajar, which both relieved me and made me nervous. Someone could've recently stepped through the entrance, and be hovering nearby on the other side.

I listened for any sounds of talking or creaking floorboards, but there was nothing, so I dared to slip through the gap. The heat of the house engulfed me, and I broke out into a sweat. I gripped my gun, trying to ready myself to take aim if I had to, but I made it several feet into the house without any ashen beasts flying at me.

When I reached the staircase, I halted, finally picking up on voices. This time, however, it sounded like they were coming from upstairs. I moved closer to the first step, gazing up, the dim gaslight allowing for deep shadows on the landing.

A creak sounded from above, as if someone was barely a few feet away from the top of the staircase.

I backed away, stepping through an unlocked door. The heat

intensified and my head throbbed. As I whirled around, I realized which room I had entered.

I barely managed to contain my gasp as my eyes fell on Ronad, lying on the floor beside the fiery hearth, on the same stretcher as before, which I now realized was more like a narrow mattress. He was wingless, and his skin had lost all hues of gray and turned a full golden tan color. And he was asleep. Or at least, completely still. If he had detected me entering, he didn't show it. The footsteps were growing closer on the staircase—someone was descending.

I eased the door shut as quickly as I could, then looked about the room wildly for a place to hide. I didn't know who it was on the stairs, but I couldn't take any chances that it might be Jethro or Ianthan.

A low coffee table stood in one corner of the room. It was the only option I had in this almost bare room. I groped through the heat and slid myself underneath it. I curled up in a fetal position, waiting for the footsteps to pass.

There were several tense moments when I wasn't sure that they *would* pass, when I feared they would enter to check on Ronad—but then they ventured deeper into the house. I allowed myself to breathe again as the creaking grew distant, and then, after another minute, dared to slide out of my hiding place.

I staggered to my feet, moving toward the door.

"No, don't!"

Ronad's voice suddenly rang out, making me leap out of my

skin. I whipped around, gun at the ready, only to realize that he was... still in a stupor.

His face was contorted with pain as he continued to yell, "Naya, it's me! Please, stay with me, don't . . . you can't . . . Naya . . ." He lost his voice then, but his face remained stricken with pain and despair, his lips moving in silent protest.

I stared at him, my thudding heart slowing a little, then softening. He was obviously having a nightmare, and I couldn't help but wonder what his story was. He looked younger than Navan and Bashrik—no older than nineteen. What had driven him to such lengths, to such pain, to undergo this radical transformation?

And hadn't Navan started to say *we've suffered*? But then he caught himself and said that Ronad had suffered a great loss. Perhaps Navan had just misspoken, though a part of me felt there was much more to the story than he was letting on.

But that was a subject for another day. Assuming I lived another day.

I returned to the door and slowly opened it wide enough to peer through. The hallway seemed empty, the voices continuing upstairs. I gathered the courage to step out, casting one last fleeting glance at the young man lying in front of the fire, before shutting the door behind me.

I moved back toward the staircase, then stopped. The voices were too muffled for me to make out what they were saying, but the more I listened, the more I pinpointed a depth and cadence that reminded me of Navan and his brother. None of the voices sounded like Jethro, who had a much older tone. Which might be good news. If I slipped upstairs now, I might be able to corner the brothers on their own.

I cringed as I placed my right foot on the first stair, my gun feeling slippery in my hands from the sweat. I imagined Navan's face as I stepped into the room. *Please don't be too pissed off with me.* Given the news I had come with, he had no right in hell to be. *I just have to be sure to spit my message out qui—*

Something sharp pressed against the base of my neck. I had been on the verge of planting my left foot on the next stair, but was instead dragged backward, before a hand clamped over my mouth, stifling my yelp. I heard heavy breathing in my ear, followed by a whisper:

*"I thought we got rid of you."*

Jethro's voice was unmistakable, and I had only a few seconds to wonder how I hadn't sensed him approach before he slammed me headfirst against the wall and grabbed the barrel of my gun. Reflex made me squeeze the trigger, and the gunshot rippled through the house. His hand loosened around my mouth—long enough for me to scream up the stairs at the top of my lungs:

"JETHRO SENT HUMAN BLOOD TO VYSANTHE!"

The next second, Jethro let go of me and took off down the hallway. I felt so dizzy from the heat and having my head bashed that I could hardly see, but I had enough sense to know that I had to fire after him. My aim was terrible, though, as my hands were shaking, and I shrieked as he raced toward the door.

Ianthan burst out from a room as Jethro rushed by, and he hurried after him.

Footsteps thundered down the staircase, and then I was face-to-face with Navan and Bashrik, shirtless, their skin back to golden-tan. In any other circumstances, I would have found it comical how closely Navan's expression resembled how I had imagined it would look—a mask of unadulterated shock—but before he could say anything, I pointed down the hallway and screamed again:

"Jethro and Ianthan are stealing your ship! GO! NOW!"

I couldn't imagine that my words made much sense to him, but something about the sheer panic in my voice jolted both brothers into action, and they darted down the hallway, toward the back door. Pounding after them, I heard Angie and Lauren's gunshots firing outside.

I made it to the door in time to see a bullet hit Jethro, who had spread his wings in mid-flight. He staggered, falling to the ground, and Ianthan, who had almost made it to the ship, hurried back for his father. But Jethro was already standing, even as blood the color of molten lava dripped from his right wing.

"GET IN!" he roared, pointing at *Soraya*, before half running, half limping after him.

"Ianthan? Jethro?" Navan's voice carried across the clearing in utter shock, as he and Bashrik raced across the yard, their wings exploding from their backs as they took to the air and shot forward.

"Lauren! Stop firing!" Angie yelled, right as Bashrik suddenly faltered in the air.

Everything had happened too fast. It had taken seconds for Bashrik and Navan to fly within my friends' shooting range—during which time Lauren's reflexes hadn't been quick enough.

"Oh my God!" Lauren's horrified voice infused the already chaotic scene. "Bashrik! NO! I'M SORRY!"

Bashrik let out an agonized groan as he fell and hit the ground, and I raced to him, giving Navan—who had stalled in the air—a furious look that told him to keep going. He hesitated only a second longer, and then went after them while I dropped down next to Bashrik. He'd been caught in the wing, like Jethro had. Only, his injury appeared to be more severe. Lava-colored blood oozed out near his right shoulder blade, the bullet having torn through both wing and the flesh in his back. Without thinking, I tore off my shirt, not caring all I had on now was my sports bra, so I could use it to stem the bleeding.

Before I could breathe a word of reassurance to Bashrik, Navan let out a curse that reverberated through the yard. I looked up to see he had reached his ship a second too late. Ianthan and Jethro had managed to lock themselves inside. The ship hummed to life, its sleek surface glimmering, and began to rise at alarming speed. It bashed into Navan, sending him hurtling back.

He steadied himself and launched after it, shooting straight for the hatch—an indent in the sphere I hadn't noticed before. His wings beat heavily as he wedged his hands around the indent, gripping the door tightly, even as the ship continued to rise. Metal groaned and creaked, and barely a heartbeat later, the hatch separated from the mainframe and plummeted to the ground, landing six feet away from Bashrik and me.

I gaped at the damage Navan had done with his bare hands. The door's metal was inches thick, and the edges where Navan had gripped had been bent as if it were silly putty. His strength was *unreal*.

I looked back up at the rising ship. Navan was no longer within view. He had hurled himself within it, and I could hear the sound of grunts and groans, violent cracks and smashing. The entire ship shuddered, and a chill rushed down my spine as Jethro let out a blood-curdling cry.

The ship plummeted, and I gasped as it crashed to the ground. Two tall figures sprang out of it, rolling onto the grass—Navan on top of Ianthan, gripping him by the throat. Lava-colored blood coated Navan's bare hands, arms and chest, and his entire body heaved as he dealt a crushing blow to Ianthan's face.

"You *bastard*," Navan snarled, his voice hoarse and thick with emotion. "I can't believe you'd do this."

"I'm sorry, Navan." Ianthan was crying. "I didn't want to go along with it—and the plan was never to betray you or your brothers personally. We were only going to use a sample to buy ourselves into Queen Brisha's good graces—that was all."

Navan's grip barely let up—if anything, it tightened. "You were my best friend!" I could hear the anguish in Navan's voice.

"I *trusted* you!" He punched Ianthan in the face again, and I heard a crack that made my stomach turn. Navan raised his fist again but stopped. "How long?" he asked. "How long had you and your father been plotting this? Scheming behind my back?!"

"My father... probably ever since he helped you build that ship. It was one of his motivations for helping you, I am sure, given that you had an Explorer license and he did not. He hoped you'd make a discovery he could take advantage of. But me? I swear, Navan. It was less than a month ago. When you first asked us to come down here for Ronad. I... I felt cornered. Father told Elida to put pressure on me to agree to his plan, and she swore she would leave me if I didn't go through with it. I-I know these are excuses but, I promise I will make it up to you. I don't expect you to ever trust me again, but I will do any—"

"You already sent off a sample?" Navan growled, releasing his grip on Ianthan and balling both blood-splattered hands into fists.

"Yes—Riley's blood," Ianthan wheezed. "My father did it, early this morning. But that wasn't part of the plan I agreed to. At least, he didn't tell me he was going to do that—"

"How far is the pod?" Navan demanded, racing back into the grounded ship, and his expression sent shivers down my spine. He was in his full-on beast mode—his eyes looked like they could burn holes through iron.

"I don't know. B-But the pod is slow compared to *Soraya*. We can catch up with it!"

Angie and Lauren reached my side, their faces drained and

pale. Lauren looked horrified as she approached Bashrik. I had Angie press my shirt against the wound and I stood up shakily, ignoring the nausea that was still roiling through me. I hurried to the ship after Navan.

I leaned my head inside the smooth steel interior of the sphere, large enough to fit ten people. Jethro was sprawled out on the metallic floor, his head separated from his body.

I turned away, vomit rising in the back of my throat. It was the first time I'd ever laid eyes on a dead body, never mind one as mutilated as this. Though it wasn't a surprise that Navan had killed him. Coldbloods were brutal, not ones to mess around. Their physical appearance alone was enough to glean that.

I managed to tamp down the bile in my throat and focus on Navan, who was hunched over, examining some kind of complex control board—or what was left of it. I didn't need to be a mechanic to see that it was wrecked. Dials had been smashed, buttons ripped off, levers mangled beyond recognition. Not to mention the fist marks that had been punched into the walls— and of course, the door was missing. I had learned how to fix cars, thanks to Roger, but this was way above my pay grade.

My breath hitched. "Navan," I said softly, "how will you go after anything in this?"

He ignored me as he opened up a compartment beneath the control board. The top half of his body disappeared inside it. I heard the crackle of electricity and saw sparks flying, and then the entire ship shuddered, before it sputtered out. He hauled himself out of the compartment a second later and stood up, his eyes blazing.

"They betrayed us," he said hoarsely, wiping his forehead with the back of his hand. I could hear the anger in his voice, but also the disbelief. "And you're right. This ship won't take off without major repairs."

Ianthan approached us tentatively. There were bloody patches where his long blond hair had been torn out, and his face was coated with blood, his nose lopsided—definitely broken.

Navan's eyes landed on him, and Ianthan stood there like a dog that knew it was about to get kicked.

"So what do you suggest we do now?" Navan demanded of him. "I could fix the door with the tools I have in the cabinets,"—he gestured toward the back of the ship, though I refused to look, not wanting to lay eyes on the corpse again —"but I'm not equipped to fix the control board. You know, I wasn't planning on being stabbed in the back by my best friend while we were here. That was actually *not* on the list of things I had expected to have happen."

Ianthan gazed around the ship and choked back a sob as his eyes fell on his father. He flinched, closing his eyes and covering his face with his hands. It took him several moments to gain enough composure to speak.

"Yes, it's a mess," he croaked. "B-But you do have the tools you need back at your main base, right? On its own, the pod will take at least three weeks to reach Vysanthe. Soraya will still have time to catch up with it, even with the delay. Fly to Alaska, grab all your tools, then return to fix the control board. Once it's fixed, you'll have access to the pod's exact coordinates and you can go straight after it."

I was about to ask what on earth they were talking about regarding Navan's "main base" and "Alaska," when the nausea I had been experiencing on-and-off for the past hour increased ten-fold, and I found myself buckling at the knees. I fell backward out of the ship, tumbling to the grass and gripping my head as a searing pain tore through my brain.

"Riley!" I heard my friends cry, and then Angie was there, by my side. Navan, too, was there, kneeling next to me. I was seeing double as he stared at my face, his brows knotted in a frown.

"Are you okay? What happened?" he asked, his eyes wide.

"We didn't take the Elysium," Angie said, and Navan's eyes snapped toward her. "Sorry!" she added quickly, holding up her hands, "but you're crazy if you think we'd be okay with just forgetting everything we found out! When we went into the house to talk, we found a bowl of vials, which Riley had spotted you drinking from earlier, so we figured that they probably wouldn't do us much harm, and we could do a switch— but don't get mad! Because if we hadn't, we wouldn't have known to come and fetch you when we overheard Jethro and Ianthan plotting—"

"Oh, for Rask's sake," Navan said, and I wasn't sure who Rask was, but the way he said it made it sound like a very bad swear word. His stormy eyes zoned in on me. "What did it taste like—the liquid you drank?"

I opened my lips to respond, my throat feeling painfully parched. "Slightly salty."

Navan swore again, and his boiling hot hands pressed against my forehead, his thumbs lifting up my eyelids, despite the fact I was suddenly overwhelmed with the need to let them close.

"Oh no," Angie gasped. "Why are her eyes doing that?!"

"Doing what?" I asked, trying not to panic.

Navan looked at me, his face blurring. "Clouding over."

My vision continued to blur, as though a blind was being slowly drawn over my eyeballs.

"And what about you two—what did yours taste like?" Navan asked Angie and Lauren, a renewed sense of urgency in his tone.

"Mine didn't taste salty at all—it was slightly sweet," Angie replied.

"Mine too," Lauren added.

Navan exhaled sharply. "That bowl of vials contained a mixture of substances. What you two most likely drank was the blood of white deer—which, although a species native to Vysanthe, shouldn't have much of an effect on you earthlings. On the other hand, it sounds like what Riley drank was silver root—a type of stimulant, similar to coffee for us coldbloods, but much too strong for human consumption. It seems like it took a while for the effects to kick in, as it's known to be a slow-acting substance, but now..." His voice trailed off, and his silence frightened me.

"Now what?" I choked, nearly blind as the mist thickened over my eyes.

"Navan," Ianthan's hoarse voice spoke up from somewhere to my right. "Go to Alaska now, and you can kill two birds with one stone. Fetch your tools and take the girl with you to fix up. You have a loaded apothecary in storage, don't you? I'm sure you can figure out an antidote with the ingredients you have there."

There was a pause and I heard Navan take a deep breath. "I can't be mad at you, because if you had taken the Elysium, we'd have no clue about Jethro and Ianthan. Also, Ianthan's right—I've got the ingredients I need for an antidote. You're going to be okay, Riley. But *you*, Ianthan." His voice took on a harder edge. "I still haven't decided what to do with you. I'm not letting you out my sight—you will travel with us. Lauren and Angie, you'll need to take care of Bashrik, as well as be here for Ronad in case he needs assistance. His treatment is mostly complete now, but it'll be several days before his strength has returned. I'll extract the bullet out of Bashrik, and then give you some medication to feed him—I have a small stock in the ship that I will leave you with, along with instructions."

"What will we tell the Churnleys?! How long will you be gone for?" Angie asked.

I heard Navan swallow. "I don't know what you'll tell them, but we won't be gone much longer than twenty-four hours...I hope."

*a*ngie helped me into a chair, and I was mostly in a daze as Navan and Ianthan darted about the yard, between the ship and the house, preparing to leave. I could tell what was going on primarily by my sense of hearing, given that my eyesight remained blurry.

I heard Bashrik groan as Navan extracted the bullet, and then Navan spoke in hurried tones regarding an assortment of ointments he was leaving with the girls.

What felt like fifteen minutes and a lot of confusion later, Navan and Ianthan had made the necessary preparations, and I sensed them approaching. Through my hazy vision, I could see that Navan had washed the blood off of himself, and had a black shoulder bag slung over his back. Ianthan was clutching what appeared to be a thick puffer coat.

Navan bent down to tug some sort of shirt over me, and then

picked me up. I flinched, expecting his unbearable heat to course through me once again and cause my head to split in two, but to my surprise, his temperature was moderate—on the warm side, but more than bearable.

"Wh-What happened?" I managed, as one of his arms slid beneath my knees, the other around my waist. He picked me up and held me against his chest, and I put my arms around his neck for extra stability. Though my vision was still blurry, I felt... inexplicably safe in his arms. Ordinarily, I would've insisted on walking on my own two feet, but I was too woozy to pretend that I could even stand, and the gentleness of his touch made my whole body relax.

"I don't want you to be any more uncomfortable than you already are," he explained. "I took a formula to help regulate my temperature while I carry you."

"Wait," I said, as his wings appeared behind his back. "You're going to fly with me all the way to *Alaska*?" I hadn't fully processed the thought till now.

"I'm afraid the last train has already left the station. It's the only way we can reach it."

"Riley!" Lauren called. She and Angie approached me, and I felt their hands squeeze mine. "Please be careful."

"If we hurry, she should make it," Navan replied, and a second later, my friends' touch left me as he lifted into the air, Ianthan by our side. My stomach dropped. I had barely murmured "Goodbye" before I felt the air rush past me as we broke through the treetops, the heat of the afternoon sun beating down on my skin.

I wanted to look down, to see how high we had flown, whether I could spot the Churnleys' little wooden house already, but I could hardly see past a few feet—even Navan's face, mere inches above mine, was a strain to make out.

But maybe that was a good thing. As we soared higher, I shivered, imagining just how many feet must be between us and the ground. Navan's speed was breathtaking, and given that there were no straps securing me to him—except for his own arms and mine around his neck—my lack of sight was probably something to be thankful for.

I wanted to ask him questions, like how long he thought it was going to take us to reach his "base" in Alaska, what he even meant by "base," and how he had one there—as well as what would happen to me if his antidote failed to work—but with each second that passed, I found myself less and less able to formulate coherent thoughts, as though my brain were disconnecting from my mind.

I didn't lose consciousness, not completely, but I felt myself slipping into a heady, almost dreamlike state. I hadn't swallowed a drop of alcohol my whole life, but I imagined this was close to how being intoxicated must feel—like I was floating on a lazy river, anything anxiety-inducing too slippery to hold on to. I closed my eyes as the pain in my head faded, and I felt lighter than my body, as though I might at any moment simply be blown out of it by the wind.

It was unnerving, and I tried to grab a hold of something, anything, yet my arms remained still—then I remembered they were already wrapped around Navan's strong neck, and while I was being held in his arms like this, there was no chance of anything bad happening to me.

Then I felt my lips begin to move, my voice coming to life, though my brain couldn't connect to what I was saying. All I was aware of was my emotions as I spoke, which began to vacillate like a pendulum. One minute, laughter was bubbling up in my throat, and the next, tears spilling from my eyes as an over-whelming anxiety gripped my chest. Somewhere in-between, a small part of me—the part that was aware of a complete stranger's eyes watching me—felt an acute sense of embarrass-ment at my behavior, but no matter how hard I tried, I couldn't regain control of myself. That was the most terrifying thing. I had no idea if this stupor I had fallen into would ever stop. I could've blurted out my entire life story to him, my deepest fears and insecurities, and I wouldn't have known it—from the myriad of emotions rolling through me, it would not have surprised me if I had.

"Riley." His voice was soft, gentle—and yet also deep, grounding. It vibrated through his chest and rumbled into mine, tethering me to him, to the security of being pressed against him.

I was grateful that he seemed to recognize the effect his voice had on me, and he continued to say my name, every now and then, reminding me of a reality outside of my own mind. Gradually, my emotions began to feel less out of control, and I managed to focus on the firmness of his body, supporting my soft limbs like a strong bed frame. My lips closed, and I stopped babbling. I nestled my head against his collarbone as a deep exhaustion settled into my bones.

Sleep somehow swooped in, enveloping my soul and dimming my senses. I dozed, while the air continued to whip around me, and when I finally came to again, it was to the sensation of extreme cold.

I opened my eyes and realized that it was dark, except for the light of a pale moon in the night sky—and I was wearing the puffer coat Ianthan had been carrying. I could also see a little more clearly. The pain in my head and the dizziness were still there, but perhaps the rest had done my vision some good.

I gazed up at Navan. His skin had returned to its grayish hue, and his dark eyes were fixed on a small platinum compass he was holding in one hand—his other arm still wrapped tightly around me. The dials on the compass were illuminated, casting light upon the strong plains of his face. Under different circumstances, it might be a dream come true to be wrapped up in the arms of this handsome man. Well, not man, exactly, but . . .

He met my eyes as he realized I had come to, and I felt the blood rise to my cheeks. The embarrassment of earlier returned full force. I wished I could remember what I had said to him. There was a sense of understanding in the look he gave me that had not been present when we had taken off—as though, during our journey, he had gotten to know me better. I wouldn't have necessarily minded that, if not for the fact that it was completely one-sided, and I had no idea *how* much better he knew me. I was as good as alone with him—hundreds of miles away from family and friends—and my life was literally in his hands. I felt I really ought to know him better, too... as well as try to gauge how much I had divulged about myself.

"Um," I croaked, uncertain of how to start the conversation.

"You're feeling better?" he asked. His voice was throaty, like he hadn't spoken in a while, as he raised a brow.

I nodded, wetting my lower lip. "A little, thanks."

"We still have to get you treated. You've undergone a serious ordeal. I don't think you realize the magnitude of . . . of what you've done." A troubled expression was etched on his face. I could hear the concern in his voice, and it made me nervous. "We're almost there now." He averted his gaze to the compass, and then looked straight ahead.

I followed his gaze. In the far distance, I could make out the twinkling of lights spread out over a small area—apparently some kind of village—but other than that, there was nothing but the glistening of icy tundra for miles. The silence was almost deafening, except for the beating of Navan and Ianthan's wings.

Ianthan was flying about ten feet away, his face a stoic mask. I couldn't imagine many words had been exchanged between the two as we'd flown. For that matter, I couldn't imagine what an ordeal Navan was going through, to have had his best friend betray him like that. I couldn't even *conceive* of either of my best friends betraying me. I trusted them with everything I had. It would devastate me to discover one of them scheming behind my back.

"Hey," I said, shaking away the thought. "I'm sorry I tricked you." I gave him a meaningful look as he glanced back down at me.

"I seem to be getting betrayed an awful lot lately," he said and shook his head, exhaling, his cool breath touching my face. "I used to think I was a pretty hard guy to fool. I'm starting to rethink that now."

I chewed on my lower lip, trying to scrape together the courage to say what I wanted to. "I hope it wasn't too weird on the way over. I . . . I don't know what came over me. I don't know why I was saying whatever it was I was saying."

His Adam's apple bobbed as he swallowed, and he looked away again, focusing on our line of flight straight ahead. I'd been hoping he'd take the bait and spill what had happened, without me needing to put myself out there and ask him directly, but his lips remained sealed.

"Because, see, I can't actually remember what I was saying. So, maybe you could clue me in?"

When he looked at me, I was surprised to see empathy in his eyes. My cheeks grew hotter.

"You said some things," he replied vaguely.

"Uh... Okay." I breathed out, deciding not to push it. If it came out naturally in conversation, then that was all well and good. If not, I wasn't going to force it. It didn't make the discomfort go away, but there was one way I could try to compensate for that... "Well, I feel like there are quite a few things you skimmed over during our first question and answer session," I said, changing the subject. I recalled the conversation I'd over-heard Ianthan and his father having, and how many question marks still hovered over that in my brain.

Navan cocked his head to one side. "Such as?"

"Such as, what's really going on back in your homeland? I overheard Jethro talking about two queens, who are going to be entering some kind of war against each other? Jethro was saying how important it is that he and Ianthan get on the side of Queen Brisha, because she's going to win the war. Which led me to assume that he—and probably you and your brothers too—are on the side of Queen Gianne?"

Judging by the dark flicker in his irises, the question made him uncomfortable. "You're right," he replied heavily. "I did hold back a lot of details when answering your questions. If you recall, I believed you would take Elysium right afterward, so there wasn't exactly much point in giving you a full back-ground... But yes, Vysanthe is ruled over by two queens. Gianne of the South and Brisha of the North. They are sisters—twin sisters—who inherited the throne about a decade ago. My brothers and I are citizens of Gianne's queendom, as are our parents, as were their parents..."

"Wow. So why do the sisters hate each other so much? Why is a war brewing?"

Navan sighed, stowing away the compass into his black shoulder bag and adjusting his grip on me with both hands. My skin tingled as his right hand accidentally slipped through the interior of my coat and brushed against the bare flesh at the small of my back. His touch was freezing—not a bit of warmth left in him.

My breath hitched and I clutched him tighter, shivers running through me, unwittingly drawing our faces closer together.

"I apologize," he said, his eyes meeting mine. The shadow of a smile crossed his lips. "As I mentioned, the 'humanizing' formula I developed allows us to become a conductor for heat, but in the absence of external warmth—and sunlight—our blood goes cold again. Like a reptile, just as you said."

"No worries." I loosened my hold on him and created a little more distance between our faces. Though I couldn't deny being that close to him felt... nice. "All in all, you're probably easier to handle as a coldblood."

"Is that so." I could tell he was trying not to smile. "I don't think anyone's ever told me that before. Anyway . . . As for your question, why are the sisters going to war? Well, it's kind of a long story... Vysanthe is a planet that consists mostly of ocean, iced over for the majority of the year. There are two mainlands —located around the north and south poles. Both of these continents were once ruled by a single monarchy—King Hektor and Queen Shari, the parents of Brisha and Gianne, their only children. But a little over a decade ago, a powerful underground rebel faction rose up, unhappy with the king and queen's dictatorship. They wished to introduce a system closer to democracy

—as you on Earth would describe it. However, although the faction managed to execute the King and Queen, the two sisters escaped the assassination, and, quickly rallied troops and formed an army to wipe out the resistance. The few who managed to escape with their lives were forced to go underground. If they made public their wish for democracy, they'd be executed, so anyone who managed to escape essentially had to disappear. So the rebellion was over, thus securing their own place as leaders, the rule of Vysanthe naturally passing down to them from their deceased parents."

He paused to glance at Ianthan, as if to check he was still following us—or perhaps wondering if he was listening in on the conversation. Ianthan's stony expression gave away nothing.

"Wow," I remarked. "Politics sounds like a bloody business where you're from."

"Isn't it like that everywhere?" he asked. "The sisters took up their thrones after the resistance was wiped out, and set about ruling Vysanthe as it had always been ruled—as one united nation, facilitating trading from the north to the south, allowing distribution of the varying resources that each polar continent produces. However, less than a few months into their rule, things began to deteriorate. As twins, one could hardly exert authority over the other. They each developed their own ideas for how they foresaw Vysanthe's future. A roundtable was established to help mediate between the two sisters and come to a negotiation, but ultimately, they failed to cooperate, and a compromise was made to divide Vysanthe into two rulerships— two governments.

"Many citizens were unsettled and upset by this, at first, as it was a complete paradigm shift that hadn't been done before in all of recorded history. Vysanthe, due to its long track record of wasting and misusing resources in general, is a planet that produces little for its own sustenance, and hence needed to be managed by one central authority to ensure even distribution of resources.

"Under the new split regime, however, it became practically each to her own. The sisters had certain agreements in place, but it quickly became clear that they were more interested in developing their queendoms individually—primarily by dragging resources from other planets.

"So, that has been the status quo for the past decade—the twin sisters ruling their queendoms separately—but... a number of us have reason to believe that the queens are growing tired of this status quo. After all, compromise means two people getting something neither actually wants—and that's exactly what happened when they split Vysanthe in two. Both wish to be the sole ruler, and both believe they are the one most qualified to do so. One of the reasons Vysanthe has become so obsessed with material advancement—including the search for immortality— is both are engaged in a game of one-upmanship, trying to outdo the other and prove how they are the more capable, forward-thinking leader, to their populace, and the populace of the other side. Each is vying to become Empress."

"It would sure make a great reality show," I said, though I knew it really wasn't anything to joke about.

"No official statement has been made yet regarding a war," Navan continued, "or anything of that sort—at present, it is merely a feeling many of us have. We sense the rumblings of discontent from both ends of our land."

"I see," I said slowly. "And where would that leave you and your brothers, if there's a war? You'd stay on Gianne's side—or try to transfer to Brisha's?"

"We'd have no choice but to stay on Gianne's side. Brisha is picky about who she grants residency to in her territory, because she thinks any outsiders could be spies. My family, especially, due to its rank. In order to be allowed over to Brisha's side, they'd have to offer something exceptionally valuable to her, to prove themselves trustworthy beyond doubt." He threw a scowl in Ianthan's direction. "Something *I* for one am not quite selfish enough to do."

"Your family's rank," I repeated, distracted by his previous statement. "What *is* your family, exactly?"

From Navan's expression, the question clearly made him uncomfortable. "My father is a highly valued... advisor of Queen Gianne. And my mother is a weak, silly woman who would never stand up for anything that didn't support her husband's status in society. That's pretty much all you need to know about them."

The disdain in his voice reminded me of how I regarded my own parents. Though, his tone was closer to vehemence—it seemed to be rawer, fresher, like a recently opened scar, rather than a closed one, like mine was these days (for the most part).

My thoughts returned to Ronad, and the anguished words I'd heard him speak back in his recovery room. Perhaps his tragedy was one of the reasons behind Navan's bitterness toward his parents, though I wasn't insensitive enough to bring up that topic now. Navan had made clear earlier that he didn't want to talk about Ronad's past.

"I'm sorry to hear that about your parents," I said.

"Nothing for you to be sorry about," he replied. "It's just free will. Everyone has it."

*Free will.* That term seemed to mean something to him, I realized, as I recalled his answer to a question I'd asked the day before. *"Every creature in the universe is born with free will. We can choose to be different, even if we share the same anatomy."* It had struck a chord with me then, and it did again now, given that free will was the only hope *I* had to carve out a life for myself that was different than my parents'. Even though this man and I were from entirely different corners of the universe, it was a sentiment we both clung to, it seemed.

Though, I imagined his daily battle had to be much more difficult than mine. After all, I hadn't been brought up to be a literal beast. He had his whole physiology to contend with, too.

It made me consider Navan's personality in a new light, and I felt that I finally understood him better. I thought back on all the behavior I'd observed so far in him, like that first encounter when he'd shown us his fearsome true form—and how, in spite of that, he'd been insistent to the point of being fanatical that we not be harmed, and that we take the Elysium voluntarily rather than being forced to. Shortly afterward, he'd engaged in a candid negotiation with me, and agreed to my terms to give us more information. Then he'd been a gentleman and arranged for us all to be placed back in our bedroom (I couldn't blame *him* for Jethro deciding to take a slurp out of me along the way). None of this behavior was characteristic of your average Vysanthian, clearly—Jethro alone had proven that, and I imagined that Jethro had to be one of the much nicer coldbloods inhabiting that world, given that Navan hung out with him. His upbeat and sometimes quirky comments, which I'd found odd at first, also made more sense now.

It was obvious to me that all of this was Navan practicing. Practicing using his free will to go against his grain, defy his natural instincts. There *was* an undercurrent of roughness to his manner, but from what I could tell, he'd learned to control it. To become a master of his circumstances, rather than a victim of them.

He'd even gone so far as to figure out how to change himself physically, with his special heating formula, to become the virtual opposite of what he was in every respect.

All of it made me wonder if he'd been like this his whole life, or if there had been a time when he was just like the rest of his kind. And if it was the latter, what had caused him to make the change...

Whatever the case, I'd gained a newfound respect for him,

because I knew how hard it was to change yourself—especially without any real support system around you. Sure, Navan had a brother and an almost-brother he was close to... and a rather questionable best friend... but the rest of the time he was surrounded by creatures who were clearly the exact opposite of what he was trying to be.

That also explained his earlier comment regarding why he wanted a ship that was better than everyone else's—so he could get away, be in his own space, think his own thoughts. He didn't have the luxury of two amazing adoptive parents, or access to a psychologist whenever he felt like having a chat. He'd had to struggle through this by himself. I couldn't imagine the strength of character that must have been required. It's what true bravery was, in my opinion. Having not only the self-awareness but the courage to recognize you ought to change, and then preparing to go to war with yourself every day to achieve it.

I only realized I'd been staring at him too long when he widened his eyes at me, as if to ask what the matter was.

I looked away, embarrassed. "I just..." I began. "I think you're very brave, that's all."

He frowned at me, apparently unsure of what to make of the compliment. And quite rightly so. It sounded totally random.

"I mean," I hurried to try and clarify, "I think the way you're choosing to use your 'free will' is... noble."

"Oh, don't get all mushy on me," he said. "I'm not doing anything... I have a lot of bad blood to make up for. I'm not actually that stellar of a guy."

I frowned. "I don't think you're so bad. You just flew me all the way to Alaska, in your arms." I thought back to all the guys that I'd gone to high school with. Not one of them—even if they'd had the ability—would've done anything even close to that. "That's pretty stellar." I paused. "And...I feel safe with you."

A pained expression crossed his face as he sighed. "Don't feel too safe. I'm not a great protector."

I would've thought he was just fishing for compliments, except that he seemed completely unable to accept a compliment, and that pained expression was still etched across his face.

I swallowed, not really sure what he meant by it, or how to reply. But even if his actions were driven by guilt, it still made him a better person than the rest of his kin—who apparently didn't even seem to *feel* guilt, and deemed it their God-given right to exploit others.

I wasn't quite buying his self-deprecation, but I let the topic go. As it turned out, we didn't have much time to continue our conversation anyway.

Barely three minutes later, he cleared his throat and nodded toward a large rock protruding from the dark, icy ground. "We've arrived, so I suggest you hold on tighter."

*I* realized as we were descending that we'd already passed over the glittering village I'd spotted earlier in the distance, and it was now behind us. My stomach lurched as we soared downward, dropping out of the sky faster than I was comfortable with. I held on tighter, while Navan's arms pressed in harder around me.

I shut my eyes for the last few feet, and opened them again only when I heard Navan's feet crunch against the snow. I was glad we'd been blackberry picking when the whole Ianthan-Jethro incident happened, since it meant I was wearing long pants and sneakers. Still, I was grateful that Navan kept holding me, since my attire was not exactly snow proof.

Ianthan's dark figure approached.

"Over there," Navan muttered, gesturing to the large rock protruding from the ice, some ten feet away.

He carried me in silence, until we reached it. It wasn't an awkward silence, though; I didn't feel the need to try to think of something to say. It felt natural, which almost made me laugh out loud—here I was, being carried in the arms of a coldblood who had just flown me from Texas to Alaska because I'd imbibed a potentially dangerous substance. Nothing about this was normal, or natural, yet being there in his arms felt exactly that.

He stopped at the rock's base and began brushing against the snow with his boots, revealing a metal trapdoor. He put me down, though made sure I held on to his shoulder for support, because my knees were shaky. I pulled the coat closer around me, and watched as Navan pulled open the secret trapdoor, revealing a storage compartment underneath that contained a steel trunk, which was about four feet by five feet in size. He heaved it out onto the snow and opened the lid, revealing a treasure chest of countless small silver vials, sectioned into dozens of compartments with exotic names that held no meaning to me.

Navan studied the assortment of vials for a few moments, before pulling three out, along with a glass beaker. He poured the three liquids into the container and shook it before pushing it toward me.

I clutched the beaker in my hands.

"Drink it all," he instructed firmly.

I breathed in, then nodded, before holding my nose and downing it as quickly as I could. I almost spat it back out as it burned down my throat, but somehow, I managed to force it down.

To my astonishment, the effect was almost instant. I felt the last of the mist clear from my eyes, the headache disappeared, and I felt... quite normal. Cold, but normal.

"Wow," I said. "That really worked."

Navan nodded, then took the bottle back from me. He wiped it with a cloth that had been tucked into one corner of the trunk, and then replaced it, closing the lid of the trunk.

He moved closer to me, and pulled out a tiny flashlight from the bag around his shoulder, which he shone into my eyes. "Seems to have worked—for now at least..." He hesitated.

"What?" I asked.

He sighed, and that same look of guilt I'd detected in him earlier when he'd talked about my ordeal returned. "I've been reluctant to say it, but... you ought to know that you will likely feel the consequences of drinking that silver root for the rest of your life."

I stared at him. "Wh-What? What do you mean?"

"Silver root is strong. It can have a negative impact on even a coldblood's brain if he or she consumes too much. A known side effect of overconsumption, aside from nausea, is increased susceptibility to stimulants in general, as it weakens resistance levels. Being a human, you only needed a small dose to be severely affected by it, and as a result, I would advise you to be very careful when consuming anything with addictive qualities in the future... Even food could become a problem, if you allow yourself to overeat." He shook his head. "I can't believe you switched the two vials like that without me noticing."

My lips parted as I absorbed his words. It felt as if he'd punched me in the gut. Thanks to my dear parents, I had no desire to ingest anything remotely intoxicating, now or in the future, but the thought that this entire ordeal had left me more susceptible, more vulnerable than I already was, played on an insecurity that was already so raw in my heart and mind, it was hard to stop my hands from shaking. My confidence was already fragile, a timid thing that I worked hard every day to nourish and protect. The idea that even *food* could end up becoming a vice if I wasn't careful was frightening.

"I'm sorry," Navan said. "It was good you caught Jethro and Ianthan, but... I wish you had just taken the Elysium like I wanted you to."

Despite the shock and the whirlwind of emotions I was struggling under, I managed to find a thread of reassurance in his empathetic gaze, and reel my mind back in. I got the uncanny sense that he understood what I was going through, but more than that, his presence reminded me of what I had just been thinking about, barely a few minutes ago—if he could maintain his character in spite of all the massive obstacles he faced, then there was no reason why I couldn't.

The thought calmed me. "Okay."

Navan took a breath, then nodded, switching his focus to a patch of snow six feet ahead of us, further around the side of the rock. "Let's keep moving," he said softly. "This was just a storage cupboard."

I kept hold of his arm as we approached the patch of ground his eyes were set on, where another trap door lay hidden in the ground.

He exhaled sharply as we reached it, his arm muscles tensing. The snow had already been cleared away from the door.

"That's not possible," Navan breathed.

He swooped down and yanked open the door, shining his flashlight to reveal a much larger space beneath—an actual room.

He withdrew his wings into his back and dropped through the hole, followed swiftly by Ianthan, and I found myself crouching, staring down after them. It was... empty.

"Where is all of my stuff? How could anyone have known about this?" he exclaimed. "Everything's gone. Every last damn thing!"

"There's a light!" Ianthan said suddenly, pointing to a door in the far corner of the room. Indeed, light was shining through the cracks—dim and warm, like candlelight.

Navan fell silent and rushed to the door, but before he could grab the handle, it swung open, spilling light into the main room. An old man with a long, bedraggled white beard and a grubby once-beige coat emerged in the doorframe, a gin bottle hanging in one hand. He looked just as surprised as Navan. Barking ensued, and a husky dog came padding out of the room, stopping beside the man.

"Who are you?" the old man slurred. "Is there a party I didn't know about?" He raised his bottle like he was making a toast, sloshing liquid down his arm. He didn't appear to notice. Nor did he appear to notice Navan and Ianthan's grayish skin.

"*Party?* No, there's no party!" Navan grabbed the old man by his collar. "Who are you? What are you doing here? What did you do with all of my things?"

"Things? Are there things down here?" The man tried to twist around but couldn't escape Navan's grip.

Navan gritted his teeth. "There's nothing down here anymore."

"I got no home to call my own, you see. Found this lil old hole in the ground—door was open and I climbed right inside!" He grinned, looking pleased with himself at the discovery, before taking a gluttonous swig from his bottle. "Thought it was my lucky day. I don't have too many of those, you can probably tell."

Navan let go. It was obvious this man, who could barely stand on his own two feet, was not the thief. "Maybe it is your lucky day," Navan said. "Why don't you take off."

"I think I will, seeing as I'm not welcome here no more," the old man mumbled, shuffling over to the ladder and climbing up it. He swayed dangerously, and I was afraid he was going to fall before he made it to the top, but he managed, and I moved aside to let him pass. He cast one lazy glance over me in the gloom, before turning back around to call down, "Mind passing Charlie up, would you?"

Navan had disappeared into the second room, but Ianthan passed the husky up to the guy, and with that, he headed off into the snow, his dog trotting along by his side, seemingly oblivious to the fact that he'd just been in close quarters with a couple of vampires. At least we didn't have to bother with Elysium with him—he had his own bottled version.

I stared after the retreating silhouettes for a moment, hoping he'd make it to the nearby town before freezing to death, but I couldn't dwell on his well-being for long; we had bigger things to worry about right now.

Such as the safety of the entire human race.

I looked back down through the trap door to see Navan had reemerged from the second room and was prowling around like a caged animal, running his hands through his hair.

He turned to Ianthan, narrowing his eyes. "A logical person would suspect you. Or at least suspect you had something to do with this."

"I swear, Navan, I have no idea!" Ianthan said. "I had nothing to do with this, and I can't imagine why my father would have either. He only wanted to escape to Queen Brisha with a blood sample; being accepted by her was his only objective. There's no reason on Vysanthe why he'd come ransacking this place. And *when* would he have done it? *How* would he have done it? What would he have done with all your equipment? There's no way!"

Navan seemed almost relieved as Ianthan spoke; there really didn't seem to be a way that Jethro or Ianthan could've pulled this heist off. I had a feeling it would've been more than Navan could handle right now, to find out his best friend had been involved in this, too.

"We've *got* to get that ship fixed," Navan said, breathing out. "It's the only way."

"Do you think it could have been other humans who found this place and raided it?" I asked softly.

There was a long pause. "It's possible but unlikely. I... I do have another idea what might've happened here."

"What?" I lowered myself onto the ladder and climbed down.

Navan set Ianthan with a dark look. "I think it was The Fed."

I scrunched up my face in confusion. "Huh? The Fed?"

"*What?*" Ianthan said. "What makes you say that?"

Navan continued to prowl, addressing me first. "The Fed is a supernatural federation that operates in this quadrant of the universe, and essentially helps to maintain peace and good relations between worlds. It's a protective and intermediary agency."

"What? I've never heard of it," I said, my mind being blown open yet again by another facet of our universe I'd previously been oblivious to.

"You wouldn't have," he replied. "Although The Fed does have a base here on Earth, they don't make themselves known to humans."

"Why's that?"

Was there the slightest hint of amusement in his eyes? "Don't take this the wrong way, but the rest of the supernatural community generally sees your kind as . . . rather primitive and immature; and a little too trigger-happy when it comes to their weapons."

"Oh," I said. He did have a point. "I guess that's fair enough."

"Humans aren't the most powerful species in the universe." Now Navan did smirk. "I mean, a good deal of your population honestly believes that they're the only intelligent life form in the universe." He and Ianthan both laughed. "Which is so ridiculous and narrow minded it's almost unimaginable. So, you can understand why your kind were never deemed fit to join The Fed, officially—and so the alliance contains no human members —but Earth is in their circle of watch, nonetheless."

"And you think they somehow found this place and raided it?"

"I know they operate on Earth because I encountered an agent here, several weeks ago." He pursed his lips, shaking his head. All traces of the previous smile was gone. "I was utilizing my holograph map, and it must've given off some strong, irregular frequencies that a nearby Fed agent picked up on. Damn. I should've known better."

"What happened?"

"I'd say it was the last thing he expected—to find a cold-blood. The Fed doesn't have much jurisdiction in our corner of the universe, and they despise Vysanthians to the core. We stand for everything they are against—they seek to preserve and balance, while we essentially seek to destroy. That agent fired at me before I could explain why I was here. I had no choice but to kill him; otherwise, he would've taken me in, or worse. Still, I feared that he might have already alerted his base to my presence. I waited for three days, expecting that if his fellow agents were coming, they would do so within that time. When they didn't, I assumed the agent I killed had not yet transmitted his findings to his base, and I needed to return to Vysanthe, so I left... Which I now realize was a mistake."

"The agent who came to get to you," I said, my head reeling. "He was... a different kind of supernatural?"

Navan nodded. "Earth's base is manned by a lycan unit."

"Lycans?"

"I guess you would be more familiar with the term *werewolf*, though they are different."

"Werewolf?" I said, again trying to wrap my brain around what he was telling me.

"What do we do?" Ianthan said. "I mean, this is bad, right? This is really bad."

Navan swallowed hard. "It's only bad if we give up. And we're not going to. We have to get my ship fixed... And the only way to do that now is to stake out the Fed and convince them to return my tools."

"That's insane!" Ianthan exclaimed. "The Fed would never negotiate with you! To them you're a filthy Vysanthian! They'd shoot you down on sight, before you could even get a word out —and that would be even if you *hadn't* murdered one of their agents."

"I know." Navan glanced at me. "Which is why we might need to try a different tactic."

CHAPTER 13 | 167

I looked from him to Ianthan, then back. "What?" I asked. "Why do I have a feeling I'm suddenly about to get a lot more involved?"

"Because if it was a human who made first contact with them, then we might at least get a meeting," Navan replied.

"And tell them *what*?" Ianthan asked. "What would a human tell them, exactly, in order to convince them? That we need those tools back to intercept a human blood sample that's on its way to Vysanthe? That would get The Fed asking serious questions, which would inevitably lead to revealing Vysanthe's search for immortality."

"Why would that be so bad?" I asked.

Ianthan exhaled. "If there's anything our Queens agree on, it's that The Fed should never be given information about our activities, because all that will do is encourage them to scrutinize Vysanthe more than they already have," he explained. "If Gianne—or her sister—found out we were behind the leak, we'd be in for a fate worse than death. We'd all be."

I could only imagine what such a fate might consist of, but from the petrified look in Ianthan's eyes, I knew I didn't want to find out.

"I didn't say it was the ideal plan," Navan said, clearly frustrated. "Do you think I want to risk something happening to Riley? But it's the only way. If we don't try, then we're never going to be able to get back, the blood sample will arrive in Vysanthe, and then they'll—"

"You're right," I said. "We've got to at least try. I mean, won't they help if we ask them to? Vysanthe clearly needs to be stopped from terrorizing other planets, and The Fed was an organization set up to do just that—maintain balance and protect weaker species."

"Unfortunately, it's not so simple," Navan said. "If we approach it like that, what we're *really* asking for is a bright red target on our backs—The Fed would not be successful in subduing Vysanthe even if it tried. If threatened, the Queens would put their differences aside to join forces and combat the threat. Take your entire planet's militaries, combine them, and you wouldn't be anywhere close to how powerful Vysanthe's military is. And our environment is too harsh; there are few who could compete with us in our own element. The Fed knows this, which is why Vysanthe has had free rein for so long. Of course, that doesn't mean the Queens will ever grow complacent—they still don't want The Fed knowing about their business."

"So what would you tell The Fed, then, if you managed to get a meeting?" Ianthan asked.

"As you said, we may have no choice but to tell them the truth—or at least, part of the truth. Our case has to be strong enough for them to be persuaded," Navan continued. "We'd also have to hope we can persuade them to keep our identities confidential... But we're getting way ahead of ourselves. Before we get to that, we have to figure out *how* to meet with them."

"What do you mean?" I asked. "I thought *I* was going to try to get a meeting with them."

"I don't know where The Fed's headquarters are... though I

do have an idea of how we might attract their attention." He swept past me and reached the ladder. "For now, let's get out of this hole."

Ianthan and I followed, reemerging in the icy world above. However we ended up meeting with this organization, I was going to have to convince a bunch of werewolves to return Navan's supplies.

The only thing I knew for sure was that we were certainly going to be gone longer than twenty-four hours.

*N*avan closed the bunker's hatch after us, and then we took to the air again, flying to the nearby village to continue our discussion. The cold had really started to get to me; I couldn't stop my teeth from chattering, and my fingers had gone numb a while ago. We landed outside a cozy little café, thankfully open at this early hour. By the looks of the dark street it was located on, it was probably the only place ever open at this time. We stood around the back of the building where vents were situated, blowing out deliciously warm air.

I shuddered, trying to sink deeper into my coat as I relished the heat. Navan dug a hand into his shoulder bag and pulled out a fistful of dollar bills. He pressed them into my hands, and nodded toward the entrance of the café. "Go get yourself something to eat."

"How did you get this money?"

"I arrived with some Vysanthian gold that a pawnshop was happy to accept."

"Ah," I murmured, "that's handy." I didn't have the interest to linger too long on that, with the prospect of food awaiting me. I hurried around the corner and entered the café, where I was delighted to find a counter filled with an assortment of warm, buttery pastries. I ordered two large croissants and hot chocolate in the largest size they sold—topped with a dollop of whipped cream.

I made my way back outside after paying for the order, and almost moaned as the warm, sweet liquid trickled down my throat. I dug into the pastries ravenously, and had eaten half of one already by the time I returned to Navan and Ianthan around the corner.

Navan's bag seemed to be becoming more and more like Mary Poppins's — the guys had been shirtless before, but, to remain inconspicuous, they had folded away their wings and donned black sweaters, which Navan must've been carrying in his bag.

As I approached them, Navan was also holding a small round gadget to his ear that I hadn't seen before—it was some sort of comm device. He must've left one back in Texas too, because he was talking to his brother, a note of impatience in his tone. "Yes, I *know* it's dangerous, Bashrik," Navan was saying in a low tone. "But what other choice do we have? Whether or not The Fed was responsible for the theft, we need their help. They will have advanced ships of their own—probably even more advanced than ours. They'll have equipment I can use to get the control board working, and hell, if we really managed to get on their good side, they might even give us a new ship. For now, just hang tight."

Navan paused as Bashrik said something, and his eyes rested on me as I continued devouring my meal. "I appreciate your concern. And you're absolutely right, of course I'd say the same if it were you. And yes, you need to tell Riley's friends—they're going to have to think of an excuse to cover her for at least another day, I suspect. We'll talk soon. Take care of yourself."

Navan removed the gadget from his ear, pressed a button, and stowed it in his bag. He ran his hands through his hair and looked at me as I extended my hand out to him to return the change. He took it, then looked over my shoulder, toward the glass bus shelter behind me. "Shall we sit?" he suggested, slipping the change into his bag.

The three of us sat down together on the bench, our backs facing the road. It didn't look like there were surveillance cameras around here, and it was still dark, so I wasn't concerned about anyone noticing their peculiar skin shade. We would likely be on the move before the sun rose.

"How's Bashrik doing?" I asked. Whatever Bashrik had said to his brother, it had sounded like he was very concerned about Navan's safety—which I found both nerve-racking and endearing. "He seemed worried."

"His wound is healing—it hopefully won't be too long before he can fly again. And yeah, he was worried, but that's what he does. Under that outgoing exterior of his is a huge bundle of anxiety."

"Well, it's good he's healing." Lauren would be relieved about that. Poor thing, she'd gone from barely shooting a bullet in her life to almost accidentally killing someone. "I assume my friends were sleeping?"

Navan nodded. "They returned home for the night." He withdrew a couple of vials from an outer zipped pocket of his bag, handing one of them to Ianthan, before unscrewing his own and downing it. He grimaced slightly as he swallowed.

"What's that?"

"Silver root."

"Ah." The pit of my stomach dropped a little at the reminder, but there were too many other things for me to think about to dwell on it. "So, the plan," I said, sipping from my cocoa.

"Yes, the plan," Ianthan repeated. "How do you suggest we go about attracting their attention in the first place?"

Navan rubbed his hands together, staring at the brickwork of the café building in front of us. "We'll have to pull off some kind of stunt that screams supernatural in order to draw The Fed out to investigate. Also, it'll need to be somewhere densely populated. I suggest a major city, possibly New York."

I frowned. "That's my city."

"Feel like a homecoming?"

"I just . . . Nobody will get hurt, right?"

"If all goes according to plan."

"How do you know Earth's geography so well, by the way? You seem to be well acquainted with the customs in general."

"Do I?"

"Yeah. You knew what a pawnshop was."

"Pawning. The universal language." Navan shrugged. "I've spent a decent amount of time on Earth since I discovered it, under the guise of exploring other planets for an immortality elixir. And I managed to find a good library."

I smiled, picturing Navan hunched over a little library table with a pile of books. "Where did you first land, when you arrived?"

"It was here, in Alaska. I was drawn to it for its temperature —given that I hadn't invented any formulas yet. But, to get back to the plan . . . I didn't actually ask you yet: are you really okay with helping us? As I said, we need a human."

I nodded. I had to help—there were literally only three humans on the planet who could even theoretically help, and the other two were back in Texas. I had begun taking risks since the moment I decided not to take the Elysium Navan had offered me, and if these were the consequences, I was going to have to accept them.

"Are you sure?" he asked me, eyebrows raised. "Obviously it's a decision I want you to come to on your own. And I want you to know that I'll do everything I can to ensure your safety, but . . ." He swallowed. "As I mentioned before, I'm not infallible. I can't guarantee it."

I nodded again, even as I clutched my cup a little more tightly. "I'll help."

Navan sighed. "I hate having to put you in this position. I really do. But if you're in, then, in that case—"

I never got to hear what he was about to say, because the sound of gunshots exploded into the night, and the glass behind us shattered. My drink slipped from my grasp as Navan slammed into me, his hands gripping me by the waist and forcing me to the ground. His body pressed against mine, and his breath came in quick pants against my neck—his eyes were wide and alert like an animal's.

"What—" I gasped.

The next second, he was picking me up again, and as gunshots continued to fire all around us, he lifted me up and we went soaring through the air so fast I could barely keep my eyes open. The bullets seemed to follow us, but we were quickly over the café building and out of range. Navan continued to press forward, flying over residential houses and gardens, until he halted and dropped us back on the ground, a few miles later.

He planted me down on a bench, gripping my shoulders. "Stay here," he breathed. "We lost Ianthan—I'll be right back." And with that he took off again, flying over the houses lining the street, and back in the direction of the café.

I held my breath, a chill running down my spine as I listened and tried to make sense of what had just happened. It sounded like the gunshots had stopped.

Who had fired them? Why at us?

It would be an absurd coincidence for that to have been a random shooting. Who would fire at an empty café in the middle of nowhere, and so early in the morning, when virtually no one was around?

I clasped my hands together and stood up, watching the dark sky for Navan's return. I kept expecting the firing to start up again, but it didn't, and I was left with the sound of my own harried breathing.

I finally caught sight of Navan in the sky, his dark wings beating hard as he lowered himself to the ground next to me. He was alone.

"I couldn't find him," Navan said, panting.

"What do you mean? Where could he have gone?"

"I don't know. As soon as the firing started, I was focused on getting us away from there. Ianthan must have flown in an entirely different direction. I looked all around the area but couldn't find any trace of him—no body, nothing. There was no sign of our attacker either—except for a lot of confused residents spilling out into the street, and the shattered remains of that bus stop."

I clasped a hand to my forehead, trying to comprehend what he was telling me. "You think Ianthan might have been taken by whoever our attacker was?"

Again, Navan looked deeply concerned—and utterly clueless. "I have no idea." He sat down heavily on the bench, and I stood in front of him, scrutinizing his face. "A part of me wonders if it was a preplanned escape attempt on Ianthan's part, but... that would be impossible. Right? Who would have been his ally? How would they have gotten in touch with him? I'd been watching Ianthan ever since we left Texas. I have no idea how he would've pulled it off..."

"But then, who shot at us?"

"I don't know." His hands balled into fists. "How did everything get so screwed up so quickly? Maybe I should've ended him like I did his father. I just... I couldn't..."

"No, no," I said softly, reaching out to place a hand on his shoulder. I could see his conflicting natures grappling, and it made me want to comfort him. "You did the right thing, Navan. He was your best friend. You did the right thing by giving him the benefit of the doubt. I witnessed firsthand during Ianthan and Jethro's conversation that Ianthan's heart hadn't been in it." *But how did that add up with his behavior now, if he really had escaped?*

I could see how hard the idea was for Navan to swallow—to have his best friend betray him not once, but possibly twice. Ianthan had promised to stick around and help with whatever course of action Navan chose next.

I gulped, wondering, if Ianthan *had* indeed deliberately escaped, what he would do next.

I hesitated before voicing my next thought, not wanting to cause Navan more pain, but also recognizing the importance of discussing it. "Do you think... Do you think he might try to beat us to the Fed?"

Navan looked off into the distance. "I don't know. That is

CHAPTER 14 | 179

apparently my new default response to everything: I don't know."

"We were just talking about the Fed being your only means back to Vysanthe. What if he tries to reach the Fed before you and comes up with a way to barter himself back to Vysanthe, in perhaps a different ship, where he could carry through his father's plan with another blood sample?"

It *did* seem far-fetched, but the timing of his departure was odd—just when we had been discussing our next move. *Could it really have been orchestrated?*

My head hurt from the sheer confusion of it all.

Navan breathed out, shaking his head and standing up. "I need time to process all of this. But I think it's safe to assume that we are in a race against Ianthan, and we don't have a second to lose." He paused, gazing down at me through his deep slate eyes. "Looks like it's just you and me now."

15

*I* wrapped my arms around Navan's neck and my legs around his waist, and he took off again. I'd never tell him how much I had come to enjoy this particular mode of transportation, but every so often I'd glance up and our gazes would meet, before he looked off into the distance again, and, in spite of everything that had just happened, he'd have the tiniest of smiles on his face, which told me he didn't seem to mind the extra cargo, either.

We flew back toward his underground base. I glanced down at the café street as we soared over it, noting the flashing of a police vehicle and the gathered crowd, as they tried to make sense of the incident. I sensed eyes watching us. I was certain that we blended in with the dark sky too well for anyone below to see us, and yet, as we flew, the feeling persisted.

Half of me was still holding out hope that Ianthan was

around here somewhere, afraid of the attacker and waiting for the confidence to leave his hiding place, but he did not rejoin us in the sky, and I saw no sign of him.

I shook the unsettling feeling aside as we landed a few feet in front of the hidden storage cupboard where Navan stored his ingredients. He stocked up on vials, piling them into his bag until it was bulging. I hoped its seams would hold together, because we had a long journey ahead of us.

He took out a map of North America, and his compass. After a minute or two of frowning at the map and consulting the compass, he stowed the map away, and we took off again.

"At least the Fed didn't find the storage cupboard," Navan said, his mouth so close to my ear I could feel his cool breath. It occurred to me that all I had to do was turn my head and our faces would basically be touching—close enough to kiss. *Has he ever been kissed before?* I found myself wondering absentmindedly as we flew. *Of course he must have, though I doubt he's ever kissed a human...*

"How long do you think it will take us to reach New York?" I asked, trying to distract myself from that derailing train of thought.

"Um, I'm estimating half a day," he replied. "Though, I'm not exactly at my peak performance, so it may take longer."

I glanced at his face, and noted the tired lines etched into it. I hadn't really considered supernaturals getting tired, but now that I thought about it, Navan had been through a hell of a lot since the last time he must've slept (in fact, I didn't even know when he had last slept). Not just physically but emotionally. The shock of discovering Ianthan and Jethro's betrayal, and then his battle with them, and then flying all the way to Alaska. He hadn't been able to doze off during the journey, like I had. He'd been so focused on getting me to Alaska, he hadn't paid any attention to what it was that *he* needed.

"Maybe we should find somewhere for you to stop and sleep a little?" I suggested, glancing toward the horizon, which was slowly but surely brightening, the first rays of the sun touching the darkness. I knew we needed to hurry now, more than ever, to get what we needed from the Fed and fix *Soraya* so Navan could chase after that pod, but there was some comfort in the fact that Ianthan would need to rest too, at some point—assuming we were in a race.

I felt Navan's chest move as he breathed out. "Maybe. But I'll keep going for as long as I can."

And so he continued to soar, over ice-capped mountains and frosty white plains, until the sun peeked over the horizon, and we reached less frozen territory, more browns and greens and blues splashing to the landscape.

I watched in wonder as Navan's skin changed with the lightening atmosphere. It didn't happen all at once—there was only a subtle difference at first. His skin transformed proportionately with the sun's strengthening rays, little by little, until that gorgeous golden tan shade had returned.

"I gotta say, that's pretty cool," I said.

He smiled. "Just call me chameleon."

We hadn't spoken much during the first hour of our journey, as I suspected we'd both been too preoccupied with our thoughts, but now seemed like a good time to start talking details. We were on our way to New York, and I still didn't know how he actually planned to pull this off.

"So what's the plan when we get there?"

"We'll have to pick a public area. I'll let you pick, since this is your homecoming. I'll have to reveal myself—my true self—long enough to cause a commotion, but not too long. I'll need to fly fast, so I'm mostly a blur on cameras, but distinguishable enough to get the Fed's backs up and get them on my tail. If they're doing their job right, they're constantly monitoring news channels for unexplained incidents, and a city like New York would be a priority for them. Who knows, they might even have a branch there. I'll be able to figure out the logistics better once we've chosen the spot."

"And what part would I play, exactly?"

"We should coordinate things so that you're the first to approach them, help soften them a little. And you'll have to tell them a blood sample is on its way to Vysanthe—I don't see any way around that. However, if they want to know more, they'll need to get us a meeting with their chief of operations here on Earth. I'm hoping that sliver of information will be enough for him or her to agree to a hearing."

"Right," I murmured. That made sense—tease them with information in order to get a foot in the door, rather than spilling everything at once. For all I knew, they could take that information and still not help us. I hadn't forgotten the fear in Ianthan's eyes at the thought of betraying his race, and invoking the Queens' ire—we needed to hold information as close to our chests as possible, for as long as possible.

My mind wandered back to 'lycans,' wondering what they looked like, how they differed from the werewolves of human lore. Hopefully, they would be more amenable to talking than Navan was when I first met him.

We continued our journey in silence, falling back into our own thoughts. I felt Navan's body becoming hotter—not too hot, thanks to his regulating formula—but enough that I started to get stuffy beneath my coat. I unzipped it to let in more air, and felt the hard lines of Navan's chest press directly against mine. The sudden lack of layers between us made my traitor of a heart beat faster. I tried to focus on what lay ahead.

The sun continued to rise, bathing us in its warmth, and although it was impossible to truly get comfortable in this position, God knew how many feet above the ground without a safety belt, I figured this was probably the closest I was going to get.

As someone who had barely traveled across a few states in her life, I had done a lot of sightseeing in the past twenty-four hours. But in spite of the breathtaking views, I sensed myself beginning to doze off beneath the sun's comforting rays.

Until my ears picked up on an odd noise behind us. I had grown so use to the quiet atmosphere, the only sounds being

Navan's deep breathing, and the rhythmic beating of his wings around us. But this... this was different.

"Did you hear that?" I asked, looking over his shoulder. There was nothing other than blue sky and clouds.

"What?" he asked.

Maybe I shouldn't have expected him to hear it, given what I knew about coldbloods' senses being impaired when they became 'hotbloods.'

It had sounded like a grunt—loud enough to have been distinguishable to me, but fleeting enough to make me think twice and wonder if I had imagined it. I held my breath for several moments, seeing if it would return, and when it didn't, I concluded that I had most likely imagined it.

Still, it left me with a vague sense of unease. "It's nothing," I muttered, not wanting to project my own paranoia on Navan, when there was literally nothing surrounding us for miles. He had enough on his plate to worry about.

But then, barely ten minutes later, I heard another noise— that I could've sworn was a distinct second pair of flapping wings.

"Navan," I murmured, my eyes going wide as I gazed around us. "I... I know this sounds crazy but, I feel like someone's following us."

"Huh?"

"I don't know." I looked around the empty sky again. "I'm hearing noises. A grunt, and then, something that sounded like another pair of wings. Maybe I'm just tired but..."

Navan did a sudden about turn in the air. I yelped and clutched his sweater tighter as he swooped upward, and then back around in a loop, so he could get a good look behind us without losing momentum.

"I don't see anyone," he said, his brow furrowing. "And invisibility is not something we coldbloods have a potion for, so it probably is your imagination." Nonetheless, he did another loop to look around, his expression worried. "Maybe we should stop for a bit—for both of our sakes." His head panned downward, and I realized we were approaching a dense area of buildings, nestled in a valley scattered with glistening lakes.

I nodded, glad for the suggestion. I had sensed Navan's speed slowly faltering. He had been doing his best to keep going, but it made much more sense to stop and rest a while, then continue with renewed energy.

"I agree," I said. "Even if we stop for an hour or two, it'll do us some good."

I had barely said the words when his grip tightened on me, and we dipped abruptly, soaring at breakneck speed toward the town. He was aiming for a large patch of trees. We descended, touching down in a peaceful forest. He withdrew his wings beneath his sweater, which was torn from our emergency exit earlier. Then, after he had adjusted the heavy bag on his shoulder, we walked through the trees and arrived at a quiet road.

We both looked up at the sky as we stepped out into the open. Even though my rational self knew there was nobody following us, my mind kept taunting me, making the back of my neck prickle. I needed some proper, uninterrupted sleep.

Above us was nothing but perfect blue sky and sunshine. Even so, we found ourselves sticking to the shadows, and taking a winding path through the town. We kept beneath the awnings of stalls as we trailed through a crowded marketplace. We were in Canada, based on people's accents. We passed a clothing stand and picked up two extra outfits for both of us, using a handful of Canadian dollars Navan had in his bag. His purchase included a new sweater, which he put on immediately, given that his torn one was attracting more attention than we wanted —especially from young tourist women. I saw them staring and heard their titters as we walked past, commenting that he didn't look like he was from around here, one of them even asking for a photo, probably assuming he was some kind of celebrity. Navan frowned at the curvy blonde who had asked, before politely declining.

I hung back a little and stole a once-over of Navan as we kept walking, allowing myself to quietly appreciate his... aesthetics from a distance, now that we weren't in immediate mortal danger. *Dang.* It was hard not to feel like a lucky girl to have had him clutching me to his chest for the past several hours. If my nerves hadn't been playing up so much on the journey, I would have appreciated it a *lot* more.

I quickened my pace as he looked over his shoulder, frowning and wondering why I'd hung back. We continued through the town, trying to avoid attention while looking for somewhere we could crash in safety for an hour or two. We ended up finding shelter in the form of "Cricklewood House." It was a small, cozy-looking hotel that bordered the bustling marketplace.

It met our unspoken criteria of being inconspicuous, so we entered the reception area. Neither of us had ID, but thankfully I persuaded the owner with upfront cash. The elderly woman seemed to take pity on our tired faces and led us to a room... which I realized, as the door swung open, contained one double bed.

"Um, actually we're not a couple—" Before I could complete my request for a room with two single beds, she had already turned to head back down the staircase. Given that we were lucky to have a room in here at all, it was best not to push it.

I looked at Navan, towering above me in the low-ceilinged corridor, and swallowed. We were going to have to make this work.

We stepped inside. Pretty floral curtains were drawn against the open window, letting in a mountain breeze that carried the scent of fresh bread from the bakery next door. My eyes fell on two large bottles of water, and a basket of fruit and sandwiches on a little table in one corner of the room, and I headed there first. Sipping from the water, I realized how dehydrated I was, and downed half a bottle, before attacking the sandwiches.

The door clicked as Navan shut it, and I glanced over at him. He stood still, gazing around our small quarters, before his eyes fell on the elephant in the room—the double bed.

"You can sleep there," I said quickly, before things could get too awkward. "I've been dozing on and off during the journey, and you need quality sleep more than me."

He looked a little hesitant, but didn't argue; he was that tired. He discarded his large black boots by the door, and tugged off his sweaters—both the old one and the new one he had pulled on top of it—hanging them on a chair. My chewing slowed as I took in his deep tanned chest, the scars crisscrossing it much more visible with this lighter skin shade. He moved to the bed and lay down on one side of it—the side nearest the door—and faced the ceiling. I wanted to ask about his scars, but now didn't seem like the right time.

I settled deeper into my chair and resumed eating, watching as Navan made himself comfortable. He didn't bother pulling the sheets or the blanket over him, seemingly content with the temperature; just stretched out his long legs, which caused his big feet to tip over the edge of the bed, and nestled his head into the pillows. The muscles in his arms relaxed, and he went still, except for the gentle heave and sigh of his chest.

I finished my sandwiches slowly, my eyes alternating between the view out of the window and the... view on the bed. I ate four sandwiches and two bananas in a row, and finished the rest of the water.

I tiptoed to the bathroom to relieve myself, before splashing water on my face and looking at myself in the mirror. It came as no surprise that I looked like a witch. Apparently, I didn't weather journeys as well as Navan. Dark bags hung under my eyes, and my hair had gone static, poking up at all angles, while my skin was parched and lips dried out to the point of cracking.

I stepped into the shower to wash my hair and scrub the general grime from my body, relishing the hot water beating down on my back. I changed into a set of the new clothes we'd picked up from the market—warm pants, a long-sleeved thermal top, and a fleecy sweater. I found a small bottle of skin cream in the bathroom cabinet and lathered it onto my face and hands, before blow drying my hair. By the time I was done, I felt perfectly ready for bed. Except, there was no bed for me to climb into, unless I planned on sharing it with a vampire.

I opened the bathroom door. To my surprise, Navan was still awake. His eyes were open as he stared at the ceiling, but flickered in my direction as I stepped into the room.

"Hey," I said. "Can't sleep?"

"I thought I'd be out before my head hit the pillow. But I can't get my mind to shut up."

I moved slowly around the bed, and sat down on the other side of it, propping my back up against the headboard and leaning against the pillows. He reached down to his bag and pulled out a silver vial. He downed it, leaving me wondering whether it was a snack of blood, or perhaps something that would help him sleep.

I gave it a few minutes before talking again, wanting him to drift off, but although his eyelids dropped every now and then, they kept opening, as if there were something on his mind that was keeping him from shutting down.

Eventually, he turned on his side and looked at me. "What else did you overhear, in that conversation between Ianthan and his father?" he asked.

"Oh, um. I didn't overhear much because I wasn't listening for long, but..." I ran through in my mind what I had already told him, trying to sift out the pieces of new information. I realized there was something important that had been troubling me. I hadn't had a chance to think about it much with so many other distractions. "Jethro said that Vysanthe will find out about Earth and humans sooner or later—that it's only a matter of time before they crack the ship technology, like you and Jethro did. So his argument was that they might as well benefit from the discovery of human blood being the elixir Vysanthe seeks, as it was going to happen anyway."

Navan exhaled, running a hand down his face.

"Is it true?" I asked quietly. "That they'll discover the technology sooner or later?"

"Of course, it's possible. Though, given my rank as a chief explorer, even if the technology developed to reach this far into the universe, I would have authority to direct teams to other quadrants, and keep them away from Earth. But that would be by no means failsafe. It would only take one rogue, one disobedient team—or a team from Queen Brisha's side—to become curious and land here..." He looked away, his jaw tightening. "Ultimately, there is little one man—or a few men—can do to thwart an entire race, especially one as savage as mine. All I know is that I have to do my part in preventing it—in delaying that day as long as possible. It's all any of us can do."

I gulped. "Right." That was worrying, to say the least. To think that we could go to all this trouble to get Navan's ship repaired, only to have the coldbloods invent their own ship and discover Earth a few months or years later. Still, Navan was right. What else could we do but try? Maybe, after we had retrieved the blood sample, we could brainstorm ways to at least prepare Earth for the possibility. Maybe we would have to tell humans about coldbloods after all, in order to allow Earth's leaders to prepare for their arrival. I could take Navan and Bashrik to meet them as proof.

But, one step at a time. The most pressing matter was the blood sample—*my* blood sample—that was currently on its merry way to Vysanthe.

Gazing at Navan, I wondered again what was driving him to help us. What was stopping him from doing a Jethro, and selling us out for an easier life. He had mentioned guilt before, but what guilt could be so strong as to drive him to such sacrifices for the sake of a species that had no connection to him? A species that, up until recently, he didn't even know existed.

"Navan," I ventured, knowing that talking to him wasn't going to help him fall asleep, but I couldn't help myself now. "Do you mind telling me why you're doing this for us? You're putting yourself out in a major way. It would be much easier for you to, you know..." I trailed off, seeing that he had caught my drift.

He sat up against the pillows, his head rising to be more

level with mine, and grimaced. "Do you remember during our first 'question and answer' session, I told you about an alchemist who came up with the Immortality Theory? The man who caused this whole frenzy of coldbloods seeking out the blood of far-flung lands?"

I nodded.

His face darkened. "That alchemist was my father."

I stared at him, my lips parting. "Oh."

"You remember I told you that originally I was an alchemist, too? Before I switched professions and became an explorer?"

"Yes," I said uncertainly.

"Well, my father was my alchemy teacher, and the first several years of my apprenticeship were spent helping him develop the theory. He was the one driving the project, but I did most of the grunt work." He sat up and turned around as if in shame, planting his feet on the floor as he turned his back on me. "I was the only one of his ten sons who decided to take up his profession, mostly for reasons of ego. My father is renowned throughout all of Vysanthe as an expert in his field, and my brothers didn't want to feel overshadowed by him. I didn't care about that, though, because I really had a genuine interest in the subject. So I took it up... only to regret it. I didn't know at the time what the theory would lead to, or even the purpose of many of the lab tasks he was having me perform—but regardless, nothing can or will ever change that I am essentially the theory's co-creator, and responsible for... all of this. I'm responsible for a lot of things that I wish I could take back."

His last sentence was spoken with a gravity that resonated through my very being. I felt his emotions so deeply in that moment, his remorse and his frustration, it was as if I were experiencing them myself. I couldn't imagine the level of pain the guilt must be causing him—especially when it wasn't even his fault.

*Okay. This explains a lot.* I wasn't sure how to respond to his revelation. I didn't sense that he wanted any kind of sympathy or reassurance from me—just that it was something he was getting off his chest, since I had asked. So I remained quiet, waiting for him to continue.

"As soon as I realized what I had helped my father accomplish, I gave up alchemy and decided to become an explorer. I wanted a ship better than anyone else because... although I didn't know for how long I'd be able to keep it hidden, given all the damage I was complicit in causing, I wanted to be the first to discover the blood, if it really was out there."

"Why do you think your father kept the theory a secret from you, when you were working on it?" I asked.

"Not because he thought I'd be against it, if that's what you're wondering—he expected me to be onboard with it. He kept it a secret simply because he didn't want a single leaky hole. He wanted to be the first and only alchemist to present the groundbreaking theory to our Queen Gianne, as it would enhance his already high status, and didn't want to risk me slipping anything to anyone, even by accident. That's how my father is. However, in an incident that I believe was not related to Jethro, but rather some other spy of Queen Brisha who managed to infiltrate her sister's palace, some of my father's papers were stolen—and the theory was leaked to the other side. Once both queens knew about the theory, it became a race to see who could discover the right blood first, and so from there, the whole thing snowballed."

Finally, he turned to look at me again, and his eyes were so intense that I flinched, barely able to hold his gaze. "Countless lives have been lost because of me, as my people go around plundering planets, seeking out the magic blood. And I will be responsible for many more before my life is done. So maybe now you can understand better why I'm doing what I'm doing. Any creature who wasn't a complete monster would do the same. It's not noble or brave... It's just a way to live with myself."

He went silent, and his words hung in the air. I didn't know what to say.

He turned over and reached for another vial and downed it, before resettling his head against the pillows, and turning his back on me again.

Navan didn't speak again after that, and neither did I. After twenty minutes, I sensed that he had finally let sleep claim him, but I couldn't sleep, not after that. So instead I watched him, trying to unpack everything he had said, everything new I had just learned about this troubled and haunted man.

16

*I* didn't think I'd be able to sleep, but after Navan had been out of it for over an hour and a half, his calm, steady breathing must have seduced me into my own slumber. I woke up to the sensation of something hard and warm beneath my cheek, and as consciousness slowly trickled back to me, I realized with a start that I was partially lying on Navan. My head was on his chest, and I had one arm slung over his waist, my legs trying to intertwine themselves with his.

I jerked backward, and then realized why I had woken up in the first place. Navan was saying my name.

The blood rushed to my cheeks, and I crawled back so fast I almost fell off the bed. "Oh my God!" I exclaimed, mortified.

He was frowning slightly, his blue-gray eyes glimmering with mild amusement at my reaction. "Gee. I didn't realize I was that horrifying."

I blushed. "No! It's not—I mean . . . I'm sorry."

"It's all right." A smile played at the corners of his lips. "I suppose you must've gravitated toward my warmth in your sleep."

"Yeah," I said breathlessly, and as our last conversation came back to me, I was glad that I had managed to bring out a smile in him, even if it was at my expense.

I gazed around the room, still feeling rather disorientated, as I realized how low the sun had dipped in the sky. "What time is it?" I asked, rubbing my forehead.

He pointed toward the clock on the mantelpiece. "7 PM, which is why I woke you. I overslept too—woke up only a minute or two before you."

"Oh man." I swept my feet off the bed and stood up, running my hands through my clean hair. "We should get going then."

"Yes."

"I'll, uh, use the bathroom real quick."

I stumbled into the bathroom and closed the door, leaning my head against it and giving myself a few moments to calm my pounding heart. I washed my face with cold water and lathered another generous layer of cream onto my face and hands, before brushing my teeth, using one of the complimentary tooth-brushes.

After I emerged, Navan took his turn, and he locked himself in the bathroom. As I heard the shower being turned on, I tried to imagine what the bathrooms were like in Vysanthe—whether they were similar, or something entirely different. For that matter, I wondered what civilization in Vysanthe looked like in general. The whole concept of other highly developed civilizations out there in the universe was still sinking in.

I made sure we had all our things together, and then ate another couple of bananas. We were about to make the last leg of the journey to New York, and I wasn't sure how long it would be before I ate again. When we arrived, I supposed we would find another hotel to check into or maybe go straight to an internet café so we could start planning our stunt. *God.* It still hadn't quite sunk in what I had gotten myself into. If all went according to plan, I was going to be coming face to face with yet another supernatural species—lycans.

Navan reemerged from the bathroom ten minutes later, wearing a fresh set of clothes, his black hair, eyebrows, and eyelashes damp.

"Ready?" he asked, sweeping his eyes about the room.

"Yes. If you are."

I put on my coat and Navan grabbed the bag. Together, we checked out of the hotel, and headed back to the same forest we had landed in, figuring that was a good place to take off inconspicuously.

When it came time for me to wrap myself around Navan again, I blushed in a way I hadn't done before, recalling the bed incident, even though it was silly since I had been squeezed up close to him for possibly over ten hours across all our travels. Still, the context of a bedroom had made things feel... different.

He glanced at his compass, consulting his map again, and

then we took off. I braced myself for the harsh wind as we broke through the treetops, and Navan zoomed forward at what felt like three times the speed of his former pace. Clearly, the rest had done him good. And though it made for a much more uncomfortable ride, as my stomach was constantly clenching and my eyes watered as I tried to breathe, it was a needed change—we had lost time to make up for.

It took even less time than I had anticipated for the bright lights of NYC to come into view—a little over an hour. Navan's skin was already resuming its gray hue as he slowed down. We approached the high-rise buildings, and I felt a slight ache in my chest on seeing home. It made me wonder where Jean and Roger were, what they were doing in this moment. At least they were blissfully oblivious to what *I* was doing. If they knew, they'd have a heart attack.

Like I almost did, as a heavy object hurtled past my right ear. A second later, a window in a nearby building shattered. What-ever that was, it had come within inches of my head.

"What was that?!" I gasped.

Another whoosh came from my left, shattering a second window. An alarm went off, followed by loud voices coming from the building, and I could have sworn someone said the word "knife." Navan dropped into a freefall, zooming down the length of the building, even as strange objects—knives?—continued to fly past us.

"What the *hell*?" I screamed.

Navan leveled out, surging ahead through the darkness, weaving a path through the maze of buildings, and traveling so fast we would have been a blur to any surveillance cameras.

The objects stopped flying after us, and I was left with the same unnerving feeling from earlier today, only amplified tenfold. There was nobody in the sky tonight, just as there hadn't been earlier. But it was either that, or Navan and I both were losing our minds. I had seen the shattered window, though, and heard the sound of surprised voices. This could not be just my imagination.

Navan flew for another ten minutes, weaving a complex trail in between buildings, as if trying to shake off an invisible follower. He finally landed on the roof of a twelve-story building, his eyes wide and alert as he set me down and gazed around the evening's sky, before pulling me toward a service door. We crouched down next to it. The worry I had noted earlier in his eyes had returned.

He didn't say anything about it, which made sense, since what was there to say? We stayed down for a long moment, scanning the empty sky, and then he pulled me up, and we took off again.

We weren't flying for long this time, as he headed straight for Central Park, which was only a few streets away. He settled us down in a dark, quiet spot, then pulled in his wings, adjusting the hood of the sweater he was wearing so that it cast long shadows over his face.

"Okay," he said, leading us toward the park's exit, and I couldn't miss the nervousness in his tone. "I have no idea how to explain that, but we should avoid the sky, for now—and we need to get straight on with the plan. The sooner we get this over with, the sooner we get out of danger."

"Do you think it could be the actual *Fed* following us?" I asked. "Do they have the technology to be invisible, and they keep picking up on our trail somehow? Could they have been the ones to fire on us, back in Alaska?"

Navan exhaled, looking deeply concerned. "They might have invisibility tech, but the Fed weren't there when we arrived at the bunker. By the looks of it, they were long gone. I don't know how they'd start tracking us... But whatever the case, we have to continue with the plan. If it's the Fed behind this, then we'll find out soon enough—though, were going to have to take some extra precautions now."

"Like what?"

"We need to be more careful. Even if they *are* flying around in some invisible machine, intermittently picking up on our trail, we probably still have a chance to make peace with the chief. At the moment, they'd simply be trying to eliminate me as a coldblood discovered on Earth's territory, and they don't yet know anything about the blood sample on its way to Vysanthe. I'm hoping that information will be a game changer. It's got to be," he added, almost more to himself.

I sucked in a breath. "Yeah, it had better be." They seemed to be more than willing to sacrifice my life, too, in order to get to Navan. "I wonder if they did get Ianthan after all?" I said in a hushed tone. "Maybe we just didn't find the body."

Navan swallowed. "Maybe... Whatever the case, let's keep moving."

"So should we go straight to an internet café then?" My voice shook a little as I realized just how much danger we were in. "We can, uh, figure out logistics," I added, trying to keep my tone calm.

"Better we do that first, then look for somewhere to rest."

We left the park and walked through crowded streets, keeping our heads down—Navan especially—looking for an internet café, which we found after a few minutes. It was mostly empty. I went in first with some cash to reserve a computer, and then chose the one closest to the window, and gestured for Navan, who had been waiting outside, to discreetly slip in. He took a seat next to me, his back facing the counter.

After half an hour searching the web, analyzing maps, and looking through lists of local events, we figured our best bet would be an outdoor music festival that was being hosted tomorrow evening. That seemed like a long time to wait, but Navan and I needed some time to scope the grounds out, as well as prepare ourselves mentally.

We printed off a detailed map where the event was being held—at a park in Brooklyn that was... kind of close to Jean and Roger's place. I had to hope they wouldn't be attending the festival in some odd twist of events—not that they were likely to find me in a sea of faces, anyway.

We left the café and began a search for someplace to sleep. We ended up in another hotel, in a cheaper area, which didn't turn us down without my ID. They had a room with two twin beds available, so I wouldn't end up cozying up to him by accident again. This time, however, we had to be a little creative about Navan's entrance. His skin was too noticeable under the bright lights of the hotel lobby, so once I had checked into the room, I came back down to Navan who was waiting outside and informed him which window he needed to fly up to. It looked onto a side alley, which made his flight up a little less noticeable, but still, I was nervous somebody would see him clambering inside. We did the job quickly, and soon, we were both settling into the room, sitting opposite each other on our respective beds.

Navan pulled his bag onto his lap, and rummaged around, before pulling out his comm device. "I should check in with Bashrik now. I'm sure his anxiety's off the charts."

I moved over to him as he pressed a button and held the device to his ear. The other end picked up after a few seconds, and I was close enough to hear that the voice coming from the receiver was not Bashrik but Angie. I leaned closer and heard her say, "Navan?!"

"Angie?" he asked, frowning. "How are you? How's Bashrik and Ronad?"

"We're all fine. Lauren and I are with them now. We

managed to slip away from the Churnleys. But listen, I gotta speak to Riley. There've been some, uh, developments."

I held my breath, instantly feeling tense. Navan handed the device to me and I pressed it to my ear. "Angie? What is it?"

"Riley!" She sounded relieved to hear my voice, as I was hers, after everything that happened since I last saw her. "How are you?"

"I'm, um, okay," I replied, figuring that now was not the best time to tell her someone had tried to kill us, again—I'd rather leave that for Navan to tell Bashrik. "What's up?"

"Well, we've kind of been having a problem with the Churnleys regarding your absence. We haven't been able to think of a good excuse to explain it other than... basically you got the major hots for one of the lumberjacks, and went off with him to Austin to spend a few nights."

My face burned. "Oh my God. You didn't tell them that."

"Look—what else were we supposed to tell them?" Angie said. "Honestly!"

I sighed. She was right. It was extremely hard to think of a remotely reasonable excuse for my sudden disappearance, and I probably wouldn't have thought of a much better one, either. Still, it was *embarrassing*.

"The main problem is," Angie continued, "they got in touch with Jean and Roger, and they're kind of freaked out. Understandably, they're worried about you gallivanting off with some guy you've only known for like, less than a day."

I swore under my breath. Crap, crap, *crap*. "What did my

parents say, exactly?" I asked, my chest suddenly feeling constricted.

"They want you to call them as soon as possible. They're worried about you."

"Right, call them." I swallowed.

"And, uh, they want you to actually go home."

*Damn.* It wasn't like Jean and Roger to be controlling, or make demands like this, but they were obviously *completely* freaked out—they might even be thinking I had been kidnapped or trafficked.

"They want me to come home," I repeated, biting my lower lip.

"Yeah. They're really, really worried. I'm guessing they're gonna call the police if they don't hear from you soon."

I exhaled loudly, staring at Navan. He was close enough to have heard every word, and he looked back at me steadily.

"Okay. Well, the good news is we're in New York now, trying to figure out how to meet with the Fed,"—I took a guess that Bashrik had already filled her and Lauren in on what the Fed was, and the fact that she didn't ask confirmed it—"I guess... I guess we could visit them tomorrow morning. We've got some time to kill anyway."

"*We?* You mean, you're gonna take Navan to see them?"

I knew how crazy that sounded, but I was going to need to buy myself at least a few days more, and I needed them to be onboard with my excuse. I had too many other things on my plate to be worrying about them calling the police. Lauren and

Angie had already fed them the lie that I'd found a summer boyfriend so... it only made sense that they should meet him. I was also strangely confident that Navan could pull it off. I'd seen that he could be a gentleman, and I wasn't too worried about him seeming out of place—he knew a lot about Earth's customs. We would go to see them during the daytime, when his skin was normal. We *would* need to have a little chat about some things in advance, though, such as the whole... boyfriend and girlfriend thing.

"Yeah," I replied.

"Okay, well..." Angie sounded totally skeptical, and I couldn't blame her. "Good luck with that."

"Is Lauren there?"

"She's with Bashrik. He's lying down."

"Okay, tell her I said hi. And you can tell the Churnleys to stop worrying—I'll figure things out with my parents."

"Okay," Angie replied.

"Do you want to speak to your brother?" I asked Navan, away from the receiver.

To my surprise, he shook his head. "I'll talk to him next time. Giving him one more thing to worry about isn't going to help him recover any faster. Just ask Angie to tell them we're okay and we'll check in again once we have more developments."

I nodded and conveyed his message, then handed the comm back to Navan, who switched it off. I drew in another deep breath and returned to the bed opposite him. We stared at each other for several long moments, until I finally broke the silence.

"So, uh, you up for meeting my parents?"

he fact that somebody seemed to be following us worried me in relation to our planned visit to Jean and Roger. The last thing I wanted to do was put them in danger. After Navan agreed to meet them, and I filled him in on some basic things about my parents (they wouldn't expect him to know a whole lot anyway, given that we had only just met), we agreed that we would avoid flight and travel there by taxi—I hoped that would make things safer.

I then dialed my adoptive parents' number and spoke to Jean, who sounded both tense and relieved to hear my voice. I told her that taking off with Navan wasn't something I would normally do but, given that it was my last summer before college, I kind of got swept up in the spontaneity of it all. I winced internally even as I said the words, knowing that it really didn't sound like me, but she seemed to buy it. Though, she still wanted me to come home so she could see me face to face, and was glad when I suggested bringing Navan along. We agreed to meet at noon the next day.

Navan and I retired to bed soon after the conversation, though I barely slept, tossing and turning, wondering what tomorrow would bring—the stunt we were planning to pull off far eclipsing any nerves I had about the meeting with my parents. It didn't seem like Navan slept much either, judging by how much he tossed and turned on the other side of the room.

We left the hotel with plenty of time the next morning, and stopped by a store on our way to the subway to buy some more suitable clothes.

"What sort of outfit would your dream boyfriend wear?" Navan wondered as we walked through the racks of clothing. "This?" He stopped in front of a purple velour suit and ran his fingers down the sleeve. "Pair this bad boy with a lime green bow tie?"

I snorted. "Um, that is *not* what my dream boyfriend would wear."

"Well, show me then."

There were suits of all sorts—linen, tweed, velour. Dress shirts with white collars folded into perfect rectangles in clear plastic packaging. Rows of ties in a rainbow of colors. He would've looked good in any of it, but we were going to Jean and Roger's, not some white collar corporate event.

We wandered over to the casual section. "How about I show

up in this?" Navan asked, holding up a gray waffle-weave bathrobe. "Really make a good first impression."

I stifled a laugh. "How about this instead?" I pulled a pair of jeans off a hanger. "Jeans and . . . this." I grabbed a plain black t-shirt.

"I like it," he said. "What about you?"

"You'll look good in it. It's classic."

"No, I meant, what about you for clothes? What are you going to wear?" He seemed genuinely curious.

"Oh. We can head over to the ladies' section. But first you should try those on to make sure they fit."

Navan held the jeans up. "Eh, I'm pretty good at eyeballing things. These are a size too small. And the legs look too short."

"Okay." I slid those jeans back on the hanger and put it on the rack. I grabbed the next size up. "You should still try them on. The dressing room is right here."

He went in with the jeans and the t-shirt. "I'll wait right here," I said, sitting down on a leather bench that was right outside the dressing room. A three-way mirror was in front of me, reflecting three of me back.

"Uh . . . I might need the next size up," Navan called, stepping out of the dressing room. The jeans fit perfectly, but the shirt was way too small—his muscles strained against the fabric and the bottom of the shirt just barely grazed the waistband of the jeans.

I laughed and went back to where the shirts were, grabbing one two sizes up. "Here you go," I said.

He came out of the dressing room again a few seconds later, arms outstretched. "How do I look now?"

I felt like whistling. *Damn good* was how he looked. "Perfect," I replied.

We made our way over to the ladies' section, where there were dresses of every style and color imaginable.

"How about this one?" Navan remarked, holding up a ridiculously gaudy yellow and white polka dot dress with a long, sweeping skirt and white bow in the back.

"That is quite possibly the most ridiculous thing I've ever seen," I announced. I went over to a rack of maxi dresses, where I grabbed a floral print racerback one. "This one will do."

"Okay, I agree that's better." He smiled, and I could tell he was genuinely enjoying himself. I wondered what the shopping experience was like in Vysanthe—if they even had shops.

"Should I come in the dressing room and help you try it on? A good boyfriend would do that, right?"

For a crazy split-second I wasn't actually sure if he was joking, but then I looked at him, and he raised a dark brow, a spark of humor twinkling in his eyes.

"I think I can manage," I replied, simultaneously trying not to laugh and not blush. I was sure getting a good dose of relaxed Navan during this little outing... I guessed there weren't many occasions when he could flex his personality like this—be whoever the heck he wanted to be. Certainly not back in his homeland. And he was clearly taking full advantage of that with me... Not that I was complaining. I found upbeat Navan incredibly cute.

In the dressing room, I was glad to find that the dress I'd chosen fit, and it looked great on me, if I did say so myself. It highlighted the curve of my waist, and the pattern brought out the blue in my eyes. I ripped the tag off so I could pay for it without having to change first, took one last look at myself, and then backed out of the changing room.

As I reemerged, Navan was standing, waiting for me, his arms crossed over his chest. And when he saw me, he froze, and I could have sworn his eyes lit up.

"Oh, that..." He cleared his throat and hesitated for a moment, as if trying to find the right words. He uncrossed his arms and took a step back, giving me a long once over. "That... looks much better on you than my shirt," he concluded, his eyes spanning the length of my legs and returning to my face, his lips curved in an admiring smile.

I grinned, accepting the compliment. "Thanks."

He kept his eyes on me as I approached him, and it was all I could do to keep my cheeks from flaming. *Damn.* I'd been on my fair share of dates during high school, and I'd never felt this girly around any guy before.

On our way out of the store, we passed by another three-way mirror and Navan held out a hand, stopping us in front of it.

"Would you look at us," he said, putting an arm around me and causing my breath to involuntarily hitch. "Not too bad on the eyes at all... You ready to go impress the pants off your parents?"

"Um . . . I hope they're not that impressed that they lose their pants. I'd very much like to avoid that, actually, at all costs."

He chuckled and kept his arm around me as we walked out of the store, and I doubted he realized the effect it had on me. My face felt thoroughly red by the time I hailed a taxi and directed it to Jean and Roger's neighborhood.

Once we were sitting, I returned my thoughts to the task at hand. Until now, I hadn't been feeling that nervous about this first task of the day. Navan was clearly in a calm mood, and I reminded myself that he could handle it, especially since we were not planning to stay for long, anyway. I'd told my parents we had plans with Navan's brother who lived in the city. Still, my palms were sweating as we arrived at my adoptive parents' street, and we approached our modest, three-bedroom house. It felt like everything had changed so much since I had last been here, my entire world spun out of control. It was going to be hard to act like nothing had happened.

I stopped at the porch and drew in a deep breath. I glanced at Navan. His expression was calm, almost contemplative, and I realized that if anyone had the right to be nervous about this, it was *him*. I grabbed a hold of that thought and tried to infuse some of that calmness into myself, right as Sally, our Labrador, started barking.

"Riley!" Jean must've been waiting right by the door, because it swung open and there was her thin face, breaking out into a smile, her crow's feet crinkling at the corners of her warm brown eyes. But as they fell on Navan, I could see the tension brewing behind them. Her eyes widened as she took in his imposing form, the image she'd had in her head of who I might've run off with was evidently very different from the man who stood before her.

I had to hide my smile as Roger appeared behind her, his blue eyes bulging, too, and his red-bearded face assuming an almost identical expression to Jean's. Roger was by no means short at almost six feet, but even he had to tilt his head slightly to look Navan in the eye.

"And this would be Navan?" Jean managed, and I nodded, suppressing a smile.

"The dashing boyfriend that swept Riley away," Navan replied, and he gave a warm smile, the hard lines of his face softening. "That would be me. I apologize if I caused you any distress. It's an honor to meet you." His smooth, polite tone was at odds with his rugged appearance, and I could see from my parents' faces that they were pleasantly surprised. He also spoke with a neutral American accent, like we had discussed—so as to avoid questions about which country he was from, as his regular accent was clearly not American. It wasn't the best impersonation, but it was passable.

"Come in, come in," Jean said, stepping back with a smile to allow us in. Navan had to duck his head under the doorway to avoid bashing it as he entered, and we left our shoes by the door.

"Again, I'm so sorry for scaring you guys," I said as we moved through the house, dodging Sally, who rushed up to Navan and started sniffing him.

"Well, the main thing is you're safe and happy," Jean replied, though there was still a note of uncertainty in her voice.

We entered the dining room, which looked out onto our small garden. Navan and I sat next to each other on one side of the table, while Jean positioned two chairs on the other. There was an awkward silence as my two adoptive parents gazed at us. Then Jean announced, "I'll bring in the brunch!"

"So," Roger said, fixing Navan with a half-friendly, half-wary look. "Where are you from, Navan?"

"Born and bred in Austin," he replied genially.

"Navan works in renovation," I explained. "He's been doing some work on the plot of land next to the Churnleys'."

Jean reentered with a tray of tea, coffee, and snacks, and I helped myself to an herbal, decaffeinated tea bag instinctively, the silver root incident still fresh in my mind. Navan went for a coffee, and I was genuinely curious to watch his reaction to the warm drink. I wasn't sure if he'd tasted it before.

"How did you and Riley meet?" Jean asked.

"Well," Navan began in a confident, almost theatrical tone, "it was a blisteringly hot day and for unknown reasons, I thought that might be a good time to chop some wood. I must've been complaining a bit loudly about it, because the next thing I knew, Riley's there, wanting to know if everything's all right. Apparently, she and her friends had been out doing some work in the Churnleys' garden, and she could hear me all the way across the field."

Jean beamed at me. "That's our girl," she said. "Riley has a good heart, as I'm sure you know. She's always concerned about the well-being of others."

"I couldn't agree with you more," Navan replied, and he made a big show of reaching over and squeezing my hand. "She sure is something."

I looked at him, feeling suddenly very awkward with all eyes on me, and he winked.

"She's also the bravest woman I've ever met," he added, and this time, the frivolity was gone from his voice, and his expression had become serious as he looked over at me.

I blushed as Jean and Roger smiled fondly. "That she is," Roger said, and I wished I could do a disappearing act under the table.

His response was well chosen, though, as it held real meaning to my adoptive parents. I could see that it instantly warmed them toward him. They were obviously thinking I'd told him a bit about my past, and what I'd been through, though I had personally never thought to describe myself as *brave*. I'd simply survived.

"Well!" Roger said, clapping his hands together. "We can certainly tell you've got charisma, Navan."

Jean smiled, and was it my imagination or was that smile bordering on coy? "I understand now why you might have wanted to go out and have a little summer fling."

I pasted a smile onto my face in an attempt to hide my mortification.

"What about you, Riley?" Roger asked. "Navan says you're the bravest woman he's ever met—and I don't think I'd dispute him there—but what do you like so much about him?"

"Um . . ." Was this really happening right now? Had it been a huge mistake to come here? I knew Roger and Jean would be scrutinizing Navan, but I didn't think they'd be asking questions like this. Navan leaned back in his chair, barely able to contain the smile on his face. They were all looking at me, waiting.

"I'm not really sure what to say," I said slowly, "other than he just . . . swept me off my feet."

Navan could barely contain his chuckle, while Roger nodded approvingly, and Jean sighed.

"Young love," she said. "Such a wonderful thing."

We spent the rest of the conversation on mostly small talk, and I could see from my parents' perspective that was intentional. They really just wanted to observe this new guy I'd suddenly developed the hots for, so they could feel comfortable about me spending time with him. By the end of our brunch, Navan had certainly accomplished that—in fact, he'd pulled this whole thing off more beautifully than I'd thought possible. It was hard to fake genuine friendliness and respect, and I knew Jean and Roger well enough to tell when they were putting on a front.

It was difficult to imagine this was the same man who, barely a day ago, had decapitated someone with his bare hands.

*Never trust a first impression,* I thought wryly.

As the hour drew to a close, I set my cup down. "I'm sorry we can't stay longer; we've got to meet Navan's brother after this. He lives in New York and has room in his apartment for us, so we were planning to spend a little time there before returning to Texas."

"Back to Texas?" Jean asked, finishing her own cup of tea. "How will you get back there?"

"Uh, we're not sure yet. I'll let you know once we've thought about it." I was about to say, *you can always call my phone, too,* when I remembered I didn't even have it with me. So far, my parents hadn't commented on the fact that I'd entered without a handbag, nor pulled out my phone once, so hopefully I'd be able to slip out without having to touch on that particular detail. "We should probably get going," I added, brushing off invisible crumbs from my knees as I stood up.

I moved over to Jean and gave her a hug and a kiss on the cheek, then did the same with Roger. When they moved to shake hands with Navan, I winced slightly, thinking about his warmth. Thanks to the formula he was on, his touch wouldn't be nauseatingly hot, but he was still warmer than the average human. Luckily, they didn't notice—or if they did, they didn't comment and chalked it up to him just being... a hot guy.

I led the way out of the living room and back down the hallway toward the front door, bending down to say goodbye to Sally as I went. But before I could reach the door, the bell rang.

I opened it and then jerked back, practically choking on my tongue as I stared at the two people standing in the doorway.

My parents. My real parents.

My stomach twisted into knots at the sight of them, and a wave of sickness surged up in my throat. I took a step back, bumping into Navan and Jean who were right behind me, and I felt Jean's hand squeeze my shoulder, her guard immediately up when she realized who it was.

"Sasha, George. Can...Can I help you?" she asked.

Their eyes flickered over Navan with some confusion and they barely even looked at Jean, before their eyes zoned in on me.

My mother wore a white and blue floral summer dress which clung to her bony frame in a most unflattering way. Her blue eyes looked bloodshot, her face pale and sagging, and her wispy gray hair was tied up in a limp ponytail. I couldn't remember the last time I'd seen her in a dress, and the irregularity disturbed me, as I realized this was probably her way of dressing up to see me. My father wore his usual attire—a pair of jeans one size too big for him, and a loose, crinkled shirt, sleeves rolled up to his elbows in the heat. His mustached face was as ragged as my mother's, his hair balding at the crown of his head.

*Why were they here? How did they know to come?*

"We wanted to check in to see that Riley was definitely okay," my mother said, her voice like nails grating against cement.

Jean shuffled next to me and gave them a forced smile. "Excuse us for a minute." She didn't give them a chance to respond as she gripped my hand and pulled me back into the house, pushing the door until it was mostly closed, so that we could have a somewhat private conversation.

"How are they here?" I whispered.

Jean gave me an apologetic look. "By coincidence, they called me last night—before you called to tell me you were okay. Your mother called wanting to verify the date of your return from Texas and, well, I was feeling extremely worried about your absence and it seemed only right for me to mention that you had gone missing from Elmcreek. Then you called me, so I called her back after I spoke to you just to let her know you had been located and were fine, and would even be stopping by to see me today at noon. In hindsight, I shouldn't have told her the time—it slipped my mind, but I honestly didn't expect them to show up uninvited like this." She paused, sucking in a breath. "Look, you don't have to deal with them. I can simply tell them you're not ready for this—"

She trailed off as I slowly shook my head. As unpleasant a surprise as this was, something told me that I couldn't keep running forever, that I had to get this over and done with. They had been trying to see me for weeks, and they were here now, right on my doorstep. I had to find some kind of closure with them, for my own sake more than theirs, no matter how painful it might be.

I met Navan's eyes briefly as I turned around, and I couldn't help but note the concern there. I shook the thought aside as I pulled open the door again and reemerged on the doorstep.

They stood there on the lower step, gazing up at me with expectant eyes, my mother especially. Her expression was so wide eyed with anticipation, it made me feel raw inside.

I steeled myself against it, and met their gaze head on.

"Mom, Dad," I said, the terms spilling coldly from my tongue. "How can I help you?"

"Oh, don't be so formal, Riley," my mother chided in her scratchy voice. She reached out to squeeze my arm, but I flinched. I was willing to talk to them, but *that* was going one step too far.

My mother looked crestfallen, but I couldn't bring myself to feel much sympathy.

"But we have good news," she said. "And we wanted to tell you in person."

"What?" I asked warily.

My birth parents exchanged a glance. "We've been saved."

"Excuse me?" I said.

"Saved?" Navan asked from behind me.

They both nodded vehemently. "There's this church we go by almost every day," my father said. "Always walked by it, barely even noticed it, if you want to know the truth."

"It does have the most beautiful stained glass," my mother said. "I did always notice that."

"Right, well, aside from the stained glass then. Other than that, it was just this structure that we walked by. Until recently, your mother and I were going by and we both felt pulled to go in there. Just felt that it was what we *had* to do. So we went right in, and we sat in one of the pews. We just sat there for quite some time, and we were both filled with . . . with . . . well, I don't really know how to describe it. We were both filled—"

"With the love of God," my mother interjected. "And that has changed everything."

"We've realized the true error of our ways."

"We want to repent for everything that we've done."

"We have found our way back to the path of righteousness."

I stared at them, my mouth hanging open.

"George, Sasha," Jean said. "That's . . . that's wonderful news."

"I know we shouldn't have just stopped over like this," my mother said. "But we wanted to share our news with you in person, Riley."

"Did you like the birthday gift?" my father asked.

"I-I... I haven't opened it yet."

They both sighed. "Riley," my mother said. "What we've been trying to communicate to you is that we are sorry. We are truly sorry for everything and if we could go back in time, we would take it all back. We would treat you the way..."— here her voice cracked—"the way a beautiful little girl like you deserved to be treated."

I glanced away, a muscle in my jaw throbbing as I tried to maintain a stoic expression. "Okay," I said. "Is that all you wanted to say? Aside from this good news of your newfound belief in God?"

"We have something for you."

My father's hand dipped into the plastic bag he was carrying, and drew out an envelope. I glanced at it, suspicious and hesitant, immediately assuming that it was going to be more stupid photographs. I took the envelope and turned it over, realizing that it was too light to be photos. It couldn't hold more than a thin piece of paper...

"It's... a little something to help you along with your college," my mother explained, looking at me through her rheumy, doleful eyes. "We saved up, and I know it's not much but we hope it'll be helpful."

As soon as it hit me that they'd handed me a check, my instinct was to drop it. *No,* I realized. I wasn't ready for this. Photographs were one thing, money was entirely another.

I pressed the envelope back into my father's hands.

"I appreciate it," I said, "but you can keep it."

I couldn't deny that money would be helpful for my education, but I wasn't willing to accept the ties that I knew would come with it. I had worked way too hard to remove the invisible bonds they'd held over me for years to allow this. Even if they had changed and truly repented for what they'd done, it was going to take time, and a lot more than words to prove it.

Tears formed in my mother's eyes as she realized I wasn't going to accept it. "Why, Riley?" she asked. "Do you still hate us that much? I know we caused you so much hurt, baby girl, and we don't expect you to forgive us, but we've been trying so very hard to change, to be the parents you deserve. Won't you let us at least *try* to make things up to you?"

"Mom, I-I can't." To my horror, I realized my mask was cracking. I felt the heat of tears rising in my eyes. I'd been handling this calmly, but watching a full-grown woman break down in front of me tore emotions out of me that I'd thought I'd locked away. It made me angry at the same time, as a part of me wondered if my mother's tears were even genuine, or just a show to manipulate me. Either way, it was working.

I stepped back and breathed in heavily, *refusing* to cry. I pressed a trembling finger to my temple, trying to find the right words to express why I couldn't accept it, and why they had to stay out of my life until further notice. I'd gone over my reasoning in my head for why I behaved the way I did with them thousands of times, but it was all suddenly much more difficult to recall now, with them standing right in front of me, looking so old and unwell and *remorseful*. "I-I..." I stumbled, and just as I was feeling I could cry out in frustration, an unexpected weight landed on my shoulder and a warm, strong hand closed around it.

I glanced up to see that Navan had stepped right behind me, his eyes fixed on my parents.

Their gazes rose to his face, their eyes widening.

"Your daughter does not hate you, Mr. and Mrs. Fenton," he stated matter-of-factly, and his deep, steady voice was the exact antidote my shredded nerves needed. "She's not rejecting you either. Her decisions these days are made in complete isolation of you—without spite or malice—merely a desire to focus on her own life and growth. And she would appreciate if you accepted that. When or if she wants to resume a relationship with you, rest assured, she will come to you. I'm sure as parents that's difficult to hear, but you have to accept that Riley has made her choice."

I gawked at him as much as my parents did. He had voiced exactly what I'd wanted to but could not, as if he were inside my very brain.

My parents took a step back, my mother's tears fading some as she stared at him. I could have even sworn that I saw a flicker of understanding cross her face.

Silence fell between us, as I gazed between my parents, and then Navan was saying to Jean and Roger, "It was a pleasure meeting you." His large hand closed around mine, and the next thing I knew, he was leading me out of the house, past my parents, and through the front yard toward the gate.

I had enough time to turn around and say, "Goodbye," before we exited through the gate and turned a corner.

"Whoa," I said, gripping his arm and pulling him to a stop. "Navan, what was that? How did you... why..." I trailed off, speechless as I stared up at him.

"I didn't want to be out there in the open like that for too long. It was dangerous."

"No! I mean, where did all that come from?" And how did he know my parents' last name, for that matter? I didn't recall telling him.

He shrugged, a smile stretching slowly across his face. "Don't give me the credit. I was simply repeating what you told me."

*Oh man.* I should have guessed that right away. Though I highly doubted I'd been as articulate when I'd been in my state of delirium, he had still been attentive and sensitive enough to interpret my words. "What else did I tell you when I was delirious?"

"I think it's probably safe to say you told me your life story, mostly things relating to your parents. You don't want to be pressured into seeing them. Deep down, you love them, but you're afraid to get close to them in case they disappoint you again. Also, you don't know if you might turn into someone you don't want to be."

His gray-blue eyes felt like they were boring into my very soul as he looked down at me, filled with an empathy that made me feel so completely understood. He put into words what I was feeling so simply and eloquently that I could tell he was drawing from personal experience. Yet it felt like he almost knew me better than myself—drawing out things I hadn't fully realized. What he'd said about me loving my parents—I hadn't been conscious that that was how I felt about them, and it made me do a double take. Frankly, I couldn't remember *ever* experiencing emotions of love toward either of them. Guilt, yes, but love? I hadn't been aware of it, and to hear that deep truth about myself coming from Navan's lips, it felt like he'd just left me with a better understanding of myself—even though he was, by many standards, still a stranger to me. It also made me feel better about my refusal of my parents' gift. Because what Navan said was true. I *did* love them, even if that love was hidden beneath layers of other emotions, and my motive was not to hurt them. And maybe their newfound belief in God would mean they quit drinking for good—assuming they were telling the truth. If that happened, maybe, just maybe, we might be able to have some sort of relationship.

"Thank you," I said softly.

He shrugged. "No need to thank me—I didn't say anything you didn't already say yourself."

"Maybe not, but you made it sound way better than I could have."

He smiled. "Maybe I should take up poetry."

I had already thanked him, but it didn't feel like enough. I didn't know what else to say, though, so I let the gratitude stay inside me, swell up in my chest. Maybe I'd find the words to better express it later.

Navan finally turned away, nodding his head toward the opposite end of the street, and set me with a serious look. "We should get going. We've got a lot to do before tonight."

18

Once darkness had fallen, we left the hotel room via the window, Navan stretching his wings and flying us to the event site. We risked flying this time, because our destination was not far, and if our pursuer was related to the Fed, we would be forcing their hand very soon anyway.

We had scoped the site out after visiting Jean and Roger, and finalized logistics. Now all that remained was action.

Reaching the park, the music and smoke drifted up from the throbbing crowds, and we stuck to the treetops. We had changed back into our dark, plain clothes, which helped us avoid notice until the time was right. After trailing above a line of trees, Navan made sure the coast was clear and then dropped down through the treetops, setting me down on the grass.

His eyes were wide and alert as he glanced toward the stage, and then back at me. "Okay," he said quietly. "You know what to do?"

I nodded, gulping. He turned to leave, but before he could fly away again, I grasped his hand. "Be careful," I whispered.

"I will," he said, giving me a meaningful look. "You too."

With that, I moved away from the trees, and looked discreetly at the sky where Navan was flying, like a shadow among the treetops, making his way toward the back of the stage. The crowd erupted in whoops and clapping as a female performer strolled onto the stage and began singing. A long fabric screen hung behind her and her band, from ceiling to floor, which was being used as a projector. That would be Navan's first stop.

He had now flown level with the back of the stage, and I watched him quickly cross the distance between it and himself, so fast I would have missed him if I'd blinked. He flew out of view, and I could only assume that he was now beginning to figure out how to infiltrate the back stage. We had managed to buy him a backstage pass earlier, but that didn't mean getting access to the projector was going to be easy.

I moved closer to the crowd, pulling my hood up to cast a shadow over my face. As the first song ended, and the second one began, I kept my eyes glued on the projector screen. I dug my fingernails into my palms for the duration of two more songs, and just as I was beginning to worry that Navan had run into trouble, he made his appearance.

His imposing silhouette became visible through the

projector screen, his large wings stretched out, and there was a collective sound of appreciation from the crowd, thinking this was part of the special effects.

That became harder to believe when suddenly, he launched forward, directly into the fabric, ripping the entire screen from its hinges. It collapsed on top of him, folding around him as his wings beat underneath and he took to the air. There was a ripping sound, and then the bulk of the fabric fell from the sky, drifting down onto the crowd, while Navan kept just enough covering him to avoid people glimpsing his body. All anyone could make out clearly now were the ends of his black wings—and that would be enough of a distinguishing feature for the Fed.

People gaped upward, though it was clear the majority still believed this to be a feature of the show, or maybe even a prank.

That all changed when Navan, spotting me in the crowd, dove down at breakneck speed and grabbed me, plucking me up into the air.

I flailed and shrieked, making a show of being petrified, while Navan was ultra-careful to keep my face mostly obscured from the crowd beneath us. He kept me facing him, covering me partially with the same fabric he was using as a cover for himself. If anyone managed to get a snap of me...well, that would be kind of counterproductive to the special visit we had made to Jean and Roger earlier today.

My acting must have been convincing because people started to scream and call for help.

"How much longer do you think we need to do this?" I gasped.

"Not too much longer," he replied, as he continued to whoosh me about in the sky. "But we want to make sure we leave an impression."

Navan did another loop in the sky, which left my head spinning. Even after all the experience I'd had so far with being carried by him hundreds of feet in the air, it was incredibly unnerving to have my feet dangling like this, but I trusted his strong grip around my waist, and I continued playing the part of distressed damsel.

When we'd first come up with this final plan of action, I'd been half afraid that the humans beneath us would start trying to shoot at Navan—but thankfully, nobody was that stupid. Leaving aside the fact that Navan was flying too fast for any human to take accurate aim, they were also more likely to shoot me than Navan.

"Okay," Navan said, after another few moments had passed. "That's enough. Now we need to get out of here and find somewhere to wait—"

Before Navan could finish his sentence, a heavy weight slammed into us—so sudden and unexpected, Navan's grip loosened on me and I almost fell from the sky. I screamed, and this time, it was for real.

He staggered in the air, gripping me harder and clutching me to his chest, and then zoomed forward, away from the park, away from whatever invisible thing had almost knocked us from the sky.

We had escaped the park and were flying low, weaving a path in and out of tall buildings, when sharp objects cut through the air, giving me a déjà vu moment of the previous night. I was expecting Navan to pour on the speed to place more distance between us and our invisible attacker, but in a move that almost gave me a heart attack, he soared toward the end of a dark alleyway and stopped at the end of it. He pushed me behind him as two knives hurtled directly at us, and in a moment when I could've sworn I saw my whole life flash before my eyes, Navan hauled me downward, the knives slamming into the brick wall behind us and clattering to the ground. I barely had time to look at them before Navan had snatched them up, and faster than I realized what was happening, he had shot the two blades forward with such breathtaking velocity I feared they would travel the entire length of the alley and reach the crowded street on the other side.

But instead they stopped abruptly in midair, less than six feet away. Two bloodcurdling cries rang out, and blood blossomed on the tips of both steel blades, one the color of molten lava, the other dark red. The next second, two figures thudded to the ground.

One was Ianthan, a knife plunged deep into his chest, and the second was a creature who must have been riding on top of Ianthan; the second blade had caught it in the neck. It looked nothing like a lycan or a werewolf—it was thin, hairless like a baby bird, and wiry, wearing an ice blue suit. Its skin was pinkish and so pale it looked almost translucent, and its long hair was almost white. Its hands and feet were far bigger than a human's, with long and bony fingers, and its bulging eyes were a deep orange color.

"Ianthan," Navan breathed, dropping to his knees before his friend. "What are you..." His eyes took in the other creature with alarm. "A *shapeshifter*?"

"Is it dead?" I stammered.

Navan ignored me as he grabbed the creature on top of Ianthan by the hair and threw him aside. He clutched Ianthan's shoulders and rolled him over, revealing the full extent of his wound. I doubted even one of Navan's formulas could fix him, but that didn't stop Navan from reaching into his bag and pulling out two vials. He poured them over the wound, and I assumed they were meant to stall the bleeding, but it wasn't enough. The blade had wedged too deeply into his chest. Ianthan sucked in a sharp breath. "I'm sorry, Navan. It forced me to..." His voice trailed off, his body going still.

Navan's breath hitched, and then he shook his friend, as if that could bring him back to life. "No, Ianthan," he rasped, and I realized from the tears glistening in his eyes that, despite Ianthan's involvement with Jethro's betrayal, Navan still loved his friend, and would have, in time, forgiven him.

Navan seemed to channel his grief into fury as he turned on the creature next to Ianthan. The "shapeshifter" was still managing to hold out, though from the looks of it, it wouldn't be for much longer. Blood dribbled from its mouth, its chest contracting erratically. Navan grabbed it by the back of the neck, and the second he did so, the shapeshifter's body morphed, and to my shock, turned into the spitting image of the homeless man we'd seen the night before, who had taken refuge in Navan's bunker. The vision flickered, and then changed again, to another human I didn't recognize. It continued to flicker and blur, from another human form and then to that of a brown Alaskan bear, and then its ability to shift seemed to sputter out, and it resumed its original pale shape. A now dead shapeshifter.

"What just happened?" I breathed, my heart hammering against my ribcage.

Navan stepped backward, unsteady on his feet as he stared down at the two corpses before us. His answer came out disjointed, as though his brain was still trying to process it all. "It was him... this shifter. Somehow, for some reason, it had been waiting for us, back in my bunker, to see if anybody was going to come back. And then... followed us, once it found out our intent? It was sent by someone, perhaps, and has been trailing us on and off. They must have kept losing us and finding us again. Using Ianthan as its carrier."

I stared at him. "What? How could it have followed us? Why?"

"Shapeshifters can adopt any form they like. They can camouflage themselves with the environment, which in effect makes them invisible. They can also impart that camouflage to others, via their touch. Somehow, it got Ianthan, which was why we couldn't find him. I just... I didn't know shapeshifters were prevalent on Earth. It makes no sense to me that they would work for the Fed, either, since as far as I've always understood, the two have a notoriously bad relationship, almost as bad as they have with coldbloods." He shook his head. "None of this makes any sense."

"Well, maybe the Fed made an exception in this case?" I had never witnessed anyone die right in front of me and, even if they weren't exactly human, it was unsettling.

We didn't have time to stand there, though, because a crowd had started to gather at the end of the alley.

I grabbed Navan's arm, expecting him to spread his wings and lift us out of there, but his eyes had fixed on two tall, heavy-set dark figures in skin-tight black suits heading swiftly toward us through the crowd. Steel masks covered their faces, and they moved with a confidence that scared me. Thick belts with sheathed weapons fit securely around their waists.

"Here they come," Navan breathed, and I felt his hand rest lightly on the small of my back in a protective gesture. "Lycans."

I sucked in a breath. Our plan had gone horribly wrong. We were the ones who were supposed to have spotted the Fed so I could make the first approach.

I instinctively stepped in front of Navan and moved toward both men. The crowd on the other end, I realized, was staying in place, watching the two men approach us, perhaps mistaking them for off-duty policemen. I could make out the lycans' eyes as they neared, vibrant shades of green and amber, and my heart was in my throat as they stopped three feet in front of us.

I held out my hands in what I hoped was a universal sign of peace, even as they eyed the two supernatural corpses behind me. Although the first question I wanted to ask was whether the shifter had been working for them, I had to be economical with my words, especially as they both reached for their belts and unhooked some kind of silver handgun.

"You've made more than a bit of a mess here, haven't you?" one of them snarled, glaring at Navan. He pointed his weapon at Navan's chest. "What's a bloodsucker like you doing on Earth? Spit it out before I put a bullet in your brain."

"Please," I said, my gaze beseeching them to listen. I could see the question whirring behind their eyes as they looked at me: *What's this human doing with a coldblood?* "I know what it looks like, but we're not here to cause trouble. We pulled off a stunt back there only to get your attention—we have an urgent message for your chief, and you need to take us to see him. Human blood is currently in transit to Vysanthe."

They stopped. It was impossible to tell if they believed it, as I couldn't see their expressions behind their masks. But they went silent for a moment and glanced at each other, which I hoped was a sign that they were at least considering it.

Then one of them reached out and grabbed me by the arm. Navan immediately stepped forward, but the second lycan pointed the gun at him.

"Don't move," the officer growled.

My ears picked up on the sound of rotors, and I looked up to see a black chopper hovering thirty feet above us. Four more masked figures, clad in black suits, dropped from the aircraft, rappelling down on wires. They landed heavily, three of them instantly moving to Navan and grabbing him, roughly locking his arms behind his back.

The lycan who was holding me shoved me toward the fourth lycan attached to a wire. He gave Navan one last glare. "Oh, we're taking you with us all right."

19

*T*he wires shot us into the night sky and pulled us into the belly of the waiting helicopter. The open hatch clamped shut after us, and Navan and I found ourselves standing within a small chamber lined with metal panels and long benches against the walls. Two lycans waited, in addition to the four who had escorted us up, and they grabbed us roughly by the wrists, fastening cold metal handcuffs around them. I wasn't sure if Navan would be able to break out of them, but it was a moot point—we'd have to cooperate if we wanted a chance of meeting with the chief.

I shot a worried glance at Navan, who was standing a few feet away from me, and although I could sense nervousness behind his eyes, he was keeping his calm. He gave me a firm, reassuring look, and I tried to latch onto it, instill some of his calm into my racing heart.

One of the lycans led me to a bench and sat me down, and the others did the same with Navan, seating him next to me. A second later, black fabric was pulled over my head and I couldn't see a thing.

"Is this necessary?" I asked nervously, but the lycans ignored me. It sounded like they were walking out, but I managed to make out one of them saying, "Sergis and Masta said they'll deal with the cleanup job."

I felt Navan's warm hand touch my knee, as if to reassure me. "It's okay," he whispered. "They just don't want us to see how to get to their headquarters."

I swallowed as the sounds of the lycans' voices faded behind the closed door. "What do they mean by 'cleanup job'?"

"I imagine they have their own memory-wiping formula," he replied. "I doubt they'll bother with the people at the concert, given that I never revealed myself fully—you'll probably see the story on the cover of tomorrow's *National Enquirer*. But that scene in the alleyway was too graphic. They'll have to go after the humans who'd gathered at the end of the street."

The hairs on my arms stood on end as the chopper propelled forward to God knew where. I felt terribly vulnerable. We had no idea what these lycans were going to do with us, or if they would even arrange the meeting we needed. They could be on their way to a remote location where they could execute us. If anything was keeping us alive, it had to be what I'd said regarding blood being on its way to Vysanthe. We had to hope that would last.

I slid closer to Navan on the bench, craving his warmth. It was chilly at this altitude, and although I knew Navan's heat would fade soon, he still held some warmth from the mild city night. He must've sensed my insecurity, as his hand touched my knee again, squeezing. "You're doing great," he said. "I mean that. You really are brave."

If those words had meant something to me before, they meant a whole lot more now. "Thank you," I whispered, squeezing him back.

It was hard to say how long the journey lasted—maybe a few hours, though with the black hood over my head, it felt like eternity.

We knew we were nearing our destination when the cockpit door opened, and footsteps spilled into the room. They stopped a few feet in front of us, where they remained, until the aircraft slowed, and then descended at a rapid speed, making my stomach flip.

When we shuddered to a stop, the footsteps moved forward and a viselike grip hauled me up. I was lofted over somebody's shoulder in a fireman's lift, and I spluttered, winded from the unexpected movement. I had no choice but to get used to the position as the lycan carrying me descended a set of stairs, and then stepped onto what sounded like rocky terrain, judging by the crunch beneath his boots. I heard more footsteps climbing down the stairs— Navan and the others following us—and my lycan continued to move forward, in what quickly became a very bumpy ride.

The air felt distinctly different from New York. It was also chilly, with a sharp wind that carried the scent of saltwater. We were by the ocean, but which ocean? Were we even still in the United States?

Finally, the lycan put me down. We walked forward, and after a few feet, the gravel turned into a sharp ridge that I would've tripped on had it not been for the strong man gripping my arm and pulling me over it. We then stepped onto a flat surface, perhaps polished stone or marble. I heard the sound of doors sliding apart in front of us, and then closing once we were through. We had stepped into some kind of hall, perhaps a lobby or a reception area, judging by the soft echoing of voices.

We stopped in front of something hard and wooden that felt like a desk, and my escort spoke up. "Is Interrogation Room 3 available?" he asked gruffly.

"It is. You can go through," a higher-pitched voice replied, which I suspected belonged to a female lycan.

We started walking again, the lycan guiding me across the room, and I heard another door slide open in front of us. He yanked me through and then after another minute of walking, we came to a stop. There was a beep, the *swish* of another door opening, and then I could sense a blinding white light. The fabric over my head was tightly woven, but this light was so bright, some still managed to get through.

I was lowered into a seat, and I heard Navan settling next to me. Then the bags were pulled off our heads, forcing us to face the full brunt of the fluorescent lighting. I had to cover my eyes with my hands, the light stinging my pupils, and was only able to look around after a minute, by which time our escorts had left the room—except for one. I glanced at Navan, who seemed to have adjusted to the light faster than me, his eyes fixed on the remaining lycan.

His mask was still on, his vibrant coral eyes glaring through. But as he lowered himself into a seat opposite us, he removed the mask, revealing a face that was... quite extraordinary. Its bone structure was narrow and angular, with eyes set deep beneath an overhanging forehead. He had ashy brown hair that was more like a mane about his face, with the longest sideburns I'd ever seen on a man, and fine brown hairs covered every inch of his face and neck. His thin lips parted, revealing two sets of jagged teeth, and as he clasped his hands together in front of him, I realized just how inhuman they were—gnarly and elongated with unretractable claws.

He looked between Navan and me, raising a thick eyebrow. "So," he said, his voice gravelly, "who would like to start?"

I looked uncertainly at Navan, but he was staring straight ahead, a cool expression on his face. "Before we begin, surely you don't mind telling us what your rank is?" he said. "I carry sensitive information that needs to be relayed directly to your chief, or whoever makes the decisions around here."

"Well, I am not the chief," he replied tersely. "I'm the head of interrogation—it is my job to decide what matters are worthy of the chief's attention. Did you honestly think he meets with just anyone we pull off the street? I suggest you start talking, coldblood, or the guards will go with their first instinct to execute you, and wipe the memory of the human girl and pack her back to her city."

A muscle in Navan's jaw twitched, but he kept his composure. I knew the potential consequences of Navan's betrayal, if any of his people back home found out that he had given information about Vysanthe's activities to the Fed.

Navan cleared his throat. "I take your point. I will explain everything, but, as I'm sure you can understand, I won't reveal my identity until I have a guarantee that you will keep what I say in complete confidence. You need to understand that I'm putting our lives in danger by coming to you and spilling secrets. My homeland would kill me for it."

The head interrogator had a good poker face, but not so good that he could pretend his interest wasn't piqued at the mention of "secrets." Navan looked at one corner of the ceiling, where a camera was positioned. "I will also ask you to switch off that camera, and obliterate the footage of us stepping in here," he said.

The lycan's eyes widened at the request, as though he couldn't quite believe that Navan had dared to ask it. He opened his mouth and I was sure that he was going to refuse, but then he seemed to have second thoughts, and instead detached a device from his belt, and issued the order, "Rus, switch off the camera in IR 3—and wipe all footage from the last five minutes."

"Are you sure about that, sir?" a gruff voice spoke back through the loudspeaker.

"Just do it."

"Camera's off, sir, and working on the footage deletion."

The lycan shut off the device.

I understood that the camera was there for safety reasons, and was a little confused as to why the lycan had bent on this request. His curiosity must be overshadowing his caution.

He looked back at Navan and nodded. "Proceed."

Navan shifted in his chair, positioning himself in a more upright posture, before launching into his explanation. From the fact that Vysanthe had become obsessed with seeking an elixir for immortality, to Navan discovering Earth, to his desire to keep it safe from his compatriots, to how he came across me, and everything that had happened since we left Texas. The main thing Navan omitted was the fact that he had killed the lycan agent who discovered his bunker—and fortunately, this lycan didn't seem to know about an agent going missing up north... which might confirm Navan's earlier suspicion that the Fed agent who came after him had been working alone.

By the time Navan was finished, the lycan was frowning, his expression unnervingly difficult to interpret. The look he was giving Navan could be either disbelief or deep thought.

"That shapeshifter who took Navan's friend hostage in order to follow us," I ventured, wanting to break the quiet that had descended, "was he an ally of the Fed? Was he working for you?"

The lycan's eyes switched to me, and he barked out a dry

laugh. "Absolutely not. We would no sooner work with shapeshifters than we would with coldbloods. Dishonest, conniving creatures."

I felt some of the blood leave my face as I glanced over at Navan. "Then who was he?" *Why had he been waiting in Navan's bunker, and why was he following us? Had it been the shifters who somehow discovered Navan's lair, and stolen all his equipment?*

Navan looked confused and disturbed by my question, but he pushed it aside, as we came to the crux of the matter. "So will you help me fix my ship or not?" he asked. The Fed might not have his tools after all, but Navan had seemed sure that they'd at least have their own advanced tech that could help.

The lycan looked away and stood up, before prowling up and down the room, his hands clasped behind his back. "The problem is," he began, and my stomach instantly dropped at his cold tone. "I have no idea if anything you have told me can be trusted. It all sounds very urgent and life threatening, but I've never come across a coldblood in my life who wasn't a scheming bastard." He paused and looked at Navan. "That's the downside of belonging to a race as sadistic and depraved as yours, you see. Everyone always expects an ulterior motive."

"Please," I urged. "You're wrong—he isn't like the others, I promise. Why would I be helping him if he wasn't acting for the benefit of my kind?"

"He could be blackmailing you, and you could be an exceptional actress." He rolled his eyes. "You could even be a shapeshifter, for all I know, who decided to ally with a coldblood."

I exhaled in frustration. "So, what? You're going to dismiss everything we've told you? Aren't the risks far greater if you *don't* help us?"

The lycan returned to his seat, and gave the two of us a considering look. "I didn't say we wouldn't help you—that decision isn't even up to me. But given that we have limited resources, which are stretched to the max at this current time, my job is to gauge the truth of information that is presented to me, before relaying it to my superiors for consideration.

"While our usual response to a coldblood would be to shoot him through the head, I admit that what you've told me is concerning, if true. It could also be designed to lead us up the garden path—perhaps even put some of our agents into danger. So, before I even consider relaying your information to our chief, I need to be damned sure of your intentions. As a bloodsucker, you'd better expect to jump through some hoops."

"We're telling the truth," Navan said. "So we'll do what you ask."

The lycan breathed in, leaning back thoughtfully in his chair, and then stood up again. "Wait here."

With that, he moved to the door and left the room.

"I can't believe this," I said, unable to keep the frustration from my voice. I was painfully aware of the seconds ticking by, that little pod containing my blood drifting ever closer to Vysanthe. We didn't have time to be doubted!

Navan, while clearly annoyed, didn't seem all that surprised by the lycan's response. "Like he said, it's what I get for being a coldblood," he replied. "He's right not to trust my word. If I were in his shoes, I wouldn't trust me either."

I flinched at his self-deprecation, knowing that it couldn't be easy to be judged like that—to be discriminated against purely on the basis of his physical appearance—in spite of how much he was risking for Earth's benefit. It made me want to reach out and touch his shoulder, reassure him that *I* knew he was a good man, but I refrained, since if there was one thing I had detected about Navan in the brief time I'd known him, it was that he didn't seek sympathy.

The lycan reentered the room carrying a black folder filled with documents, which he dropped on the floor in front of Navan.

"I'm going to give you an opportunity to prove your intentions with action," the lycan announced. "A little task that will help me buy into your motivation. Now... on the subject of shapeshifters, it's coincidental that you happened to run into one. We have reason to believe that there has been a recent infestation of them here on Earth, in spite of Earth being forbidden territory to them—the Fed made that clear decades ago.

"This folder contains evidence suggesting that the shapeshifters have established—or are in the process of establishing—an organized base here. Their motives are yet unknown. What I'm asking you to do, with the help of these files, is two things: one, uncover the coordinates of their base, and two, gauge an approximation of the base's size. We want an estimation of how many shapeshifters we're up against. Then, you will report these two pieces of intel back to me. Fairly straightforward."

Navan paled. "That is no small task, lycan. It's going to take time to uncover their base, given their camouflage abilities, and that's the one thing we don't have—time. Not to mention there's no guarantee I'll return alive. Until a few hours ago, we were being hunted by one with a clear intent to murder."

"It won't necessarily take a lot of time—it depends on how smart you are," the lycan replied, "but I'm not saying it will be easy. We will equip you with weapons and equipment, however, which will lessen the risk, as well as provide guidance in the form of these files. Either way, if you want to gain our trust, these are our terms. If you succeed, I assure you that our chief will be much more likely to take a chance on you, and trust what you have to say."

Navan glanced down at the folder for a moment, then exhaled, his breath uneven. "Okay. I'm willing to do whatever it takes to get you to listen. But in addition to providing me with equipment, you also need to return my bag to me."

"That is not a problem," the lycan replied, and I realized only now that Navan didn't have his bag with him. It must have been confiscated when we were in the helicopter.

Navan nodded curtly, though the concern in his eyes remained, setting my nerves on edge.

The lycan gave him a brief, wolfish smile, then rubbed his hands together. "Then let's get moving."

*I* didn't have a chance to exchange another word with Navan before the lycan called two guards into the room. They pulled bags over our heads, then escorted us out, back through the hallway, into the lobby area, through the sliding doors and into the chilly air. As I was once again lofted into a fireman's lift, I realized we were heading back to the aircraft.

"What about the bag and the equipment?" I heard Navan ask tensely.

"Don't worry," the interrogator lycan's voice replied, and I realized that he had caught up to walk alongside us. "I have already arranged that."

As we reached the stairs to the aircraft, I couldn't help but wonder again where this HQ was located. I wished I could've caught a glimpse of our surroundings before I was carried into the aircraft and sat back down on a bench.

"Where are we going?" I asked, as Navan sat beside me.

"Remote Siberia," the interrogator replied. "They've been swiping humans from villages in a certain area for several months now, so it's quite clear they have some affiliation with it."

"Wait, swiping humans?" I asked, alarmed. "You never told us that's what they're doing." I hadn't really considered till now why the shapeshifters were such a nuisance in the Fed's eyes, but now it made perfect sense.

"That's because everything you need to know is included in the folder."

"Why do you think they're taking humans?" I bit my tongue before I could add, *Isn't that something coldbloods would do?* There was enough tension between Navan and the lycans as it was.

"We suspect it's for their flesh, though we don't know for sure yet. You're going to help us find out."

I sighed and leaned back, resting my head against the aircraft's cool metal wall.

A door clattered open at the back of the ship, followed by the sound of something heavy being loaded into it. I turned my head in the direction of the noise, and the interrogator explained, "That's all your equipment being loaded, as promised."

I then heard his footsteps retreating, out of the aircraft and down the stairs. A moment later he called out, "You're ready to go. Good luck. Perhaps we will be seeing you again soon."

His last sentence lingered ominously as I heard the hatch close. A minute later, the aircraft rose, then launched forward, picking up speed.

"When will you take these bags off our heads?" I asked.

"Once we're an unrecognizable distance from our headquarters," the guard replied tersely, and I huffed, sealing my lips.

Navan was being exceptionally quiet, and I sensed his nerves, coiled like a spring. But I couldn't think of much to say to break the tense silence, since at least one guard remained in our compartment, and I didn't feel comfortable with him listening in.

So I sat and waited, bored out of my mind with nothing to look at, for what felt like an hour. After that, the guard approached us and removed our bags, which made things more tolerable. I looked at the guard first as he resumed his seat opposite us. He was wearing a mask, concealing all but his tangerine-colored eyes. Then I looked at Navan, who was staring straight ahead at the wall opposite him, his jaw clenched. He glanced at me, doing a once over as if to check that I was okay, and then resumed staring at the wall, making it clearer than ever that he was in no mood to talk. And to my disappointment, there were no windows in our compartment, so all I had to look at for the next several hours of the journey was the bare interior of the chamber.

I breathed out in relief when we finally began descending, and on touching down, the guard removed our handcuffs.

The hatch opened and a waft of icy air engulfed me, leaving

me shivering. Climbing down the stairs, I realized we had landed atop a snowy cliff, which overlooked miles of forests, fields, and several small settlements clustered at varying intervals around us. It was evening, the sun setting in the distance.

I groaned, not looking forward to freezing my butt off again. I had been appreciating the milder temperatures since we left Alaska. I guessed shapeshifters had a penchant for the cold like coldbloods, given the first one we'd come across hanging around in Navan's Alaskan bunker... It was still sinking in that the old homeless man I had taken pity on had been a shapeshifter all along. And the question still swirled in my head: *Why?*

I shook the thoughts aside as Navan reached the bottom of the stairs. The guard led us around the back of the ship, where Navan's bag was waiting on the ground, along with, to my surprise, some kind of small flying contraption. It reminded me of a mini jet, about eleven feet in length, and narrow, with a tiny cockpit that didn't look like it could hold more than two or three people.

I got my coat out of Navan's bag, wrapping it around me while the guard opened up a compartment at the back of the ship, which was about big enough for one fully grown man to lie curled up inside. Within it was a metal toolbox, with an array of equipment—guns and other survival gear, including a tough metal wire, rope, candles, a gas stove, a thick sleeping bag, and knives. The folder was also there, but there was no food, though I noted they had provided some rubles in a plastic bag that I could use to buy food in one of the villages. I knew Navan would be okay, too, now that he had his bag of vials.

"This is the standard pack we issue our agents—you can use or discard what you will," the guard explained. Navan and I gathered around him as he picked up one of the guns, what looked like a silver long-barreled pistol. "I trust you know how to use these," he said, looking at Navan, who nodded. "There are bullets here." The guard set down the gun and gestured to a side compartment. He then slipped his hand into a second side compartment and pulled out a beige, skin-tight suit that looked like it was made of silicon. "You have one of these, and it may come in use. It must be worn under the clothes, and, when activated"—he tapped an odd little button-shaped bump on the right wrist of the suit—"it will allow the wearer to become invisible. It's expensive technology, so be sure to take care of it."

I stared at the suit in awe, and I couldn't deny I was eager to try it out. I also wondered what other mind-blowing technology this supernatural organization had stowed away.

"And this ship," Navan said, his eyes traveling along the length of it. "You're lending this to me?"

"You need somewhere to store all the equipment, and it will also serve as a shelter at night. It's not powerful enough to launch you into space, so don't even try—it's only designed for Earth's atmosphere. And don't bother trying to run off with it. It's fitted with a tracker, and we will be able to locate it easily."

Navan nodded. "Understood."

"If you have any questions as to its functioning, I suggest you ask me now."

Navan walked to the cockpit and pulled open the side door. He seated himself behind the controls and examined them for a moment, before pushing gears and pressing buttons. A minute or two later, he'd successfully managed to bring it to life, and began to hover it in the air.

Navan's eyes were wide as he gazed around the interior of the aircraft. "This is... astonishingly simple to navigate," he said. "Clearly, your tech is very much advanced compared to ours."

The lycan grunted, and then glanced back toward the main ship, apparently impatient to head off. "The control board is equipped with a communication device," he said. "It'll allow you to contact our HQ, should there be an emergency. Otherwise, I believe you're set. Whatever happens, we'll send out an agent to check back here in three days, same time, same place. I suggest you get to studying those files now, perhaps get a bit of sleep, and then set off to begin scouting in the early morning."

Navan lowered the aircraft back on the snow. "Very well."

The lycan nodded and turned, hurrying back into the main ship, and a moment later, it was rising, then zooming forward at an alarming speed, confirming my suspicion that it was no ordinary helicopter. I stared after it as it became a small dot in the sky, and then looked at Navan, sucking in a deep breath of the frigid air.

"So, we're alone again," I said, and gave him a small smile, attempting to lighten the mood even a little.

"Under different circumstances, I'd be thrilled to hear that," Navan replied. His eyes were on the ship, though, and I could tell that part of him really was in awe of the thing. "And we've now somehow found ourselves tracking shapeshifters." He seated himself in the cockpit, shoving the bag behind him and placing the folder on his lap. "You ready to get reading?"

I lowered myself into the passenger seat and closed the door.

"Actually," he said, the second I had shut myself inside. "Let me rephrase that: Are you ready to go back to Texas or New York? Your choice." He patted the control panel. "At least you'll show up in style."

I stared at him. "*What?*"

The idea of returning home and leaving Navan to deal with all this alone had not even occurred to me. To be fair, it was a logical option. Probably even a sensible one. Of what use would I be to Navan out here, as a human girl? We'd already made contact with the Fed, which was what he'd said he needed me for initially. Yet, every fiber of my being rejected the notion, and I realized that I simply cared too *much* to abandon this mission —and him—now.

"I'm not dragging you into this, Riley," he said. "No way. You've done your part. Mission accomplished. Thank you. I couldn't have done it without you. I mean it."

"Well, thanks for the compliment, but it's not over yet. I'm not just going to leave you."

"You are," he replied. "Let's not make this any harder than it has to be. If you won't tell me where you want to go, I'll choose for you. So . . . what'll it be? Texas or New York?"

"Neither. I'm staying here."

He sighed. "Then I'll choose." He pressed some buttons and then the ship lifted off the ground. I jumped up and yanked the door open and leapt out, falling the three or four feet to the ground. I rose to my feet and shook myself off, then crossed my arms over my chest and glared up at Navan through the open door as he lowered the ship.

"Are you *crazy*?" he exclaimed. "You could've hurt yourself! Get back in here and stop being stubborn."

"You can't force me to go back," I shot back. "Besides, it's dumb. We're here, all the way in freaking Siberia, and you're proposing to fly me *all* the way back to the US, and then come back? The Fed are tracking this aircraft—don't you think they'll find it weird if you immediately take off in literally the opposite direction? They'll think you're trying to make some kind of escape attempt with their equipment and come hunting you down, and then you'll have no hope of..."

I trailed off as Navan leapt out of his seat. He stalked around the ship toward me, and I spread my feet, digging them deeper into the snow while eyeing him warily, unsure of what he was going to do.

He stopped in front of me, a frown creasing his face. "While I appreciate your concern, if the Fed finds the behavior suspicious, they'll attempt to comm with me first. I'll explain I decided to take you back home—given that they didn't offer to do it for me—and I'll be returning to Siberia post haste. I really don't want to have to drag you back onto the ship kicking and screaming, okay? That's not who I am. But I'm not letting you get yourself into anymore danger than you've already been in."

Before I could reply, Navan's comm device started beeping in his bag. He exhaled and whirled around, striding back to the ship to get it. He ripped out the device and held it to his ear.

"Bashrik," he said. Tentatively, I closed the distance between us, enough that I could hear Bashrik's distorted voice carrying through the still atmosphere.

"Hey, man. What the hell's going on? Why haven't you been picking up?"

Navan's back heaved as he sighed. "I'd tell you not to worry, but I know how pointless that would be. We're alive, and we managed to make contact with the Fed. I was just separated from my bag for a few hours, and couldn't pick up your calls. Listen, I don't have a lot of time—"

"Whoa. Wait. Tell me everything that's happened since we last talked."

Navan reluctantly filled Bashrik in on what had happened with the shapeshifter and Ianthan trailing us, and by the time he was done, Bashrik seemed to be in a stupor of stunned silence. "I-I don't believe it," he stammered.

"I know. It's... I'm still processing it myself. But I don't have time to talk more now."

"What are you doing now? Where *are* you?"

"We're in Siberia, and I have to complete a little task in order to gain the trust of the Fed and ensure their agreement to assist me."

"Wait, what do you mean 'a little task'?" Bashrik pressed.

"It doesn't matter," Navan replied. "I'll tell you once it's finished. How's your injury healing?"

"No, Navan," Bashrik persisted, "tell me what the task is."

Navan paused. "There's been an infestation of shapeshifters in the area, and all I have to do is pinpoint their main location and report back an estimation of how large it is."

I frowned at how Navan was downplaying the task, when only a few hours ago he had been telling the lycan how difficult and dangerous it would be. Bashrik wasn't buying it either. In fact, he exploded. "Navan, no. Forget that! You're taking this whole Earth-saving obsession *way* too far. You were almost *killed* multiple times on your way to the Fed! Ianthan *was* killed. That should be a sign that you need to stop and turn around, if nothing else."

"Bashrik—"

"No, listen to me, brother. I was nervous when you set out on this trip that you'd end up doing something like this. You just admitted a shapeshifter was trying to kill you. Now you're suggesting actively seeking out a whole infestation of them? You've finally taken this to the level of *suicide!*" His voice cracked. "I've already lost one sibling—I'm not going to lose another."

My heart skipped a beat at his words, and I wondered what he was talking about. There was a long pause, and when Navan replied, it sounded as though he'd lined his voice with steel,

CHAPTER 20 | 261

closing himself off from Bashrik's emotions. "You weren't the only one to lose a sibling," he replied coolly. "I have no intention of putting you through that again, either. I've got equipment that will help me, including a fast aircraft that I suspect is also knife and bulletproof."

"But Navan—"

"No," Navan finally snapped, and I realized that his hands were shaking slightly. "I can't deal with you being stubborn, too." And with that, he pressed a button on the side of the device, shutting it off completely, before tossing it back into his bag.

His face was contorted with agitation, and he was breathing heavily as he turned and set his eyes back on me. "I can't deal with all of this," he said. "So I'm going to count to three to give you an opportunity to walk back to the ship by yourself. One."

"Navan, no—"

"Two."

"I'm not—"

"Three."

As soon as he uttered the last word, he launched forward and grabbed me by the waist. His hard chest crushed against mine as he hauled me back to the ship. Anger boiled up in me to a level I hadn't felt in a long time.

As he reached the cockpit and began to wrestle me into the seat, my right hand reached out, as if on its own accord, and slapped him hard across the face. So hard my palm left a mark where it had landed.

His hold on me immediately loosened, and he stepped back and stared at me. Judging from the flicker of surprise in his eyes, he clearly hadn't been expecting that, which bought me a few seconds to catch my breath.

"What about free will?" I asked. "Aren't you all about that? I'm adopting this as my responsibility too, and you're not going to stop me. I've already come this far. I've already put myself in a lot of danger. I can agree to sit in the aircraft for some of the time if that's what it takes for you to accept this, but I am *not* leaving you here alone. What if you got into trouble and needed someone to call for help? Just let me help you!"

There was a long pause. "I'm not used to relying on others for help," he replied. "And I'm certainly not used to getting slapped in the face."

"Yeah? Well, I'm not used to getting manhandled and forced to do something against my will."

We glared at each other for several moments. "You're right," he finally said, his voice low. "You do have free will, and if you're going to insist on staying, I can't force you to do anything. I just . . . I don't want anything bad to happen to you, okay? I've got enough guilt hanging over my head, and I honestly don't think I could handle it if you got hurt under my watch. Don't you get that?"

"Of course I do," I replied. "And I don't want anything bad to happen to either of us. But there's no way you're sending me back now, so you might as well hand me some of those files so we can get started." I held out my hand expectantly, trying to keep my gaze firm and resolute.

Navan hesitated, but then went and got the file. He opened it and took out half the papers, which he passed to me, our fingertips brushing.

He sighed again, and gazed down at me. "I guess we really are in this together."

21

We quickly decided that we'd be better off sitting someplace warm down in the nearby town to examine the documents, so I slipped the file into my coat, along with the plastic bag of rubles. Navan picked me up and we flew toward the town. Luckily, there was enough daylight for Navan's skin to absorb and change to a more normal-looking color, though his temperature was much colder than I would've liked.

The restaurant we arrived at was something of a tavern, sparsely furnished with wood tables and chairs. Our waitress looked like she'd been working there for the past century, and if she was at all surprised to see two faces she didn't recognize, she wasn't letting on. I was famished though, and ordered a plate of dumplings, which was one of four main dishes on the menu.

"This place sure is hopping," Navan said as he glanced

around the near-empty space. Aside from us, there was one other occupied table, and it was an old woman, who had a teacup and saucer in front of her and nothing else.

I divvied the papers up and we started to go through them. It was mostly reports detailing the missing villagers, along with some maps with black X's indicating the exact location where people had disappeared from. The reports were chillingly similar, though the shifters did not seem to discriminate when it came to their victims. Young and old, male and female—so long as it was a human, that seemed to be the only criteria.

Navan threw his papers down. "Riley," he said. I stopped reading and looked at him. He had an agitated expression on his face.

"We're going to figure this out," I replied. "I know it seems like a lot, but we'll figure it out."

"That's not it." He shook his head. "Well, it's part of it, sure, but . . . about what happened back there. I shouldn't have dragged you onto the aircraft like that."

He still had a mark on his face from where my palm had made contact. "It's okay," I said. "I know you did it because you didn't want anything bad to happen to me. And I appreciate that." I hesitated. "For the first half of my life, I didn't really have anyone looking out for me. So . . . it means a lot that you're concerned about my well-being. Even if maybe you didn't go about showing it in the best way. Slapping you wasn't really my finest moment, either. *I'm* sorry for doing that."

"I'd never be able to forgive myself if something bad

happened to you," he said. "I've got so much guilt about everything that sometimes it doesn't seem like I can withstand any more. How dramatic can I sound, I know. But it's true."

"You shouldn't feel guilty," I said. "What good is that going to do? You had no idea what your father was up to. You can't blame yourself for that."

"It's not just that."

"What is it, then?"

He glanced around as though he was expecting someone to be eavesdropping. "I'm not trying to relive the past or anything —once was enough—but I should be honest with you about why I'm here on Earth to begin with."

"Didn't you already tell us that?"

"Well . . . yes. Sort of. But there's more to the story. Like you with your parents, there's been a part of me that thought not talking about it might somehow lessen the pain. I think we both know it doesn't always work that way."

I nodded. "You're right. And if you have more that you want to tell me, I'd be happy to hear it." I thought back to when I'd inadvertently spilled my guts to Navan and how he'd helped me better understand myself. Maybe I could help him in the same way.

He took a deep breath. "It's been a while since I've talked about this. I had a little sister named Naya. She was my pal. When she turned sixteen, she started dating Ronad, even though our parents—and a couple of my brothers—were completely against it."

"Why?"

"Well . . . for a few different reasons. Some of my brothers were because they felt like Ronad *was* our brother. Our parents had taken him in and they didn't think it was appropriate for him to be dating Naya. Which was stupid but at least understandable. My parents didn't want Naya involved with him because he was basically an orphan, and they didn't think he was good enough for her. They both care very much about the opinions of others, and they felt that their daughter dating someone like Ronad wouldn't reflect well upon the family."

"How long did he live with you guys?"

"I think he was maybe ten? His parents were never around. They pretty much left him on his own, so he'd always come around. Until one day my parents just said he could stay."

"Sounds familiar," I said.

Navan nodded. "Yeah, I didn't even think of that. But Naya and Ronad had been friends long before he moved in—they'd been playing together since they were little. To me, if anything, it seemed kind of obvious that she and Ronad would eventually wind up together."

"So what happened?"

"What happened was my parents forbade her to see him, and told Ronad he had to move out. They of course continued to see each other in secret. Though it's all but impossible to keep anything a secret from my father. So what brilliant idea did he come up with? He concocted this elixir similar to Elysium, except much stronger—and with the added kicker of black root, which is basically Vysanthe's version of deadly nightshade."

I widened my eyes. "He was trying to *kill* him?"

"No. He didn't want to kill him, but he wanted to make him sick enough that he'd have to be bedridden for a while, and since the elixir had similar properties to Elysium, he wouldn't remember Naya anyway. And while he was away recovering, my parents assumed Naya would move on—I'm sure they planned to parade a bunch of more eligible suitors in front of her. Anyway, Ronad's birthday was coming up, so my father sent him an early birthday present—a vial of ramphastide blood."

"I have no idea what that is."

"It's a bird. It's like a toucan, except on Vysanthe, they're six feet tall, with beaks that are more than half their length. The blood from the beak of a ramphastide is a rare delicacy and very difficult to come by. So maybe Ronad should have known, when it arrived, that there was something suspicious, because my father was not a generous man like that. But Ronad is kind and trusting and the thought never occurred to him. And unbeknownst to my parents, Naya had snuck out again to be with Ronad, and he let her have the vial. He didn't think he'd ever have his hands on a vial of ramphastide blood again, and he wanted her to have it."

My stomach twisted. "Oh no."

Navan nodded, a grim expression on his face. "My father put in the exact amount of black root to injure Ronad. But Naya was much smaller than Ronad, and so it ended up being a fatal dose.

It worked quickly, and she died in his arms." Navan stared off into the distance. "Because it was a variant of Elysium, it wiped her memory clean, so she had no idea who he was."

"Navan." He blinked, and his focus returned to me, the pain in his eyes undeniable. I didn't know what to say—*sorry* seemed completely inadequate. "That's awful."

"What's awful," he said slowly, "is that I happened to run into Naya when she was sneaking out. I could have demanded that she march herself right back into the house, but I didn't."

"You had no way of knowing."

"She was my little sister, and I was supposed to protect her." He took a deep breath. "I completely and utterly failed at doing that. I am not going to fail now. All Naya ever wanted was to get away from Vysanthe—she hated how we just used resources like there was a never-ending supply, how we exploited those that were weaker. That's not who she was, that's not who Ronad is, that's not who I am, if you can believe it."

"Of course I believe that," I said. "You're here, putting your life on the line to try to save Earth when you could easily just go somewhere else and not let it be your problem."

"You should eat," he said, pushing my plate toward me. "They're probably cold by now. And we should get back to this paperwork."

He picked up one of the pages and started looking at it. He clearly wasn't someone who could take a compliment or any sort of praise at all. I wondered why that was. Perhaps it had something to do with his father.

I watched him for a second as he read, the way his eyes scanned the lines, the intense expression on his face. Everything about Navan made more sense now, and thinking about Ronad made my heart ache, especially when I remembered how he had called out Naya's name so desperately, back when I'd hidden away in his room. That must've been so awful for him, to have the love of his life die in his arms, unable to remember who he was. I felt a flare of anger toward Navan's father. Why were some parents so messed up?

Navan cleared his throat, and for a second I thought he was about to say something, but he didn't, just continued to read, so I turned my attention to my food. The dumplings might have been sitting there for a little while, but they were still delicious, the dough buttery and flaky. I ate the whole plate, and washed it down with two cups of hot tea. *Ahh.* That felt better.

"The shifters certainly have been busy," Navan said. "According to these reports, the villagers think it's the work of the *tonrar,* or the devil." He shuddered. "Which isn't too far off the mark when it comes to shapeshifters, vile little things. In everything I've read so far, people have reported hearing wolves or seeing some sort of furry, four-legged animal. No one's actually seen one of them try to take someone."

"But what do you think they're doing to the people?" I asked, thinking about the one that had been riding Ianthan, the way it had looked lying there dead in the alley.

"I don't know." Navan frowned at the paper he was looking at. "I've got some guesses, but I don't think there's any way to know for sure until we're actually able to find one and question it."

"We're going to question it?"

"We're going to try. Having the ability to shape shift, of course, certainly comes in handy when trying to evade capture."

We went back to our piles, and I sipped my third cup of tea. The wind had picked up outside, and it rattled the panes of glass. The ship would at least be shelter from the wind, but I didn't know how warm it would be, and I wanted to soak up all the heat that I could now.

I wasn't sure how much time had passed, though I had long ago finished that third cup of tea when the old woman that had been sitting at the other table approached us. She and the waitress looked as if they could have been sisters. She wore a faded head scarf that had slipped back, to reveal her thick, steel-colored hair. Her skin was deeply lined and her eyes appeared milky, though she had made her way over to our table perfectly fine, without assistance.

"I heard you speak of *tonrar*," she said. I glanced at Navan. How had she been able to hear that, all the way across the room? "Bad things have been happening here. People whisper that it's the work of tonrar, but they are wrong. They make offerings to try to appease him, but people still go missing. Just a fortnight ago, my closest neighbor was out tending his sheep and he did not return for his evening meal. Gone, just like that. People are afraid. No one knows what to do." She reached down and touched Navan's hand. He tried to pull it away before she could make contact and feel that his temperature was not that of an average human, but she must've been stronger than she looked, because her fingers closed around his hand and didn't let go. "But you do," she said. "You know what to do. And you will do it." And then she let go of his hand, patting it, like he was a little boy and she was his grandmother. She turned and walked away.

Navan and I stared after her as she made her way to the door and then walked out.

"She's a seer," he said finally.

I looked at him. "Like a psychic?"

"Yeah. She knew what I was—notice how she didn't react when she touched my hand?"

"I did notice that."

"There's actually a lot more of her kind on Earth than people might realize," he said. "Humans seem fond of stigmatizing the people who claim to have a sixth sense like that. Shunning them or medicating them or institutionalizing them."

"Well . . . I think that's because a lot of the time they seem crazy. Or they're saying stuff that people don't want to hear."

"Humans seem to have a very narrow field of what they deem possible."

"Not all of us."

He smiled. "I know."

We stayed in the restaurant for a while longer, but then we left. The wind had died down some, but it was still bitingly cold, and when Navan picked me up to fly us back to the ship, I nestled against him.

When we got back, Navan said he was going to leave me at the ship to do a quick fly around over the area and make sure that it was safe.

"How will you know?" I asked. "I mean, if there are shifters around, couldn't they be in the form of something you wouldn't even suspect, like a bird or something? Or what if they're invisible?"

"They could be," he said. "But I should be able to sense them, and I'd sleep a lot better tonight if I at least look around before we turn in for the night. You'll be fine here."

"I'm not worried about that," I said.

He smiled. "I've noticed."

Though I knew he wasn't going far, there *was* a part of me that wanted to jump into his arms before he took off, to go with him, to never leave his side. The feeling almost overwhelmed me, but I stayed in the ship and watched as his powerful wings beat back and forth, lifting him higher and higher into the sky. A shooting star arced across the darkness, and I blinked, marveling at the fact of everything that had happened in such a short period of time. Not too long ago, I'd been standing under the sweltering sun in the middle of a corn field with my two best friends, and now here I was, at the edge of the world, watching a coldblood that I was most certainly developing feelings for, fly off into the night sky.

An electronic ringing sound jolted me from my reverie, and I looked around, confused at first, until I realized it was Navan's comm. I went over to his bag and picked it up. It continued to ring, and I pressed a button, bringing the device up to my ear.

"Hello? Hello, Navan, is that you?" came Bashrik's voice.

"It's Riley," I said.

"Riley! Where's Navan? Is everything all right? Why didn't he pick up? Did something happen?!"

I suppressed a smile at the anxiety in his voice. "Everything's fine," I said. "Well, relatively speaking. Navan's just checking out the area, so he's not here right now. I know I probably shouldn't have picked up, but I had a feeling it might be you, and I didn't want you to worry."

"Well, it's a little late for that. We've all been worried sick, quite frankly. You don't know my brother the way I do, and he can get himself into situations that are way beyond his control. I know Navan's downplaying the whole thing but if you haven't noticed yet, that's sort of the way he goes about things. It's not a big deal—until it is. And, I'm not trying to be an alarmist or anything—but this is a very big deal. And it's just the two of you? It might be different if I was there but as it is, you two are both in a lot of danger. In fact—"

"Is that Riley?!" Angie's voice came through loud and clear, almost as if she were right there in the ship with me. In a way, I wished she was. There was the sound of rustling. "Riley? Is that you?"

"Hey," I said, smiling at the sound of her voice. "It's good to hear your voice."

"When are you coming back?" She sounded as anxious as Bashrik had. "Is everything okay?"

"Yeah, we're okay," I said. "And I'm not sure when we'll be back. Hopefully soon. We've got to take care of something out here first. But we're going to get back there as soon as we possibly can."

"I can't say that's the most reassuring thing I've ever heard," Angie said.

"I know. I'm sorry I can't give you a better answer. But try not to worry, okay?"

"Okay. Lauren says hi. I'm going to give this thing back to Bashrik. Stay safe, Riley."

"I will."

Bashrik continued to grill me when he got back on, and though I tried to answer him as best I could, I knew my responses weren't going to satisfy him; the only thing he really wanted to hear was that Navan and I had given things a second thought and were on our way back.

"You might have noticed he gets a little obsessed with things," Bashrik said. "And by *a little* I mean a whole heck of a lot. He's got this idea in his head that he's somehow going to be able to protect Earth, like it's his sole purpose in life."

"He told me about your sister," I said. "I'm sorry."

Bashrik paused. "He did?"

"Yeah."

"That's . . . surprising. I didn't think he'd ever bring that up with anyone outside the family." He sighed. "Well, Naya would've been all for this little recon mission you two are on. And I know that plays a role in all the decisions he's made, too. He thinks that he can somehow make it up to her, even though she's dead. Like if he saves Earth, he's somehow atoned for the fact that he couldn't save her. Even though none of that was his fault."

"He doesn't think so."

"Of course he doesn't." Bashrik sighed again, and when he spoke, his tone was softer, resigned. "Navan's always been the biggest, strongest brother. The smartest, too. Some of the brothers resented him for it, though I never did. How could I? But that doesn't mean Navan is immortal—not yet, anyway. Sometimes he acts like he is, but we both know that he's not. I don't want him to get himself killed. You've got to watch out for him, Riley. I know he's going to be focused on keeping you safe, so maybe you can figure out a way to make sure that means he's safe, too."

"I'll try," I said, though what I really wanted to ask was how did he expect me to do that? I was just a human, after all—inferior in every way to a coldblood. But if there *was* something that I could do, some way that I could help, then of course I would try my best.

"Thank you," Bashrik said. "Losing Naya was hard enough—I don't know if I can deal with losing Navan, too."

"We'll be in touch soon," I said.

Bashrik said goodbye, and I disconnected the call, placing the comm back into Navan's bag. A gust of wind whipped the side of the ship, rattling something on the outside, and I shivered. I peeked out—there was no sign of Navan.

How long had I been on the call for? Didn't he say he was just going to fly around and be right back? What if something had happened to him? I had no idea how to operate this ship to go after him. I'd be stuck out here, helpless.

My heart started to beat faster, and I took several deep breaths, telling myself I was getting carried away, that everything was probably fine, and I just needed to stay calm.

But several more minutes passed, and still Navan didn't appear.

*He should be back by now.* Finally, I could no longer ignore the thought.

I climbed out of the ship and stood outside, looking up at the sky, doing my best to ignore the wind that whipped through my hair. It was so cold, and the darkness seemed to go on forever. Like there was nothing else out there.

"Navan?" I said, and it felt as if the wind snatched the word right out of my mouth and carried it away. I stumbled away from the ship. If I kept moving, that would at least get the blood flowing, and maybe I'd warm up a little, and at the same time, be able to find Navan. Maybe he was wrong about his ability to sense the shapeshifters, especially if they were invisible. What if they had ambushed him, or he was injured and couldn't get back?

"Navan?!" I yelled, a note of fear tinging my voice. Aside from the wind, though, there was nothing.

I kept walking, until the vastness of where I was suddenly hit me, and I turned, realizing that I had gone farther than I thought. I couldn't see the ship anymore, though I wasn't sure if that was because it was dark or I'd gone too far. I stopped, paralyzed by both fear and the cold. It was stupid to have left the ship. I'd acted out of panic, and even though I knew acting out of panic was never a good thing to do, I hadn't been able to help myself this time. The thought of that vampire being in trouble just seemed to have scrambled my brain.

I turned, hoping to follow my footprints back. But the snow was old and had a crust of ice over it, so there were no tracks. I could only hope that I was going in the right direction, though with no point of reference, I couldn't be sure. I widened my eyes, then squinted, trying to make out anything in the darkness.

I had to force myself to start walking again; the cold had seeped into my bones and made my joints feel as if they no longer worked. I took as many steps as I thought I had taken away from the ship, but when I looked, all I saw was darkness. Somehow, I had gone the wrong way, and now who knew how far I was from where I wanted to be.

*Needed* to be. I gritted my teeth and forced myself to keep going, but I knew my situation was becoming dire. Hadn't I just promised Bashrik that I would try to stay safe, that I would try to keep Navan safe? And now here I was, completely alone, lost in the freezing tundra. I would have been mad at myself, but I was too scared.

My foot slipped on the ice and I went down hard, the impact

jarring every last bit of breath out of me. I lay there, unable to move, unable to get my breath back for a few terrifying seconds. But then my chest unlocked and I sucked in a cold mouthful of air, which burned my lungs and made my eyes water. I couldn't stop shaking, but a heavy feeling suddenly overcame me, like I was more tired than I'd ever been in my entire life. I could barely keep my eyelids open.

My eyes had almost closed all the way when a surge of anxiety shot through me, and with that anxiety came a jolt of adrenaline. I tried to scramble up, knowing that if I let my eyes close now, I'd probably never open them again. But my limbs didn't want to cooperate; it was like my brain was telling them one thing and they were doing the opposite. I flailed and thrashed but I couldn't get my feet underneath me. I couldn't get up.

I lay back, looking up at the dark sky. Another shooting star streaked across it. Was that my imagination? Had I ever even seen a shooting star before tonight? And now I'd seen two? You were supposed to make a wish when you saw one, right?

That heavy feeling returned, lurking like a stranger at the edge of my vision. All I could hope now was that Navan was okay, that nothing bad had happened to him, that he'd be able to continue the mission and be successful.

I made a wish that this would not be my final hour, but let my eyelids close, unable to fight their weight any longer.

The wind blew around me, and though I wasn't sure what would happen next, I expected it to be something like falling, maybe a tunnel, my whole life flashing before my eyes. But there was just . . . the sensation of the cold, which felt as though it had worked its way into my blood, was coursing through my veins. Suddenly, though, there was the sensation of ascension, of being lifted somewhere, the wind rushing around my face. I struggled to open my eyes, half-expecting to look down and see my body still there on the ground, my spirit lifting off to who-knew-where, but instead, I saw an arm, wrapped around me, the ground getting further away.

"What the hell are you doing?" I felt Navan's voice more than heard it, though the realization that he had found me, that I wasn't going to die out here alone in the cold, gave me a burst of energy and I struggled to sit up. "Hold still," he said. "Or you're going to fall. What are you doing out here? I got back to the ship and you were gone!"

"I'm sorry," I tried to say, though no sound really came out of my mouth. I started shivering uncontrollably and I tried to nestle myself against him as best I could. His grip tightened around me, and his voice was hoarse as he spoke.

"What if I hadn't come back when I did? What if I wasn't able to find you? You'd be dead right now, you do realize that, don't you?!"

It seemed only seconds until we were back at the ship. Navan set me down gently and spread the sleeping bag out. He pulled my shoes off and then helped me lie down, wrapping the sleeping bag around me. My teeth continued to click, my whole body shaking. I tried to get it to stop by taking deep breaths, but

I was just so cold. Being in the sleeping bag didn't seem to make a bit of difference—it was like my body didn't have enough heat left in it.

I opened my eyes when I heard Navan light the gas stove. I watched him for a moment, confused as to what he was up to. He had a pot on the stove and was melting down two of the candles. He dipped one hand, then the other, into the hot, melted wax. That must *hurt*.

I tried to sit up, but it felt like every ounce of strength had left me. "Wh-What are you doing?" I managed to ask, but my voice was barely more than a whisper and he didn't seem to hear me. The wax hardened around his hands and he broke it off, dropping the pieces back into the pot. He turned the burner off, and then came over to where I lay. He positioned himself behind me, pulling me to him. His hands emanated heat from the hot wax, and my body immediately melded against his, warmth finally radiating into the sleeping bag, enveloping me in what might have been the most wonderful sensation I had ever felt. And though he didn't have any heat of his own, outside of the candle wax, he seemed to absorb the heat that my own body was finally capable of generating, and the warmth swirled around us, making me feel as though we were both safely cocooned.

There wasn't a need to say anything, though part of me wanted to thank him, not just for this small gesture to keep me warm or saving my life after I'd all but resigned myself to the fact that it was over, but for being open with me earlier about what had happened with his sister, for being willing to risk his life to save a planet that he didn't even live on.

22

*J* wasn't sure how long I slept for, but when I woke up, I was alone in the sleeping bag. It was still deliciously warm inside, and though I wondered where Navan was, I was in no rush to get up and face the cold again.

I let my eyes close and I dozed for a few minutes, before I heard a noise and then Navan was re-entering the ship. He had a brown paper bag, which he brought over to me when he saw that I was awake.

"It's early," he said. "Luckily, bakers start their morning before the sun even rises. I figured you'd be hungry after your little adventure last night." He sat down next to me as I shifted in the sleeping bag and sat up, pulling the paper sack toward me. It was full of croissants, still warm.

"Oh my God, thank you," I said. I might have filled up on dumplings the night before, but right now I felt as though I hadn't eaten anything in weeks. I took three huge bites, reducing the first croissant to half, before looking at Navan. "I'm sorry," I said, after I'd chewed and swallowed. "I wanted to apologize last night, but I wasn't really able to get it out."

"Right," he said, scowling. "Because you had basically frozen to death. What the hell were you thinking? Why would you run off like that? I was on my way back and then I get here and you're nowhere. That really freaked me out! What were you thinking?"

"I . . . I don't know. I mean, I wasn't trying to run away. I just realized that you'd been gone longer than I thought you were going to be gone for, and I started to get really worried. I didn't know if maybe something bad had happened, or . . . I just wasn't sure. I panicked and went out, but then I lost sight of the ship. I wasn't planning to get lost, though. I was trying to . . . help."

"While I appreciate the go-getter attitude, *please* don't do something like that again," Navan said. "Promise me you won't."

"I promise." I took another bite of croissant and chewed slowly.

"In fact," he continued, "for the rest of this 'mission,' you're going to stay right in here."

I stared at him. "What do you mean?"

"Exactly what I said. It's safer if you're in here—we're not going to be heading to a warmer climate any time soon. You really shouldn't have come here in the first place. It's not the right climate for you, and if anything, it's just going to be dangerous. Taking all that into consideration, it's just best for everyone if you stay here."

"You can't just order me to stay in here. We've been over this, remember? Free will and all that? Besides, how is me staying here going to be helpful?"

"It'll be helpful because I won't be out there worrying about you. Trust me—that'll be more than helpful. How am I supposed to pull this thing off if I'm thinking about you the whole time?"

"I take it that's a rhetorical question." Still, I couldn't help but smile at the idea of him thinking about me all the time, and it sent a warm tingling feeling down the length of my spine.

"What?" he said, eyeing me. "Why are you smiling like that? Are you plotting your next near-death experience?"

"No," I said, scowling. "You make it sound like I'm some sort of adrenaline junky."

"Well . . . are you?"

"I don't think so. I was just . . . I don't know. I don't want to say I was enjoying myself, because we're in Siberia, hunting shapeshifters, but . . . there is a part of me that is kind of enjoying this."

He grinned. "See? I told you—adrenaline junky."

"But really, though, you can't force me to stay in this ship the whole time. I want to help. I want to do something productive. I might not know exactly what that is, but I have a feeling it's going to require me getting out of the ship at some point." I grinned. "You never know—I might just end up saving your life."

"You sure are stubborn."

"I'm not trying to make things more difficult. But I'm here, so you can't just force me to stay inside the whole time. I have free will, and I am *choosing* to be here and participate and help out in whatever way I can. And nothing you say is going to change that."

Navan sighed. "Fine! Fine. I was studying some of the maps while you were sleeping. And it seems that there's a bit of a pattern with the villages that the shifters are hitting."

"There is?"

"Yeah. Enough so that I feel pretty good about going to this one—" Navan unfolded a map and pointed. "I think if we went here today, we'd probably be able to intercept at least one shifter. That's my feeling anyway. It's not too far from here, either, so it won't take long to get there."

"What do we do once we get there?"

"We'll want to find you something to eat, maybe somewhere to get warm. We can take things as they come and see how it's going. But before we do any of that, we've got some preparations we need to see to first."

"Like what?"

"We've got a whole cache of weapons here that you've probably never encountered before."

I raised an eyebrow. "You're going to let me use them?"

"I'm not saying that—but if the situation comes up, I think it'd be good if you were at least a little familiar with them."

I followed him over to the back corner, where a large metal toolbox sat, the sort a construction worker might have permanently installed in the back of a pickup truck. Navan opened the lid and stood there, staring down at its contents. I stood next to him and peered inside.

There wasn't much that I hadn't seen before, or at least some variation of it. There were boxes of bullets, two of the silver long-barreled pistols, something that looked like an assault rifle, a sword, and a stack of knives.

"What are these?" I asked, pointing to the knives. They weren't regular-looking knives, like the kind you'd see in a kitchen—they were more like daggers, long pointed triangles with a slender handle and a hollow ring at the end.

"Those are throwing knives," Navan said. "They're very sharp, and you should stay away from them."

"But you said you were going to show me how to use some of the weapons." I reached out and ran my fingertips along the handle of one of the knives. There was something about it that seemed to be calling to me. "I want to try this." Navan opened his mouth as if he were about to say something, but then stopped. "I'll just ignore that look on your face," I said.

His eyebrows shot up. "What look?"

"That look that says you don't think I have any clue what I'm doing, and that I'll probably end up hurting someone if I try to use this." I picked up the knife I'd just been touching. "Do you know how to use these?"

"I do," he said. "And that's because it's something that I've practiced. It's not something that you'll instinctively know how to use." He held his hands up. "I'm not trying to discourage you. Well, maybe a little. I was thinking you might try something more like . . ." He looked at the weapons laid out in front of us. I waited, curious to hear what he thought I might be drawn to, but a second passed, then another, and it became clear that he didn't know what to say.

"I get it," I said. "You think I can't do this, or that because I'm a girl or something I shouldn't be handling a weapon. Well, let me try this thing out." The knife had a nice weight in my hand. It felt balanced, like this was just the thing I should've picked up. I might've been nervous to hold the gun, or that samurai-looking sword, but for whatever reason, the knife just felt right.

"Easy there," Navan said, reaching down into the box. He handed me the rest of the knives and pulled out the rifles and the sword. "Let's go outside. These sorts of things aren't meant for close quarters."

Outside, the sun was just starting to rise, a glowing orange illuminating the pale blue sky. We crunched across the hard snow, heading toward a copse of fir trees. I followed Navan beyond the trees, into a clearing.

"While I doubt anyone's going to randomly stumble upon us out here," he said, "it's better that we're a little hidden from view. Now, you have those knives?"

"I do."

"Why don't you put them down over here. We'll get to them in a minute. I want to first show you some self-defense moves. Hopefully, you won't have to use them. But it will give me slightly better peace of mind if you know a couple basic things."

"Sure," I said, though I hoped I wouldn't have to end up grappling with a shifter—the thought of having to touch one of those things made my skin crawl.

"On Vysanthe, we have a form of martial arts called Aksavdo. The closest thing you have here would probably be Krav Maga. Aksavdo is a military self-defense system, and everyone on Vysanthe is expected to master it by the time they're eighteen."

"Really?" I said. "That's pretty cool."

"Well," Navan said, something of a chagrinned look on his face. "All the boys are, anyway."

"That sounds a little less cool."

"But plenty of girls on Vysanthe know Aksavdo. And I'm just going to show you some blocks and how to break certain holds. Again, I really hope that we're not in the situation where you have to use it, but . . . just in case. Now, the problem with fighting a shapeshifter is they can change shape. When you're fighting, you want to attack the most vulnerable areas, and if your opponent is constantly changing shape, that can certainly be a challenge. So that's one of the main things when fighting a shifter— you must stay alert at all times. The eyes, throat, nose, groin . . . Those are the spots you want to go for. If the shifter is, say, in wolf form, and you manage to bash it on the nose, it's probably going to be stunned and change back to its regular form, at which point it will be a lot more vulnerable. You saw that one in the alleyway—they're ugly creatures, and they don't have much in the way of natural defenses, except for their teeth. So I'm going to come up behind you—" Navan stepped behind me, his body pressed up against mine, his arm going around my neck. "Let's just say you get caught like this. How would you escape?"

I strained forward, feeling his arm tighten against my neck. Then I tried dropping my legs out from under me, but my head couldn't slide out from his grasp.

"No," Navan said. "You're not going anywhere, and that's just giving me more time to lock the hold in. Grab my arm."

I reached up and put both my hands on his forearm. "Good," he said. "Now pull on my arm as hard as you can—you want to get some space between my arm and your neck." I squeezed with both hands and gave his arm a jerk. "The moment you feel the pressure let up a little, turn your head so your chin is down —yeah, just like that. Now I can't get the hold back in place even if you let go of my arm. And now, move this leg back behind me, like that, and sit down."

"Sit down?" I asked, feeling as if we were playing some sort of bizarre version of Twister. I was trying to focus and do what he said, but the very fact that we were this close and his arms were around me was making it extremely difficult to concentrate.

"Sit right on down," he said. "Just drop your weight."

I did so, and he toppled below me, and I landed on him with

a thud. "Good," he said. "And at this point, you can use your elbows, your knees, your feet, and you want to look for whatever vulnerable spot you can reach."

I twisted around to look at him, raising my elbow as I did so, gently touching his cheek with it.

"Like that?"

"Very good."

I knew I was supposed to hop up so he could show me another move, but sitting there with him like that felt . . . truly wonderful. Like it was exactly the thing I was supposed to be doing, and in that moment, it was easy enough to forget that we were out in the middle of nowhere, doing self-defense training because we were in the middle of a potentially dangerous mission to locate shapeshifters. The cold air seemed to crackle between us and we were close enough to kiss. His gaze went to my lips, and my whole body tingled as I could have sworn I saw a flicker of longing in his eyes, but then he shook his head and was pushing me off of him, leaving me to wonder if I had just imagined it.

"All right," he said gruffly, clearing his throat. "That was pretty good, but let's try it a little faster now. Real time."

"Right," I murmured, jumping up and hoping I wasn't blushing too badly.

We probably spent close to an hour working on different self-defense skills, and I was winded and a little sore when Navan said we could move on to the weapons. But I felt good, as though I had really learned something new, something that if I had to, I'd be able to remember and put to good use.

"So you seemed drawn to the throwing knives," Navan said. "Why don't we start with those." He cast a gaze around and then pointed at one of the trees that had a swatch of bark missing, exposing the pale, smooth wood underneath. It was about twenty feet away. "Think you can hit that spot on the tree?"

"I'll try."

I'd never thrown a knife before, but there was something about it that seemed familiar. I squared my stance and looked at the spot on the tree, then lifted my arm and threw the knife. It rotated once and then stuck into the tree, a few inches above the spot where there was no bark.

Navan whistled. "Okay," he said, "so clearly you've been keeping your identity as a professional knife thrower a secret from me." He went over to the tree and retrieved the blade. "Your aim was only a little off, but for a first try, that was damn impressive. Try it again."

I took the knife from him and readjusted my stance, then aimed, a little bit lower this time, and threw the knife. It stuck right in the middle of the spot without the bark.

"All right, then," Navan said. "I don't think we'll have to spend too much time on this part."

"I swear I've never done this before, but it just feels . . . like it's familiar or something."

"You have a natural affinity for it. Let's try a couple of the other weapons."

He set up a few log targets and had me shoot one of the pistols, from both a standing position and lying down. My aim was not as accurate, though I did manage to hit the target several times. There was power in the gun, but I liked the throwing knives.

"I feel less worried after seeing you with those," he said.

I smiled. "I'll take that as a compliment."

"You should. You've got some real skill. It's too bad we don't have more time to practice."

We made our way back to the ship. "Now," Navan said, "my hope is that you're going to stay in the ship. In fact, I'm almost tempted to forbid you to get out of the ship."

"*Almost* being the operative word there," I said. "Because you know that even if you were to do that, I probably wouldn't listen; if it looks like you need help, I'm going to be there to help you. What was the point in doing all this training just now if I have to stay in the ship the whole time?"

"The training was more for my peace of mind," he said. "Like I told you, it's going to be easier for me to focus on what I have to do if I'm not worrying about you. I mean, I'll still be worried about you, but a little less so knowing that you've got those knives."

My face flushed and I tried to hide my smile. He seemed to have no qualms expressing how worried he was about me, which I found both endearing and a little irritating. I sure as hell didn't want to be some damsel in distress, though my actions last night had certainly portrayed me as exactly that. It made my heart beat a little faster thinking that he cared about me, because after all that we had been through, I realized I cared about him, too. *Really* cared about him. The feelings had shifted in the time since we'd left Texas. It was more than just thinking he was handsome—it was something deeper than that, something I couldn't easily describe. I hadn't forgotten that almost gravitational pull I'd felt when I first looked into his eyes, nor that sensation of us being the only two people in the world.

Part of me wanted to say screw subtlety and voice my thoughts to him, but I didn't, because maybe he didn't feel the same way. Maybe he was just concerned about me in the same way that he'd be concerned about a little sister or something— and in a way, after everything he'd told me about Naya, that would make sense. If anything, I wanted to show Navan that I could be useful, that I could take care of myself, that I could play an important role in what we were about to do.

When we got back to the ship, he gave me the invisibility suit. "You need to put this on under your clothes," he said. "I'll just step outside while you do that."

After he left, I pulled my shirt off but then stopped. Was I supposed to take my bra and underwear off, too? Probably— they were clothes, after all. I stripped down and quickly slipped the suit on, then put my clothes on over it. The suit fit snugly, and once my clothes were back on, I barely even noticed it— except for the small button on the sleeve.

I opened the door and stuck my head out. Navan glanced at me, raising a brow. "You decent?"

"Yeah." He hopped back into the ship and looked me up and down. "Okay. To activate the suit, you just press the button on your sleeve."

I did as he said. "I can still see myself," I replied, looking down at my legs.

"But I can't see you." Navan nodded. "And the shifters won't be able to see you, even if they're invisible themselves. The other good thing about a suit like this is that it significantly blunts the ability of something—like a lycan or a shifter—to detect you. Only a very evolved individual will be able to sense you. And I doubt we'll be encountering many of those."

"And do I just press the button again to deactivate it?"

"Yes. You've got to hold it down for a couple seconds."

I did as he said, and the air seemed to shimmer around me. Navan looked right at me and smiled. "We've got a few more things to do and then I think we'll be ready to go."

"What's that?"

"For starters, I've got some darts that I need to coat with this drug called dakhye."

"What does that do?"

"It'll incapacitate any shifter we happen to come across. It will also prevent it from being able to change into a different form."

"That would probably be helpful," I said.

"We could put some on the blades of those throwing knives. That way, even if it wasn't a fatal strike, it would still knock the thing out." He grinned. "Not that I don't think you could hit the bull's eye every time after what I saw today. And then we've got to teach you how to navigate this ship."

I raised an eyebrow. "Are you thinking if you show me how to fly this thing that I'll be so enamored I won't want to get off?"

"Ah, you've seen right through me. Us coldboods and our ulterior motives," Navan said wryly. "Flying this thing is fairly straightforward, though."

"Yeah? That's a little surprising."

"Come on, I'll show you now, then I'll do the darts."

We went up to the front of the ship. Navan had me sit down in the driver's seat while he sat next to me. There was a steering wheel, similar to that of a car but slightly bigger, maybe more like what you'd see on a boat. There was also a myriad of buttons and levers, as well as a gear shift. I moved my feet around on the floor and felt two pedals.

"I feel the pedals," I said.

"Right's for go, left's your brake."

"Okay. And do I have to shift gears?"

Navan shook his head. "You don't need to shift gears on this. The gear shift actually controls your altitude. Rev up to go higher, rev back to go lower. The pedals are for speed. Just like a car or a bike, you jam it too quickly, the ride's going to be jerky. First things first, though—you've got to turn it on. It's that button right there." He pointed to a circular button, opaque turquoise in color, to the right of the steering wheel. "Go ahead and press that."

I did so, and the ship hummed to life the second my fingertips put pressure on the button.

"If you want to hover, you're going to rev it forward just a little. Go ahead and try."

I moved the gear shift forward, surprised at how fluid it was. The ship responded instantaneously, lifting a few feet off the ground. A smile spread across my face. "This is so cool," I said.

"The steering wheel's pretty self-explanatory, though you do have to be careful when you make turns at high speed," Navan continued. "Obviously, you wouldn't sustain the same sort of damage you would if you rolled an automobile, but there's still a chance you could hurt yourself or the ship if you try to turn too quickly while you're in the air. The only other button you really need to concern yourself with now is here." He tapped his fingers next to an opaque green button, which was maybe six inches from the turquoise button. "This activates hyper-speed and should only be used if you need to escape. Why don't you cruise around a little and get the feel for it?"

He didn't need to ask twice. I gripped the gear shift and moved it forward so the ship lifted higher, and I pressed my foot down on the right pedal and the ship accelerated. I had an almost 180-degree view. I turned the steering wheel just a bit, and the ship glided to the left. When I pressed down a little harder on the accelerator, the ship responded beautifully.

"You're a natural," Navan said. He leaned toward me, pointing. "Why don't you try and fly between those two trees right there."

The trees were two tall evergreens, and they were spaced far enough apart that I knew I'd be able to get the ship through, but I still felt a wave of nervousness as we approached. I had to maneuver around a few smaller trees in order to slip through the gap, but I did it, and when Navan pointed to another group of trees and told me to try to navigate up and over them, I did it with ease, a smile on my face the whole time.

When we brought the ship back, Navan had a smile on his face, too. "Well," he said, "I don't have to worry about you flying this ship, that's for sure."

And as he smiled at me, I felt that surge in my heart rate again, and I suddenly had the urge to reach over and pull him to me and discover what his lips felt like against mine. But I fought to regain control over my thoughts. To say that now wasn't the right time would be an understatement—even if I could find the courage to make a move like that.

We had to finish getting ready so we could leave for the village.

he village was small and quaint, with a bakery, a market, a few shops, a post office, and a tavern, along with two churches, one at either end of town. Navan left me and the ship with a good vantage point of the town; we were on a small hillside that overlooked the area, though we were out of sight behind a copse of trees, just in case any of the villagers glanced our way.

"I'm going to check things out," he said. "So for now it would make more sense if you stay here. We don't want to draw any more attention to us than we need to."

I nodded, though part of me wanted to go with him. He was right, though—he'd be able to fly quickly and be relatively inconspicuous. Being in the ship was safer, though it did put me at something of a disadvantage in terms of getting around undetected.

He took off, and I sat at the front of the ship, my eyes glued to him. For several hundred yards, he flew in a straight line, low, barely above the tree line. Nothing seemed out of the ordinary.

Then Navan stopped suddenly and changed direction, zooming toward the edge of the forest. I could tell by the way he moved that he had sensed something—that something was happening—and almost as quickly I got the ship in gear and raced down after him, trying to keep him in view the whole time. His zigging and zagging made it difficult, but the ship was remarkably agile; it was almost like it knew where I wanted to go before I had even turned the steering wheel.

He was headed for a clearing in the forest, and I saw that he had the dart gun out, and he was aiming it. But at what? I couldn't see anything—the shifters must be invisible. Navan landed, sprinting forward, taking aim with the gun. He stopped, though, and didn't take a shot. I landed the ship at the edge of the clearing and jumped out, but not before taking two of the knives with me. I doubted I'd actually use them if the shifters stayed invisible, but it made me feel better to have them with me, just in case.

I could hear sounds, but I couldn't see anything. A shiver of fear coursed down my spine. The noise was terrible, like a pack of hyenas in a feeding frenzy. On top of that was agonized screaming, distinctly human. First, yelling for help, then just yelling. But where? I looked all around, and above me, I could tell Navan was doing the same.

He lifted the gun and took a shot; the dart arced through the air and then stopped. There was a thud and the air shimmered and a shifter suddenly appeared, lying on the ground, the dart stuck in its flank. The screaming continued, though, and Navan shot another dart. Another shifter appeared on the ground, blood dripping from its mouth. The dart had lodged itself into its eye.

Navan let the dart gun drop and pulled out one of the pistols. He took careful aim and then fired off a shot; another shifter seemed to appear out of thin air and slump to the ground. Navan fired once more, and my breath caught in my throat. A man appeared, underneath the shifter Navan had just shot. The shifter was dead, and the man was, too, his throat torn out, his torso ripped open with entrails trailing.

Navan landed, his wings spread, trying to block my view. "You don't want to see this," he said. He went over to where the first shifter he shot lay. He pulled the dart out. "It's still alive," he said, looking down at it. "Judging by its shallow breathing, though, it's not going to be waking up any time soon. I might have been a little too liberal with the dakhye."

"What do you mean?"

"It's either going to die or stay asleep for longer than I had planned." He squinted, scrutinizing the thing's face. "I don't think it's dying. Yet. Come on—let's get it back to the ship."

Navan picked the shapeshifter up like it was nothing more than a pile of wood and slung it over his shoulder. He tied its hands and feet together and then handed me one of the pistols.

"I'm going to bury the bodies," he said. "It won't take me

long. And I'm about one hundred percent certain this thing will be in dreamland for quite some time, but just in case, keep your eye on it and hold onto this pistol until I get back, okay?"

"Okay," I said. I took the pistol and sat down, wondering how long it would be until the thing woke up.

The shifter showed no signs of stirring. I stared at it. If you had told me two weeks ago that I'd be sitting here, in a lycan ship in Siberia, watching over a drugged shapeshifter . . . no way in a million years would I have ever believed it. There was still a part of me now that was having a hard time believing it.

The shifter hadn't moved a muscle by the time Navan returned, so he said that we should head down into the village.

"You're probably starving. It's been a while since you had anything to eat."

"I . . . I don't have much of an appetite," I said, an image of the dead man flashing in my mind.

"I know it's not easy to see," Navan said gently. "And I'm obviously not going to force you to eat. But you do need to keep up your strength, so we should at least go down to the village."

I looked at the shifter. "Can we really leave it here?"

"Yeah. We'll close up the ship and even if it wakes up, it's not going anywhere. It can't change shape. But I really don't feel like sitting in the ship staring at it all night, so I think heading down to the village would be a good idea."

"Okay," I said. "If you think we should."

There was a surprising amount of activity down in the village, which I hadn't been expecting. Everyone seemed to be in good spirits; several people smiled and waved hello, and a woman selling noodles from a food cart asked us if we were just visiting or had decided to make our home here.

"Just visiting," Navan replied with a smile. "Though this is certainly a lovely place."

"Believe it or not, this used to be a very popular tourist destination, for people from all over the world," the woman said. There was a note of pride in her voice. "We have some of the very best hot springs in the world here. Only in recent years has word gotten out that . . ." Her voice trailed off.

"That what?" I asked gently.

"That bad things have happened here. An American tourist disappeared two years ago and was never found. It wasn't the first time such a thing happened, but it certainly got the most press. Him being American and all. We had a lot of Americans here, actually. That's how I perfected my English. Oh, well, those times have gone. We're thrilled that you're here now!"

"Thank you," I replied. "I'll try a bowl of the noodles," I added, watching as the steam swirled from the big pot on the portable burner.

"Gladly," the woman said. She dished me up a brimming bowlful, and I paid her with money from my plastic bag. "It's not too often we see new faces here, as I'm sure you can imagine. Will you be going to the festival?"

"Festival? I didn't know there was a festival." I glanced at Navan, who was shaking his head.

"There was some talk about not holding it this year," the

woman continued. "On account of the disappearances. People are scared, you see. But life goes on, now, doesn't it? No matter what else is happening around you, you've just got to keep on living. So it was decided that we weren't going to stop doing something that has been a tradition in this village for generations. It's not supposed to start until dark, but people usually begin gathering early. It's a lot of fun—you should come."

"We would love to," I replied, and Navan could barely contain his eye roll.

"Seriously?" he said, once we were out of earshot. "What have you signed us up for now? This isn't a *vacation*; I don't care how good the hot springs are. We've got a shifter tied up back at the ship."

I slurped up a noodle, and then took a sip of the broth. "Can we find a place to sit? And I *know*. But you said yourself the shifter was probably going to be out for a long time. And didn't you also say you didn't want to be in there staring at it the whole night?"

He pressed his lips together. "Fair point. I don't dance, though. So don't get any ideas."

"Why do I feel like you're probably a really *good* dancer?"

"You must have me confused with Bashrik."

There was an unoccupied bench outside of the tavern, so Navan and I sat down while I finished the bowl of noodles. We walked around for a little while, and then got swept up in the crowd and went a few blocks to where the festival was being held. It was outside, on the green at the center of town. As the sun set, it gave way to a clear, dark sky, a nearly full moon appearing on the horizon. Millions of stars pinpricked the sky. Strings of paper lanterns adorned the low-hanging tree branches, and there were several roaring fire pits. The band had set up near one of the pits—there were several fiddlers, a primitive drum set, an accordion. The music was lively and everyone was in high spirits. Even Navan seemed to relent, and I caught him smiling beneath his hood at the people dancing in front of him.

"This music is great!" I said.

"It's all right."

I elbowed him. "Come on—let's dance. Just one song!"

Navan shook his head, but before he could reply, someone stepped in front of him. He was handsome, with dark eyes and a square cut jaw, probably no older than I was.

"Did I hear someone say 'dance'?" he said. He extended his hand. "My name is Dolan."

"I'm Riley," I replied, shaking his hand.

He didn't release me though. "And would you care to dance, Riley?"

Navan was standing behind Dolan; in fact, it had seemed as if Dolan hadn't even registered that Navan was there.

"I do like to dance," I said, enjoying the annoyed look on Navan's face. "And this music *is* great . . ." The smile on Dolan's face got wider. From behind him, Navan's scowl deepened. "I'd love to dance," I said, suppressing a smirk. "This might be my only opportunity to do so tonight."

"Not if I have anything to do with it," Dolan said jovially, and Navan made a face like he was about to throw up.

Dolan was a good dancer—the song was fast, upbeat, so he clasped my left hand and put his other hand on my waist. We did a sort of side-stepping skip through the other dancers, and every so often Dolan would twirl me around, or put both his hands on my waist and lift me up. The whole time, I was aware of Navan, standing there on the periphery, his eyes following my every move.

I was nearly out of breath when the song finally ended, and everyone clapped as the band started up again.

"I'm going to take a little break," I said to Dolan.

"You're an excellent dancer," he said. "We must dance again." His gaze moved past my shoulder. "That guy's been staring the whole time," he said. "Is he your boyfriend?"

"No," I said. "Just a friend."

"Is he . . . sick?"

I looked at Dolan. "Sick?"

"He looks . . . I don't know, a little . . . off-color? And pissed. He definitely looks pissed. Is he anemic?"

Navan's hood was doing a decent job of casting shadows over his face for the most part, but if you really looked, his skin did look odd compared to others.

"He's definitely not anemic," I replied.

Dolan continued to eye him warily. "He looks like he wants to kill me."

"It's possible," I said. Dolan gave me a confused look and I laughed. "I'm just kidding. He's just cranky. I'll go talk to him."

Someone handed me a cup of hot cocoa as I made my way back over to Navan, and I took a sip, savoring the rich sweetness.

"Have fun?" he asked, his voice laced with sarcasm. "Lover boy over there looks like he's got two left feet."

"Do I detect a note of . . . *jealousy* in your voice?"

He snorted. "Please."

"I'd be more than happy to go back out there and dance with you, if you'd like. That offer still stands."

He looked at me, an amused expression on his face. I set my hot cocoa down and grabbed Navan's hand, pulling him out to the makeshift dance floor. He was strong enough that he could have easily resisted me, but he didn't, so I took it as a sign that he wasn't totally against the idea.

The band had started playing a slower song, though, and the couples dancing stopped cavorting and settled into each other's arms, moving their feet slowly back and forth.

"Was this part of your plan?" Navan said.

For a moment, I thought he was going to walk away and leave me standing there, but then he moved his hands down and rested them lightly on my waist. I put my arms around his neck, and we swayed to the music.

"I wasn't expecting the music to slow down," I said. "Really."

He raised an eyebrow. "Uh-huh. I totally believe you. This isn't so bad, though. How am I doing?"

"You're doing great."

And he was right—this wasn't so bad at all. It felt like the most natural thing in the world, being out here with him, underneath the dark sky, the music filling the air. I wanted to tell him right then how happy I was, how just being near him filled me with a joy I had never experienced before, but part of me remained afraid of voicing my thoughts aloud. The possibility of being rejected was still enough to paralyze me from acting on the happiness I felt—I couldn't bear the thought of opening up to him, only to find out he didn't feel the same way. Part of me did think the feeling was mutual—the glances we'd shared, his open concern for my well-being, the way his look could make me feel like I was the only person on the planet—yet doubt still loomed over me. I knew what it was like to love someone, only to have those feelings not be reciprocated—how many times had my birth parents rejected me because alcohol was more important?

So instead, I just smiled up at him, and enjoyed being so close.

avan and I stayed at the festival a little while longer, but then he whispered to me that we should head back to the ship.

"Do you think it's awake?" I asked.

"Yeah, I do. And I know it won't be able to escape or anything, but I'd still like to get back there before it starts trying to get away."

We slipped away from the festival, the music, the laughter, the warmth from the fires fading into the distance as we walked away.

"That was fun," I said. "I'm glad we went."

"It wasn't on the agenda, but yeah, I had a good time."

My arms swung back and forth slightly as we walked, and my hand brushed up against Navan's. His fingers interlaced with mine, sending a surprise rush of pleasure up my arm. He glanced at me.

"This okay?"

"Yes," I said breathlessly.

"Good." He nodded. "I want to keep you close. Can't risk Donnel trying to whisk you away again."

I laughed. "It was Dolan."

"He wasn't that good of a dancer."

"Hey, it's an open invitation—whenever you feel like impressing me with your dance moves, I'm all for it."

He squeezed my hand. "Don't hold your breath."

When we got to the ship, I was forced to let go of his hand and followed him up to one of the ship's windows. I pressed my face against it and peered inside.

"It's still asleep," I said.

Navan stood next to me, a slight frown on his face. "No, it's not," he said. "It's pretending to be asleep."

"How do you know? It looks asleep to me."

Navan continued to stare at it. "I can sense its energy. If it were sleeping, its energy would be at a much lower frequency. But what I'm picking up right now is basically off the charts, which tells me this thing is going to attempt to pull off some sort of ambush. Stay right here—I'm going to open the door."

I stayed by the window and watched as Navan slowly opened the compartment door. The shifter suddenly sprang, though it didn't get far because of the ropes it was tied up in. Navan gave it a kick and sent it sprawling. I went inside.

"Well, well, well, look who's awake," Navan said. "Good morning, sunshine. Damn, you things sure are ugly."

The shifter growled, and its eyes swiveled to me. Navan was right—it *was* ugly, like a giant newborn bird, with its pale, wrinkled skin. Instead of a beak and fused-over eyes, though, it had a wide, flat nose, a gaping mouth full of shark-like teeth, and huge red-veined eyes that seemed mostly made up of iris.

"Give me the antidote," it said. "And I'll change into something more aesthetically pleasing."

"Ha!" Navan's laugh was like a bark. "Yeah, sure, let me get you that antidote, and while I'm at it, how about a bubble bath and a foot rub? You're not getting anything. Nice try, though. We've got some questions for you."

The shifter stretched its mouth into what was probably supposed to be a smile, but looked more like a terrifying grimace. "I'm not answering your questions."

"Then you don't get the antidote, and you're forever doomed to be an ugly little sewer rat."

The shifter stared at him, and I could see it weighing the possibility of having to spend life forever in one form. "At least untie me enough so I can sit up," it finally said.

"Fine," Navan replied after a moment. "But I swear, if you try anything, you're going to wish I had killed you."

"Does making idle threats to your victims make you feel more powerful, bloodsucker?"

"Shut up," Navan said. "We're not talking about me right now. We're talking about you. I'm untying you on the condition that you're going to answer my questions. If you don't, these ropes are going to get a whole lot more uncomfortable."

Navan undid one of the ropes, and the shifter sat up. Its skin gathered in loose pools of flesh around its elbows and knees. It saw me looking and it grimaced.

"Hey!" Navan snapped, kicking it. "Look at me, not her. Pay attention. Here are your first questions: How many shifters are out here in these parts? And what are you doing with the people that are disappearing—what do shifters want with humans?"

"Oh... I'd say there are a good few hundred of us," it replied, smiling eerily. "And coldbloods aren't the only ones with a taste for blood, you know. Human blood is particularly satisfying." It looked right at me, baring its sharp teeth. I wanted to look away but I didn't.

"Maybe we should just kill you," I said. "No more human blood for you."

"If you kill me, I won't be able to answer any more of your questions. And that's what this is all about, isn't it? Your little lover here getting all the answers so he can swoop in and be the hero who saves the day?"

"He's not my lover," I replied, my cheeks heating.

The shifter smirked. "Yeah, right... A human and a cold-blood," it sneered. "I'm sorry but I have to say, I don't see that being a long-term relationship. Considering how valuable human blood is to your kind."

Navan frowned. "What the hell do you know about that?"

"She is pretty, though," the shifter said, ignoring his question. "I can see why you'd be ... *attracted.* You've probably spent many nights thinking about how good it would be to have a little taste."

Navan lashed out with his foot, catching the shifter right in the side, sending it sprawling.

"You coldbloods certainly are bad tempered," it wheezed as it sat back up.

"We're done talking about this," Navan said, and was it just my imagination, or were his cheeks a little flushed too?

He pushed a map in front of the shifter's face. "Where is your base?" he asked gruffly. "Show us on the map."

The shifter looked at the map, as though studying it. Navan and I both held our breath, but then the shifter shook its head.

"What is this?" it asked, pushing the map away.

"It's a map," Navan snapped. "I just told you that. We're here." He jabbed a finger at the map. "And *you're* going to show us where your base is."

"I'm not familiar with maps. This looks like a bunch of gibberish to me. I would be guessing if I tried to show you on here."

Navan exhaled loudly. "Are you kidding me?"

"Amongst my kind, I am known to be one of the funnier ones. But I am not kidding here. I cannot read this map you have."

"We're not letting you go," I said. "Just because you're claiming you can't tell us where the base is, that doesn't mean we're just going to set you free."

"Do I look stupid?" the shifter asked.

Navan snorted. "Do you really want me to answer that?"

The shifter ignored him. "There's nothing I'd like more than a nice taste of some young, virgin blood. Seems a bit torturous that I should be so close to it yet unable to do anything about it. But I'm still willing to help. I can take you there. I might not be able to read this map of yours, but I know the route by heart. I will take you there."

Navan raised an eyebrow. "Really. And why would we trust you to take us there? You'd probably lead us into some sort of trap."

"You have reason to trust me because my offer comes with a few conditions. The main one being that you give me the antidote to restore my shapeshifting abilities. What a lonely and disgraceful life I would live if I were doomed to inhabit no other form but this one for the rest of my days," the shifter muttered. "It would be better that I just off myself now, if that were to be."

Navan and I looked at each other. As much as I hated to admit it, the shifter's bargain seemed fair.

Navan retrieved a length of chain, which he wrapped around the shifter's neck. Once that was done, he undid the ropes.

"Okay," he said. "Take us there."

## 25

*M*avan went over to the door and opened it, looking at the shifter expectantly. The shifter looked back at him, confused.

"You're not staying in here," Navan said. "You're going out there."

"And you're not afraid that I might run off?"

"Oh, I'm not afraid . . . But just to be on the safe side, you're going to be attached to the ship." He gave the chain a yank and the shifter lurched forward, nearly falling. He pulled the shifter to the door and then gave it a kick, sending it sprawling onto the ground.

I almost felt bad for the thing, though I knew if given the chance, the thing wouldn't think twice about sinking its disgusting teeth into my flesh.

I settled down next to Navan at the front of the ship, and we started the journey, the shifter moving slowly beneath us. Navan kept the ship low, though every couple of minutes he'd move it higher, so the shifter was lifted completely off the ground, the chain tightening around its neck like a noose. It coughed and gagged, spit flying, body spasming until Navan lowered the ship enough that it could reach the ground.

"You think I'm being cruel," he said, glancing at me.

"No." I shook my head but then reconsidered. "Well . . . maybe a little. Isn't it good enough that it's chained up and being pulled along by the ship?"

"That thing has done more evil than you could even imagine," Navan replied. "Don't think for a second that it wouldn't hurt you, too." A muscle in his jaw twitched. "You heard it say how they've been feasting on human blood, right?"

"Yeah... That part was kind of hard to miss."

"Shifters are crafty, and they're also sadistic. If they're drinking blood, they're keeping their victims alive for as long as possible, because they want fresh blood—they're not interested in carrion. They kill slowly, dragging it out for as long as possible. Any humans they've taken, they've tortured—trust me. Think about a horde of those things taking you apart piece by piece. So jerking it around a little bit here and there—it's not cruel at all."

I shuddered.

We continued at a slow pace, the shifter slipping and sliding along the icy surface. Suddenly, we jerked downward, as though the shifter had suddenly gained superhuman strength and was pulling the whole ship.

"What the—" Navan started. He peered out the window, his eyes widening.

A pack of wolves had appeared out of nowhere, it seemed, and were attacking the shifter, who was trying to out-maneuver them but failing. Suddenly, one of the wolves changed into a bird and flew up before dive bombing the shifter, its sharp talons spread.

"It's a pack of shapeshifters," Navan said, gritting his teeth. He threw the ship into neutral, and we hovered there, above the melee. He opened the door and yanked on the chain. "They're going to tear that thing apart if we don't get it up here."

I got up to help him—the bird had changed back into a wolf, though a few of the wolves had changed into their regular form, like our shapeshifter, and they were tearing at its pink flesh.

"Why are they trying to kill it?" I stood behind Navan, pulling on the chain, leaning all my weight back.

"These things don't care," Navan grated out, giving the chain a hard pull. "Get me one of the guns, will you? Shifters don't have any loyalty to each other. And they probably knew this one would give up their secrets to save itself." He lunged forward and grabbed the shifter as it came level with the ship's door. One of the wolves had clamped its jaw around the shifter's foot; Navan leaned over and punched it in the nose. It changed shape as it fell, howling in pain. I handed him the gun, and he took several shots.

Navan slammed the door shut once the shifter was inside. It lay there, groaning, jagged lacerations running the length of its body.

"Great," Navan said. "I guess you're going to have to ride in here with us for the rest of the journey."

I looked out the window and saw that the shifters had changed shape and were now all a flock of birds, with hooked beaks and talons.

"Uh, they're still coming for us," I said nervously.

Navan went over to where the weapons were stored and grabbed one of the rifles. I picked up one of the throwing knives and went over to the door. There were only a few of the birds left; the rest had been killed by Navan's rifle shots. I took aim and let the knife fly. It spun end over end through the air, the blade sinking deep into the bird's side, right below the wing. It plummeted, changing back to its original form as it landed on the ground in a lifeless heap.

Navan gaped at me. "Wow... That was . . ." He peered out the open door at the ground where the dead shifter lay in a widening pool of blood. "Impressive."

We didn't have much time to admire my knife-throwing skills, though, because the ship shuddered and dropped a few feet. My stomach flipped at the sensation.

"Something's wrong with the ship," I said, grabbing the steering wheel. I tried to steady it, but the ship shuddered again. "We're going to have to land."

Our landing was heavy, and the ship slid along the ice for several hundred feet before finally coming to a stop.

"This was really not part of the plan," Navan said. He glared at the shifter. "You stay here."

I followed Navan out of the ship. The exterior looked all right, but there was an acrid smell in the air and a billow of smoke rising from the back of it.

"That can't be good," I said. "I wonder if one of those birds got into the engine or something."

"This seems to be a recurring theme," Navan muttered. "Did I do something to deserve being cursed with all these broken-down ships? We don't have time to fix this!"

"We don't have much of a choice, though, do we?" I asked. "How are we going to get anywhere if the ship is broken?"

Navan sighed. "I guess we'll have to comm the Fed for help. Who knows how long *that's* going to take."

"Maybe I could look at it. I *am* going to school for mechanical engineering."

It was a stretch, I knew, to think that I could go from fixing the drive train on a bicycle to fixing whatever was wrong with this ship, but I wanted to at least try. I wanted to feel like I was actually contributing something to this mission, other than just being a liability that Navan had to worry about.

"You can try," Navan said. "But I doubt even I could fix it, and I have experience with these types of machines. I think you'd have to be a magician, since we don't have any parts. The Fed will have to supply us with the parts at least."

There was a cackling, hacking sound, and Navan and I both turned toward it. The shifter had dragged itself to the door and was halfway leaning out of it.

"Where do you think you're going?" Navan growled.

"You two are both fools," the shifter said. "I can hear everything you're saying."

"Yeah, well, we're not the one who's chained up and bleeding," Navan retorted. "So I suggest you shut up. Go make yourself comfortable—we're going to be here a while."

"Coldbloods always want to act a lot smarter than they really are," the shifter said. "We're basically here. It's maybe a ten-minute walk."

Navan narrowed his eyes. "I don't believe you."

"Suit yourself," the shifter said, "but you're the one who's going to end up looking like a fool if you sit around here waiting, only to find out you were right next to your destination."

"Just go back inside!"

Navan waited until the shifter had disappeared back into the ship before he looked at me. "What do you think?" he asked in a low voice. "Do you think it's telling the truth?"

"I don't know. Maybe? Why would it lie about that?"

"It could be a trick. It might want to get us off the ship and in the woods so the others can attack us." He frowned. "But the thing is right—I'd feel pretty stupid if the place we're looking for really is right nearby."

"Well," I said, "I guess there's only one way to find out."

Navan ran his hand over the lower part of his face and then

took a deep breath. "You're right. But I'm not going empty-handed. I'm going to take both of the guns. I think I saw a holster in there with the rest of the weapons. It'd probably be a good idea to have both guns with us."

It was hard to read the shifter's expression when we told it that we'd walk the rest of the way. It only swiveled its eyes back and forth and then nodded. "Maybe you're not as stupid as you look," it finally said.

Navan flicked the chain. "You're staying on this," he said. "And if this turns out to be some ill-conceived little trick of yours, you're going to wish that group of shifters really had torn you apart. The first thing I'll do is rub salt over each and every one of your cuts, and then I'll—"

"Okay!" I said. "Why don't we get walking?"

The wind had picked up, and I shivered even though I had the jacket zipped up all the way. The shifter seemed unaffected by the temperature, and I hated that I was the weak link here, that I was the one who couldn't deal with the cold.

"You okay?" Navan asked, his brow furrowed in concern.

I gritted my teeth in an attempt to keep them from clacking together. "I'm fine."

"You're cold," he said. He looked at the shifter, who was probably about ten feet in front of us. "You better be taking us the right way," he warned.

The shifter cast a casual glance over its shoulder. "Don't worry," it said. "If the girl dies out here, I'll happily dispose of her body."

Navan jerked the chain so hard the shifter fell back, gagging. "Keep moving, or I'm going to dispose of *you*."

The anger ebbed on Navan's face as he looked back at me, and though his protectiveness was comforting, a larger part of me didn't like feeling as though he needed to take care of me. I tried to think of being in a hot tub, of drinking tea, a warm bubble bath, wool sweaters, down comforters. Anything that might help generate some body heat.

Luckily, we didn't have much further to walk. After several more minutes, the shifter stopped.

"We're here," it said. "See? That took about fifteen minutes. We would've made it in ten if you hadn't been walking so slowly."

"Where is it?" I asked, ignoring that last comment. All it looked like was another forest clearing.

The shifter sneered. "We've protected the area with an invisibility shield. I highly doubt that any humans would be intelligent enough to stumble upon our settlement, but we knew the Fed might be lurking."

I glanced at Navan, who was staring straight ahead, as though he actually could sense something there in the clearing.

"It's telling the truth," he said finally.

The shifter grinned, clearly pleased with itself.

"Great," I said sarcastically. "So you told the truth. Now what?"

"Now," the shifter said, "you are going to have the chance to look inside. And I can all but guarantee that you are not going to believe your eyes."

Navan rolled his eyes. "I highly doubt that."

The grin on the shifter's face widened, exposing those yellow shards of teeth. A wave of revulsion washed over me, and an uneasiness rose in my stomach, though I wasn't quite sure why. Our mission was almost complete—shouldn't I be feeling something closer to relief?

The shifter took a few steps forward and then stopped, holding a hand up. It pressed its palm into the air, and though I couldn't see anything, it was clear that its hand had come to rest upon something.

"Here," it said, and suddenly, the air started to shimmer, and I could see the outline of a huge dome. The shifter swiped its hand to the side and a gap in the dome appeared. "Have a look."

I started to step forward but Navan put a hand out and stopped me. "Let me look first," he said. "We don't know if this is some sort of trick."

He leaned his head in first, but I was right behind him. With our heads inside the boundary of the invisibility shield, we could suddenly see everything that had been previously hidden. Navan inhaled sharply, his whole body going rigid. There were plenty of shifters, all wearing the same blue uniform the one in the alley had been wearing, all with the bulging eyes and broken glass teeth. It was a repulsive sight, but all things considered, not that unexpected.

It took me a second to realize why Navan had reacted like that.

There were coldbloods mingling with the shifters.

I blinked, but the picture didn't change. The coldbloods were walking amongst the shifters, their black wings out, on full display—also clad in blue uniforms.

"What the . . ." Navan said, before yanking his head back. I pulled my head back too, and the gap in the invisibility shield closed.

"Were those *coldbloods*?" I asked.

Navan nodded slowly. "That wasn't just my eyes playing tricks on me," he said. "You saw it, too."

"But . . . but . . ." I let my voice trail off, not wanting to state the obvious, but unable to quite wrap my head around it.

"But there aren't supposed to be any other coldbloods on Earth," he said.

"Surprise!" the shifter shrieked, and it lunged toward Navan, tearing at his wings. Navan stumbled back and lashed out at the shifter, but it had managed to catch him by surprise and Navan's swing missed. While Navan and I had been looking through the invisibility shield, the shifter must have managed to free itself, because the chain now lay in a pile on the ground.

"Navan!" I gasped, rushing toward him. The shifter jumped back and evaded another of Navan's swings. It cackled as it slipped through the invisibility shield, disappearing from our sight.

"Oh my God," I breathed, "are you okay?"

He nodded, a grim expression on his face. "We've got to get out of here," he said. "*Now*. And activate that suit."

"But—"

"Just do it!"

The urgency in his voice sent a shiver of anxiety up my spine, so I pressed the button and we took off. He had a gaping tear in his right wing that slowly oozed blood. As we ran, I saw another shooting star arc across the sky . . . And then another. The second one was closer, close enough that I realized it wasn't a shooting star at all.

It was a ship.

Much like Navan's ship, actually. And they were headed straight for us.

Or for Navan, rather.

"Look out!" I screamed as one of the ships zoomed precariously close. It seemed unfathomable that it could have caught up to us so quickly, but there it was, its unearthly surface shimmering.

Navan tried to take flight, but with his injured wing, he couldn't. He landed heavily on the ground and tried to run, but the ship was upon him. I raced over right as two coldbloods flew out and grabbed Navan. He managed to pull one of the guns from the holster, but one of the coldbloods knocked it from his hand before he could shoot. He tried to fight them off, but they easily overpowered and disarmed him, then threw him onto the ship. It started to lift away, but I lunged at the last second and caught hold of the door, pulling myself in right before one of the coldbloods slammed the door shut.

They threw Navan down on the ground and fell upon him, thrashing him. He fought back, but he was no match for them. I hid underneath a bench, scanning the interior of the ship for something, anything, that I could use to help him. If only I'd had more knives! But the space we were in was almost sterile in its emptiness, and there was nothing, except for my bare hands.

But I couldn't just sit there.

No sooner had the thought crossed my mind did Navan look across the floor toward me. His coldblood senses must have been particularly sharp compared to the others, because he seemed to detect me in spite of the suit. He lifted his head, even as the blows continued to rain down, and looked right at me, shaking his head. It was such a slight gesture it was almost imperceptible, but it came across loud and clear. If I got caught by the coldbloods, they'd kill me, and Navan would be defenseless.

Right now, there was only one choice: I had to stay where I was.

26

The ship flew through the invisibility shield and landed in front of a bunker that looked like it had been there for centuries. It was a low concrete building with no windows. Jagged cracks like scars ran down the sides of the building. The two coldbloods dragged Navan out, and I scrambled out from under the bench, anxiety coursing through my veins. I followed them into the bunker and down a hallway lit with flickering fluorescent lights.

They kicked open one of the doors off the hallway, which led into a room with nothing but a metal table with a couple chairs, and a bench—much like the one I'd just been hiding under—shoved up against the back wall. They shoved Navan into a chair, one of them tying his hands behind his back with something that looked like red twine, but glistened in such a way that it made me think it had come from something living. I slipped underneath the bench.

"Loser," one of the coldbloods snapped, and it spat, the globule hitting the side of Navan's face before it slowly dripped off. Navan didn't flinch, though; he barely reacted. He stared straight ahead, unmoving, except for his hands, which were behind his back. His hands opened and closed into fists, and I could tell he was straining against the ties, but they weren't budging.

The two other coldbloods looked toward the door as it opened. A large, imposing figure stood in the doorway for a moment, retracting his enormous black wings so he could fit through. His hair was the color of mud, and his eyes were dark and seemed to reflect the light.

"That's enough," he said.

"We can't stay?" one of the coldbloods asked.

"No." The big coldblood didn't even look at them as he pulled the second chair out from the table. He didn't sit, though; instead, he walked the perimeter of the room, coming to stop right in front of the bench. He was so close, I wouldn't even need to extend my arm all the way to touch him.

"What is your name?"

Navan stared straight ahead. His lip was split, and a dark bruise was forming on the side of his face.

"Let's start this a different way," the coldblood said. "I'll tell you *my* name. I am Ezra, and like you, I am originally from Vysanthe. I hope that you will recognize that we can be on the same team here. We can work toward the same objective." He moved away from the bench and sat down at the table.

"How do you know what I'm working toward?" Navan asked. His voice was low, a throaty growl.

Ezra smiled. "Well, that's the problem—I can't completely know what it is you're working for if you don't tell me. That's what this is about right here. Think of it as getting to know each other."

"What is this—a date?" Navan shook his head. "Not interested, sorry."

I could tell that Navan was struggling to keep his cool. His look of confusion and anger made it clear he really couldn't believe there were other coldbloods here. I remembered how adamant Navan had been about keeping Earth a secret for as long as possible, about doing whatever was necessary to prevent the other coldbloods from finding out we were here—yet they'd been here all along.

"What is it you're doing here?" Ezra asked, leaning forward.

"Sightseeing."

Ezra took a deep breath. "I'll ask you again—what is it you're doing here?"

Navan rolled his eyes up toward the ceiling, as if he was going to find the answer there. "I took a wrong turn. I meant to take a left at the Andromeda galaxy and I ended up going right, then I got caught up in a really turbulent plasmapheric wind and was blown right here to Earth."

"Likely story."

"If you think I give a damn whether you believe me or not, you are mistaken."

Part of me wanted to run over to Navan and shake him, tell him to just answer their questions. He didn't have to tell them everything, but he needed to reveal enough to satisfy them—otherwise, they'd probably kill him. Ezra was being amicable enough right now, but who was to say that wouldn't change in a second? Who knew when his patience would run out, and if he decided that Navan wasn't going to give him the information he wanted, what would prevent him from killing him right then and there?

"Look," Ezra said. "I can understand that you're not thrilled to be here right now, and that for you to open up, I'm going to have to extend a bit of trust. So again, I'll go first."

"You're acting like I actually care about who you are or what you're doing here."

Ezra laughed. "But you do," he said. "You're *very* curious—and quite perplexed—as to what all these coldbloods are doing here on this planet. We found your base in Alaska, you know. We detected irregular frequencies—frequencies that indicated Vysanthian technology. That was our first clue that there was a coldblood here who had arrived on his own, not with the rebel faction, and we sent our shifter allies out there to investigate... and, if necessary, assassinate."

Navan swallowed. "Rebel faction? You mean the ones that the sisters banished from Vysanthe?"

"The very one. Brisha and Gianne should have done a better

job of killing us, but they were too wrapped up in the idea of ruling that they didn't consider some of the finer details of democracy."

"Well, democracy would not involve killing dissenters."

"Ah, but it would. You seem to be a learned fellow—I'd guess a fairly smart one, given that you've figured out a formula to camouflage your skin." He eyed Navan, taking in his human-colored tone. "What democracy isn't based on bloodshed and tyranny? It's simply the way things are done. On this planet and every other. And of these innumerable planets, Vysanthe is indisputably superior."

Navan snorted. "I know some who might disagree."

"Vysanthe deserves to be united," Ezra said. "None of this ruler to the south, ruler to the north nonsense. There should be one leader that all of Vysanthe can rally behind. This is not just an individual desire—this is for the greater good."

"And you're going to see to that from here . . . how?"

"Our plan has always been to return to Vysanthe, once we regrouped, strengthened our forces, organized our faction. We want everything to go right, the first time."

"Because it worked out so well for you before."

"That's exactly my point. Things didn't work out so well for those who wished to see democracy on Vysanthe, and so we must be more diligent this time around to ensure that our vision is realized. This takes time, this takes resources. Would you not like to see a united, peaceful Vysanthe?"

"Of course I would," Navan replied. "And the probability of that happening is about . . . oh, I don't know. Zero?"

"The probability is actually much greater than that. The numbers grow in our favor with every individual we recruit to the cause. We are not out to do harm, we are not malicious. Violence is kept to the minimum."

"Oh yeah? You should tell that to the two thugs who decided to use my face as a punching bag."

Ezra smiled thinly. "Rey and Xander can be a bit too enthusiastic at times, I admit. They shouldn't have done that, or they should have at least stopped after they managed to get you aboard the ship. But we're not here for a philosophical debate, are we? Why don't you tell me your name."

"Navan Idrax. My father is Jareth Idrax."

Ezra did a double take. "Your father is Jareth Idrax? One of Queen Gianne's advisors? *That* Jareth Idrax?"

A sour smile appeared on Navan's face. "He'd be thrilled to know he had such an ardent fan. Yeah, that's the one. Good old Father. If you let me go, maybe I can get you his autograph."

I could see Ezra struggling with whether to believe him or not. He steepled his fingers together and stared at Navan. "If that's true, it makes sense why you'd be skilled with potions... and this really is our lucky day. I'm glad our shifter failed to kill you. Your father would likely go to great lengths to see your safe return... Excuse me a moment," he said, pushing back the chair from the table and standing up. He exited the room quickly, closing the door behind him.

Now was my chance. I didn't know how long he'd be gone for, but I slipped out from underneath the bench, pressing the button on the sleeve as I did so. I knew it would've been smarter to stay invisible, but I'd looked around and hadn't seen any cameras. I knew I could talk and he'd hear me, but I wanted him to see me—I didn't just want to be some disembodied voice he was hearing. I materialized beside him, and he jumped when he saw me.

"Riley!" he hissed. "What are you doing here?"

"I'm going to help you get out."

"Unless you've figured out a way to get that invisibility suit to melt metal, you're not," he said. "Now, get back into invisible mode before Ezra returns and sees you. We're in enough trouble here as it is without them realizing there's a human in the equation, too."

"I'm not leaving you," I insisted. "And there's nothing you can say that's going to change my mind." I touched the side of his face. "They hurt you," I whispered, using my fingertips to wipe away the wet mark where the coldblood had spat on him.

"It's fine."

"It's not fine. I heard everything that Ezra said! And did you see the expression on his face when he found out who your father is?"

"How could I miss it? My father's reputation precedes him, even all the way here on Earth. I wasn't kidding when I told Ezra how delighted he'd be to find out something like that."

"I don't care about your father's ego! They're going to try to use you as a pawn, Navan. Did you hear what he said about your father going to great lengths? They don't really care about you. They're going to try to get what they want, and if you end up dying in the process, that's not going to matter to them one bit. So we've got to get you out of here." I bent down and tried to untie him, but it was like the knots had fused over; there was nothing to grab onto, nothing to untie.

"You're wasting your time." Navan sighed. "You can't untie it."

"What the hell is it?"

"It's inselo gut."

I stood up. "It's *what?*"

"It's the cured intestine from an inselo. It's an animal like a leopard seal. If they cure it a certain way, with a special binding potion, it becomes a 'live wire,' which means it's only unlockable by the person who cured it. Which I'm assuming is Ezra."

"How am I supposed to get you out, then? What should I do?" I glanced at the door, which was still firmly shut. I looked back at Navan.

He looked exhausted, and it tore me up on the inside. "If they're going to use me as a pawn, then they need to keep me alive. So maybe take some comfort in that. But if they find *you*— who knows what they'll do to you." He shuddered. "I don't even want to think about it. You need to press that button and get invisible again. And then *stay hidden*. They very well might have the technology to detect you, and if they do, there's not much I can do to help you."

"I'm going to figure out a way to get you out of here," I promised. "I know you don't believe me, but I'm going to."

We looked at each other, neither of us saying anything for a moment, then another. The air around us grew thick, and I suddenly felt a magnetic force drawing me to him.

"You need to press that button," Navan repeated.

"I will," I whispered. "But... first, I need to do this."

The words came out of my mouth without my brain fully registering them; it felt as if something had taken over my body and was propelling me forward, though there was nothing more I wanted in that moment. We were here, prisoners, but all I could think about was kissing him. If I was honest with myself, I'd wanted to do it for a while, but I'd held back because I'd been afraid, because I thought there might be a chance that he'd just laugh and push me away. There was still a small part of me that harbored that fear, but it was eclipsed by a bigger fear—that one—or both—of us wouldn't make it out of here alive. I put my hands on his shoulders and leaned down, my face right against his, our lips just millimeters from touching.

He inhaled slowly. "What a time for my hands to be tied behind my back," he said softly.

My entire body felt electrified when our lips finally touched, and I breathed in his scent, one of my hands going around the back of his head, as though I could pull him even closer to me. The other rested against the side of his cool face, my fingertips running lightly along the taut skin of his stubbled jawline. His mouth responded to mine hungrily—so much so that it took me aback. His tongue parted my lips, and I felt his desire for me with its every stroke, his every hitched breath.

As his firm lips caressed mine, I felt myself light up, my body feeling weightless. He was kissing me back, burning for me just as much as I was for him, and I mentally kicked myself for not allowing myself a taste of this sooner, for delaying it so long.

Everything seemed to fall away. Nothing else mattered. I let that kiss completely consume me. We were prisoners trapped in this bunker, but the rush of happiness that flooded through me made my heart feel like it was going to explode. Kissing him was like coming home, like arriving at the very place I'd always wanted to be but had been unable to find until now. I would have been content to stay there forever, but Navan finally pulled back, his eyes still half-closed, an anguished expression on his face.

"We've got to stop," he whispered, groaning. "Believe me when I say it's the last thing I want to do." He tilted his head and we kissed again. "But we've got to." His lips moved lightly against mine as he spoke. "You need to be safe. Please. If you end up getting caught, we won't be able to do this again."

It felt as though I was being torn in two. I knew he was right, that I needed to activate the invisibility suit again, that I needed to hide because who knew when Ezra or another coldblood might come back into the room? But the thought of having to leave Navan was unbearable.

"Riley." He had pulled back and was looking straight into my eyes. "Please. Press the button and hide."

"Okay," I breathed. I pressed my lips to his once more, savoring the feel of him for what I prayed would not be the last time.

Then I pulled back and pushed the button on my arm, activating the suit. My heart pounding, I slid back underneath the bench I'd been under, right as the doorknob turned and Ezra, along with another coldblood that I hadn't seen before, re-entered the room.

"This is Jareth's son," Ezra was saying. My brain was still locked on Navan's and my kiss, and I had to force myself to focus on his words, bring myself back to the scene around me.

This new coldblood was taller, and more refined-looking, except he had a deep scar running down the side of his face, right below his eye to the corner of his mouth. His eyes were almost completely black. He didn't look much older than Ezra, but there was something about him that emanated an ancient aura.

"An even better development than we could have hoped for," he said, eyeing Navan, whose expression was a combination of awe and wariness. Did Navan know him? They clearly knew Navan's father, and the way Navan was looking at him made me think that he knew who this guy was, too. "You've got a role to play in all this, son. You'll be an important bargaining chip." He made like he was going to tousle Navan's hair or pat his head, but then he froze, his hand hovering in the empty air. His eyes swiveled around, and he tilted his head back, sniffing the air. His gaze landed on the bench, a slow smile turning up the corners of his mouth.

"What is it?" Ezra asked.

The smile on the coldblood's face grew, exposing a pair of sharp, white fangs. I tried to flatten myself against the back wall as best I could. "Someone else is here," he said.

# READY FOR MORE?

**Ready for the next part of Riley and Navan's story?**

Dear Reader,

I'd like to thank you for taking a chance on *Hotbloods*. I hope you enjoyed it.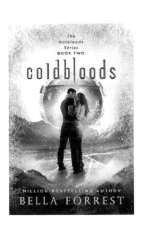

Book 2 of the series, *Coldbloods*, is available now!

Visit: www.bellaforrest.net for details.

I'll see you on the other side...

Love,

Bella x

P.S. Sign up to my VIP email list and I'll send you a personal heads up when my next book releases: **www.morebellaforrest.com**

(Your email will be kept 100% private and you can unsubscribe at any time.)

READ MORE BY BELLA FORREST

HOTBLOODS

Hotbloods (Book 1)

Coldbloods (Book 2)

Renegades (Book 3)

THE GIRL WHO DARED TO THINK

The Girl Who Dared to Think (Book 1)

The Girl Who Dared to Stand (Book 2)

The Girl Who Dared to Descend (Book 3)

The Girl Who Dared to Rise (Book 4)

The Girl Who Dared to Lead (Book 5)

THE GENDER GAME

(Completed series)

The Gender Game (Book 1)

The Gender Secret (Book 2)

The Gender Lie (Book 3)

The Gender War (Book 4)

The Gender Fall (Book 5)

The Gender Plan (Book 6)

The Gender End (Book 7)

# A SHADE OF VAMPIRE SERIES

A Hero of Realms (Book 20)

A Vial of Life (Book 21)

A Fork of Paths (Book 22)

A Flight of Souls (Book 23)

A Bridge of Stars (Book 24)

**Series 4: A Clan of Novaks**

A Clan of Novaks (Book 25)

A World of New (Book 26)

A Web of Lies (Book 27)

A Touch of Truth (Book 28)

An Hour of Need (Book 29)

A Game of Risk (Book 30)

A Twist of Fates (Book 31)

A Day of Glory (Book 32)

**Series 5: A Dawn of Guardians**

A Dawn of Guardians (Book 33)

A Sword of Chance (Book 34)

A Race of Trials (Book 35)

A King of Shadow (Book 36)

An Empire of Stones (Book 37)

A Power of Old (Book 38)

A Rip of Realms (Book 39)

A Throne of Fire (Book 40)

A Tide of War (Book 41)

**Series 6: A Gift of Three**

A Gift of Three (Book 42)

A House of Mysteries (Book 43)

A Tangle of Hearts (Book 44)

A Meet of Tribes (Book 45)

A Ride of Peril (Book 46)

A Passage of Threats (Book 47)

A Tip of Balance (Book 48)

A Shield of Glass (Book 49)

A Clash of Storms (Book 50)

**Series 7: A Call of Vampires**

A Call of Vampires (Book 51)

A Valley of Darkness (Book 52)

A Hunt of Fiends (Book 53)

A SHADE OF DRAGON TRILOGY

A Shade of Dragon 1

A Shade of Dragon 2

A Shade of Dragon 3

A SHADE OF KIEV TRILOGY

A Shade of Kiev 1

A Shade of Kiev 2

A Shade of Kiev 3

THE SECRET OF SPELLSHADOW MANOR

(Completed series)

The Secret of Spellshadow Manor (Book 1)

The Breaker (Book 2)

The Chain (Book 3)

The Keep (Book 4)

The Test (Book 5)

The Spell (Book 6)

BEAUTIFUL MONSTER DUOLOGY

Beautiful Monster 1

Beautiful Monster 2

DETECTIVE ERIN BOND (Adult thriller/mystery)

Lights, Camera, GONE

Write, Edit, KILL

For an updated list of Bella's books, please visit her website: www.bellaforrest.net

Join Bella's VIP email list and she'll send you an email reminder as soon as her next book is out. Visit: www.morebellaforrest.com

Printed in Poland
by Amazon Fulfillment
Poland Sp. z o.o., Wrocław